French Leave

FRENCH LEAVE

FRANÇOISE BARTRAM

Book Design & Production
Columbus Publishing Lab
www.ColumbusPublishingLab.com

Copyright © 2018 by Françoise Bartram
LCCN 2018946063

All rights reserved. This book, or parts thereof, may not be
reproduced in any form without permission.

Print ISBN: 978-1-63337-216-0
E-book ISBN: 978-1-63337-217-7

Printed in the United States of America

1 3 5 7 9 10 8 6 4 2

To my husband Bill.

CHAPTER ONE

My neighbor Ruth liked change about as much as chili peppers in her morning oatmeal. "Why can't they dress like us?" she asked as a group of Somali women in hijabs walked past the porch. The women lived in a rented duplex, just three of a newly arrived group of refugees.

Their arrival had rocked the neighborhood, pitting people who embraced change against those who feared it. Personally, I liked the boldness of color in the women's clothing, the exotic sounds of their chatter. Clayton, Ohio, population 50,000, had gone global.

I pushed on my heel to keep the porch swing going. "What do you mean *like us*? Look at that guy," I said, gesturing at a man heading in our direction whistling a vigorous rendition of "The Bridge on the River Kwai." The song was as dated as his

FRENCH LEAVE

outfit. With thin legs, cargo shorts and a bush hat shading his weathered face, he was Crocodile Dundee hitting Medicare. "Is he like us?"

Ruth leaned forward for a look. "Maybe." She turned her attention to two other men, big guys with bodyguard builds and dark glasses. They weren't walking fast, but the way they moved suggested they were in a hurry.

"Them, I don't like the look of," Ruth decided, reverting to the Appalachian speech of her youth. Wraparound dark glasses and shaved heads weren't her style.

"Me neither."

The men passed the porch without sparing us a glance, too busy looking at Medicare Dundee.

He seemed to sense their interest and stopped whistling, tilting his hat in their direction. The three men paused to look at each other until the Whistler broke the staring match. He looked me straight in the eye before pivoting on his feet to dash up the nearest driveway.

"The man can run," Ruth said appreciatively.

The two others took off running and darted past the end the porch in hot pursuit. We got off the swing to watch them go.

Medicare Dundee slipped inside the open garage at the top of the driveway and disappeared from view.

What happened next caught us both by surprise. One of the men stopped abruptly, whipped out a gun and fired a shot into the garage.

Ruth cawed like a startled crow. Out on the street the Somali women fled, hijabs flying. When a second shot rang out, Ruth and I hit the deck. I landed on my knees, she lay on the ground, face down, arms spread like a penitent, bunched housecoat exposing skinny white calves.

Running footsteps thumped on the walk alongside the porch, the sound muting when they hit the grass. I crawled over to the railing. The guys with the gun were leaving.

Ruth struggled to her knees. "Get down, Claire! They'll see you."

But the men ran past, made a sharp right on Ferguson, the nearest street that bisected ours, and disappeared.

Minutes later two patrol cars from the Clayton PD screeched to a stop in the middle of the street. A couple of uniforms, guns drawn, ran up the driveway to the garage. One of them motioned for us to take cover as he went past. We moved to the house to watch the action from one of the side windows. After what seemed like a long wait, the two uniforms strolled back down the driveway. One spoke in the mike clipped to his shoulder, the other holstered his weapon. They parted at the bottom of the driveway and walked off in opposite directions.

Ruth offered to make coffee while we waited for further developments, but I declined and walked home in search of something stronger. I didn't understand violence. It scared me. I crossed the driveway that separated our yards and unlocked the side door. The tranquility of the sunny kitchen with its line of white cabinets and reflective surfaces steadied me. It was good to be in my own space.

I took the bottle of Chablis out of the refrigerator and poured some into a glass. Someone knocked on the door. It was one of the patrolmen I had seen earlier. Fresh-faced and eager, he couldn't have been more than twenty. His eyes zoomed in on the wine glass in my hand.

"Rough day," I said.

He nodded, his eyes non-committal, and explained that he was looking for witnesses to the shooting. "Did you see what happened?"

"Yes, I was on my neighbor's porch. We saw the two men run past."

He produced a notebook. "Can you describe them?"

"Both were white, tall with heavy builds. They had shaved heads, dark glasses and they were quick on their feet."

"What about the gun?"

"I was too far to see what kind it was, but I wouldn't have known anyway. I'm not familiar with guns."

"OK. Can you describe their clothing?"

I closed my eyes to recapture the image of the two men running past Ruth's porch. "The guy who fired the gun had on khaki shorts and a tight black top. The other one wore blue jeans."

The patrolman wrote the description down. "Any logo on the shirt? Any tattoos?" he asked, raising his eyes from the notebook.

"Not that I could see."

He nodded. "What about their voices? Any accent? Did they say anything?"

"Not a word. They went after the guy in the bush hat the minute he started running."

"OK. Did you know the man they were shooting at?"

I shook my head. "I've never seen him before. All three were strangers to the neighborhood."

When I asked about the fate of Medicare Dundee, the young cop shrugged. They hadn't seen him. He thanked me for my time and left, heading in the direction of Ruth's house.

I felt a connection to Medicare Dundee. I wasn't sure why. Maybe it was the unconventional wardrobe or the man's laid-back attitude. Or maybe it was the fact that he had looked at me.

Or had he been looking at Ruth?

I went back to the kitchen for a refill.

The shooting didn't make the news that night, but it did three days later when the garage where it happened was set on fire.

***

"I don't pay you to sleep, Claire," Sally said, catching me with my head on the computer keyboard, felled by an onslaught of purple prose. She rounded the desk to glare at me, her moon face with its explosion of red curls floating above the screen.

I sat up and stretched. "You don't pay me, Sally. You give me pocket change." I got pennies to her dollar for helping her write popular bodice rippers. That and inherited wealth put her on easy street, but that didn't make her generous.

FRANÇOISE BARTRAM

The phone rang. The man on the line asked for Sally, punctuating the request with a dry cough. "Howard," I said, handing her the receiver. The guy never talked to me, preferring to cough his way out of a conversation.

She took the phone. "Darliinng." She dragged the endearment, her voice intimate and full of promise.

I got up and went to the kitchen for coffee. The darling had gray hair and looked like a well-dressed broomstick. He was contrary to type. Sally liked her men brash and broad, twins to the ones who seduced the swooning heroines in her books. After five years on the job, I learned that a sexy boyfriend almost always inspired a bestseller. It wouldn't happen this time. The new man was about as exciting as mud.

I heard Sally clomp up the stairs to her bedroom on the second floor of the Georgian-style brick house where she grew up. It was an elegant, spacious structure with a central hall leading to high-ceilinged rooms: parlor, formal dining room and a sitting room she turned into a home office. The room had floor-to-ceiling built-in mahogany bookshelves, an Oriental rug and two reading chairs, a library table and the walnut pedestal desk that belonged to her father. Sally never worked there. I did when she needed me close at hand. Otherwise, it was kept at the ready in anticipation of a photoshoot featuring the famous author sitting behind the antique desk.

I was working at Sally's house that morning because the book in progress, *Mischief in Michigan*, had hit a roadblock. Sally blamed me for the problem, claiming I neglected her after adding two new authors to my short list of clients. I hadn't. She made the claim because she didn't want me working for anybody else. Sure enough, it wasn't long until she offered to promote me to office manager with a substantial raise if I agreed to work exclusively for her.

I could have used the money, but the promotion meant working nine to five under her supervision and facing a slew of additional tasks.

I told her I would think about it.

After she left I slipped on the headset and started the voice recorder to transcribe the latest chapter. Sally's talent was in storytelling. Each plot was based on the same premise: man meets woman, woman rejects man only to succumb in the last chapter. She provided the template; I described the action. The only scene I transcribed word-for-word was the ingénue's glorious surrender at the end of the book. Sally knew more about sex than a Victorian madam.

She'd had scores of lovers. I had never personally met Howard of the dry cough, but once watched him climb out of his late-model Mercedes as Sally stood on the front porch waiting for him to pick her up. Norma, Sally's housekeeper, and I watched from behind the living room drapes as Sally ran up to him, arms stretched out. He avoided what promised to be a passionate embrace by putting his hands on her shoulders and pecking her on the cheek.

"A peck on the cheek. Give me a break!" Norma muttered. "Look at Mr. Hot Pants here. He's been around for what—a month? And he didn't even make the moves on her."

I raised my eyebrows. "And you know this how?"

"Cleaning ladies know more than God, Claire. I just don't understand how he can resist the woman. I mean, look at those curves! She has a great body and perfect skin. What's not to like?"

Yes, Sally was sexy, but she also had the self-confidence and the arrogance of a diva. It took a special kind of man to appreciate her.

"There's got to be something wrong with the guy," Norma insisted. "If she doesn't turn him on, what does he want from her?"

I wondered about that myself.

CHAPTER TWO

Joe, longtime boyfriend and occasional irritant, spent five days on the road as a sales rep for an agricultural equipment company, and came home Fridays or Saturday mornings depending on his route.

A reluctant cook, I baulked at cooking dinner when he showed up. He didn't ask to be fed, but telegraphed the want by looking pointedly at the cold stove and making a show of searching the refrigerator for sustenance. Every week he sent the same message and every week I ignored it.

It wasn't that I didn't care for him. But sharing space wasn't easy, and neither was conforming to someone else's schedule. I was on my own five days a week. So was Joe. The weekend's twosome often turned into a tango of missteps.

Ruth knew of the Friday standoff. Fond of Joe and firm in her belief that a woman's duty was to feed her man, yet aware that I couldn't be persuaded to share her view, she solved the problem by inviting us for dinner most Fridays.

I came home from work that evening looking forward to starting the weekend without the usual crisis. I was always glad to get back to my own four walls. My house, a one-story frame with white clapboard and black shutters, was a far cry from Sally's brick Georgian. It was about four times smaller, including the breezeway that led to the two-car garage. Every house on my street was the same size. Cookie-cutter was anathema to some. Not to me. I found anonymity soothing.

Joe came home shortly after I did. We walked over to Ruth's house at five. The street had its Friday feel with smoke rising from backyard barbecues, kids shooting hoops, a dog barking at a Frisbee flying across a lawn. The elm on Ruth's front lawn dropped a flurry of yellow leaves as we walked past, possibly to warn us of his coming demise. In the early days of the development a double row shaded the street, but over the years disease and storms felled the majority, leaving a few to break the straight line of bungalows.

"Heard from Gladys lately?" I asked Ruth as we joined her

and her two boarders at the picnic table on the back porch. The August sun filtered through the vines clinging to the lattice, crisscrossing the oilcloth with shadows. We ate out in summer, in the kitchen when the weather turned cold. It was the most welcoming room in the house. In the seldom-used living room and pocket-sized dining room, furniture lined the walls like soldiers standing at attention. No pictures graced the walls, no knickknacks stood on lamp tables eternally free of dust. There was little softness in Ruth, and what there was stayed hidden.

She nodded in response to my question about Gladys and speared a pork chop from the platter to drop it on my plate. "She called this morning."

Cal, sitting across from me, went into a sulk. A railroader, he went up to Toledo every two days and back east to Clayton at the end of his run. As Ruth's first boarder—her second was Orville—Mr. Macho expected to be served first. Cal was a short man with a bull neck, wide shoulders and a vile temper. He was also the poster child for male chauvinists, anti-everything with liberated women at the top of his list.

"She complained about her grandson," Ruth said. "After the shooting and the garage fire he doesn't think she should live alone."

"Oh, please!" I lifted the bowl of green beans and passed it to Joe. "Gladys needs a watchdog like Bill Gates needs tech support. What about the shooting—any news?"

"Not that I know of."

Cal spoke up, "Gene who lives on Ferguson told me the shooters parked their pickup in front of his house."

Ruth snorted. Cal had been known to make stuff up.

"Honest! He was outside when the two guys came running back. They told him they were bail-bond agents after a guy who jumped bail. When he asked them about the shooting and if anybody was hurt, they said they were just warning shots."

Ruth jabbed a fork in his direction. "They lied! That man was hurt. Gladys found blood in her garage."

I'd found some on my back porch as well. Quite a puddle. I was horrified to think the guy had huddled there, scared and in pain.

"Did Gene tell the police?" Orville asked Cal.

"He said he did."

"Guns ought to be outlawed," Orville announced, reaching for the green beans. He counted twelve before sliding them on his plate. The man never forgot he was a bookkeeper. "Policemen should be the only ones authorized to carry," he said.

Cal, a lifelong member of the NRA, turned red. Joe heaved a sigh, anticipating a fight.

"Clayton sure isn't what it used to be," Ruth rushed to say, nipping the argument in the bud. "Too many strangers. We aren't safe anywhere. Last week two women got their purses stolen when they left the supermarket."

Orville said, "I blame fracking." He stabbed one green bean with his fork and held it aloft. "There's too much money floating around in town these days. It draws drug dealers. The man who got shot was probably moving into someone's territory."

Orville had a point about excess money. The discovery of Utica shale deposits in our area had changed Clayton from a backwater into an oil town. Big companies fought each other to acquire oil and natural gas leases. The influx of workers brought the kind of money Clayton hadn't seen in a long time, along with a surge in crime.

"He didn't look like a drug dealer," Ruth said.

"How would you know what a drug dealer looks like?" Orville argued. "They come in all shapes and sizes. But I'm thinking the two men who chased him could've been truck drivers. The tanker trucks carrying fracking water are all over the place. They'd make a good cover for someone dealing drugs."

"Naw, the drug dealers here, they're part of Latino gangs," Cal argued. "Everybody knows the majority of drugs come from Mexico."

"Can anybody come up with even more bad news?" I asked, irritated by the general gloom and doom. "Like maybe terrorists standing at our door wearing suicide vests?"

"Well?" Ruth said, rolling her eyes in the direction of the Somalis' duplex. The reference started me on a slow burn.

Joe elbowed me in the side. "Eat!" he said before I could climb on my own soapbox. "Food's getting cold."

I did as told. A breeze ruffled the vine leaves and fluttered the oilskin on the picnic table. Silence spread, occasionally broken by the click of Cal's false teeth and the hum of a bee threading its way through the morning glories.

I was still brooding over the pessimistic mood when I looked up from my plate to my garden stretching beyond the fence. A straw hat bobbed between two rows of tomato plants. It dipped, disappeared from view, only to pop up again. I dropped my fork and yelled, "Hey!"

The exclamation startled Orville who squealed; Cal clutched his chest; Joe choked on his iced tea.

"Lord have mercy!" Ruth said. "What got into you?"

I gestured at my backyard. "Someone's picking my tomatoes."

She got up so fast her chair fell back and crashed to the floor. Thin and wiry, Ruth had more leg power at seventy than people half her age. She was halfway to the gate giving access to my yard before I started moving. "Hurry up!" she yelled over her shoulder.

But the straw hat was gone by the time we reached the garden.

"We almost had him."

"No, we didn't," Ruth objected. "And he had a friend. There was a cap running alongside him. If you hadn't called out the way you did, we could've caught them."

And done what?

But I understood why she was upset. The vegetables from both gardens, mine and hers—hers covered her whole backyard—helped feed her household during the winter. A smaller crop would mean a bigger grocery bill. The rent she charged her boarders was barely enough to meet expenses, so I occasionally bought family packs of chicken or beef to stock her freezer. But my budget didn't often allow for such largess.

After dinner Joe and Orville played Scrabble while Cal looked over their shoulders clicking his teeth and making useless suggestions, and I walked down the street to the brick double where the Somalis lived to teach Faduma English.

A thirty-year-old widow, she came to the United States with her sister and her sister's family to escape the civil war that had ravaged Somalia since 1991. They had lived in Columbus for two years, working to repay the cost of their trip before moving to Clayton and the relative peace of small-town America.

I started tutoring Faduma on the advice of a friend who came to Ohio from Spain as a bride when her GI husband was transferred to the army post ten miles out of town. The post eventually closed, but all through the Vietnam War and beyond it served as an ammunition depot. "Imagine not being able to communicate," Carmen had told me. "To lack the words to ask for directions or tell a doctor what makes you sick. I was lucky, I spoke English fluently before I came to this country. But the Somalis are isolated here."

"Teacher, teacher!" Faduma called. She stood on the steps of the double waiting for me, a slim figure in an ankle-length, rust-colored skirt. A beige hijab framed her face, accentuating level brows, tea-colored skin and well-defined lips. She had beauty and talent. A seamstress back in her country, she made all her family's clothes.

We sat on the porch to work. The side of the duplex where she lived with her sister's family and an elderly aunt was crowded and noisy. The porch was quieter, though it didn't offer much privacy. Her small niece and nephew looked out the window at us, hands splayed, noses and foreheads squashed against the glass.

I turned away from their unrelenting curiosity to listen to Faduma's laborious reading of a sentence in her workbook. "Many beoble like dogs," she said.

I loved the sound of her English. While my American voice strung words, sliding them like beads on an abacus, Faduma threw hers on a trampoline. I corrected her pronunciation of the "p" in people, but minutes later she looked up to ask, "Who beoble with guns?"

I didn't bother correcting her. "I don't know. No one does, not even the police."

She wrinkled her forehead. "Why they come? No like Somalis?"

I remembered the two Somali women taking flight. Did they think they were the target? "They didn't come to shoot at the Somalis, Faduma. They were chasing a white man, an American."

Her hand tightened on the workbook. "White man? Kill him?"

The shooting had been my first brush with violence, but not for her. Her husband had been killed by insurgents. In Somalia death was a daily occurrence.

I shook my head. "No, he ran away."

Her face cleared and she pulled the exercise book closer. "Work now. More work."

Faduma had goals. In her culture, childless widows and unmarried women could be at the mercy of their families with little say over their future. Stuck between a macho brother-in-law and a demanding elder, she craved freedom. Moving to the States had given her a chance to gain independence. Her brother-in-law, the spokesperson for the family, knew only a few words of English and understood even less. Mastering the language would be an asset and Faduma knew it.

I envied her hope, the rainbow future of her life in the US. I have everything she wanted, I thought as I walked home an hour later. What had I done with it?

"Hey, Claire!"

Joleen, Pete Jensen's wife, was waving at me from the sidewalk. They lived across the street, two houses down from mine.

Inside their garage, Pete and a man I didn't know were bent over the engine compartment of Pete's lovingly restored '67 Mustang. People came from all over to look at it. He had a website and a blog. Joe was nuts about his Mazda Miata, but his degree of infatuation hadn't reached this level. Not yet anyway.

Joleen crossed the street. "This thing flew off your mailbox and landed on our lawn," she said, handing me a folded square of yellow paper. "It was stuck behind the flag."

I took it and put it in my pocket. "Thanks. One of Pete's buddies?" I asked, looking in the direction of their garage. "Or is it one of yours from the diner?" Joleen worked in a diner just off the freeway. She got big tips from truckers who liked her aging Barbie looks and easy disposition.

"Are you kidding? I'd never give those jokers my address. The guy saw Pete's website and came out to look at the car." She rolled eyes rimmed with mascara. She had just come from work and her pink nylon uniform smelled of fried food. "He waited at the curb until Pete showed up. The Mustang people drive me nuts, particularly the ones old enough to remember the car when it was new. If we had five bucks for every old guy who came by to reminisce, I'd be rich by now."

"Get a tip jar."

"Good idea."

After she left I pulled the paper from my pocket. Big rambling letters scrawled across half a page torn off a yellow legal pad to ask something I didn't understand.

Ou té, blanc?

What the heck did that mean? I couldn't even identify the language. Blanc was white in French. I knew that much from wine bottles. But the first two words had me stumped. A stick man drawn in pencil strutted to the left of a string of numbers, seven in all. A phone number? The drawing was crude enough to be the work of a child. I looked up to find my neighbor Marlene's oldest leaning against his bicycle watching me. When he saw me looking, he jumped on his bike and pedaled away.

Was he the author of the message? He could be, but how would he know French? He was six, way too young to read wine bottles. I put the paper back in my pocket and went up the driveway to see if Joe was home.

CHAPTER THREE

The temperature shot up to ninety over the weekend. After making a quick trip to the grocery store on Saturday morning, I did laundry and a spot of cleaning to fool Ruth into thinking the place was clean. She had been known to let herself in while I was at work to check my housekeeping. She's had a key ever since her brother Raymond built the house forty years ago for Gin, my grandmother.

When she was thirty-five years old, Gin, short for Virginia, left the small West Virginia mining town where she was born to settle in southeast Ohio near Ruth and Raymond, her lifelong friends. She went north with $5,000 in cash and her sixteen-year-old daughter, Cora, who was three months pregnant. The money bought their silence. The boyfriend's father, a prominent judge, made it clear he wasn't interested in raising a bastard grandchild. After finding a job in a supermarket, Gin used the sin money as a down payment on her house and helped raise my sister Mirabelle until my mother met and married my dad. My parents divorced when I was five and Gin took a turn raising me. Cora didn't have much luck with men, but the third time was charmed. The last one, Richard, an attorney, had stuck around.

I spent a quiet afternoon in my semi-clean house bracing for Sunday's ordeal, a family gathering at Cora and Richard's house.

Cora was the sandpaper of my life. She resented me for being the spitting image of my father, the bane of her life, and I resented her for resenting me.

***

My mother and stepfather lived in a custom-built ranch that overlooked the river. A driveway cut across the carefully tended lawn to the three-car garage at the side. My sister Mirabelle's Chevy was parked on the pad near the double front door. Joe stopped his beloved Miata beside it, leaving enough space between the two cars to safeguard its fenders. We had drinks in the sunroom overlooking the great expanse of lawn that sloped down to the riverbank. I sat down on a chair facing the river and half closed my eyes against the glitter of sun on water, imagining drinking my morning coffee with a view.

Cora and Richard had just returned from a cruise to the Bahamas. During the main course, a rotisserie chicken and canned peas, Cora regaled her captive audience with a day-to-day account of their life on board. Richard, for his part, said nothing, but had the good sense to open an outstanding South African Merlot. The wine reduced Cora's monologue to a buzz.

"We ran into Sheriff Gunner on the way back," she said, smoothing her hair in an unconscious gesture.

Mirabelle aimed an amused look in my direction. Cora always had an eye for good-looking men. Her present husband didn't fall into that category. His face, with a wide soft nose, large upper lip and brown eyes, would have looked fine on a camel. But he had good bearing, impeccable manners and an expensive tailor, attributes that made him attractive enough for a lifelong union. I glanced at him to see if he was aware of his wife's interest. Eyes half closed, he was sipping the Merlot with the reverence of a wine devotee. He either didn't care or was lost in the moment.

Mirabelle switched her gaze from me to Joe and let it linger. Cora wasn't the only family member with an eye for good-looking men. I could have told her she was wasting her time with Joe. He had given his heart to a beauty named Miata, enamored of her leather bucket seats and turbocharged engine. *Mirabelle's* bucket was starting to slip a little, I noticed. But then she was six years older than I, well into her thirties. She had been steadily and irritatingly gorgeous since hitting puberty. A tall, blue-eyed blonde wasn't a comfortable sibling for a skinny, brown-haired girl. I was always jealous of her, though not so much these days. Aging was a great equalizer.

I took another sip of wine to mute Cora. She was praising our newly elected sheriff, a man who believed in sealed borders and a valid driver's license in every hip pocket. "Sheriff Gunner was on his way from a sheriffs' convention in Arizona."

I squirmed, anticipating a long lavish of praise for her favorite lawman.

Sensing my irritation, Joe put his hand on my leg to keep me quiet. No good came from criticizing Cora's pet sheriff. She firmly believed a ham-fisted policy was the only way to protect us from terrorists and drug dealers. Get them before they got us was her motto.

"Something has to be done," she insisted. "There are so

many strangers in town that I feel as if I live in a foreign country. What about the families on your street, Claire? Are they here legally?"

"They are refugees, Cora," Richard informed, emerging from his wine moment. "They were granted visas because the violence in their country made it impossible for them to live there."

"If you say so, dear. But who can tell the difference between the legals and those who aren't? Sheriff Gunner is right. It makes perfect sense for authorities to arrest suspicious individuals."

"Easy to say knowing you'll never be one of them."

Joe stepped on my foot to shut me up. "Hopefully none of us will."

Cora smiled at him. Joe was her idea of the perfect male—handsome, smart, and unfailingly courteous. Rich would have been even better, but she didn't think I had the right kind of looks to catch a man of wealth.

He smiled back. "I understand your concern about strangers, Cora. But I strongly believe most of the newcomers in town are here to work. Only a few are illegal."

"More than a few," Cora argued. "But perhaps not as many as there used to be. Sheriff Gunner says that the E-Verify system that allows employers to check the status of new employees is somewhat effective and Bernard told me—" She stopped abruptly.

We all looked at her. Bernard was my biological father and her first husband. As far as I knew no one had seen him or heard from him in twenty-five years.

"Bernard says what?" I prompted when silence lengthened.

Cora didn't answer. Richard got up and reached for the bottle. "More wine, anyone?"

Cora took advantage of the diversion to leave the room, and I didn't have a chance to ask the question again.

***

Monday found me back at work in Sally's fancy office. Howard the broomstick called in the middle of a heated discussion over the antics of the principal character. I left the room to give Sally privacy.

In the kitchen I took a mug from the cupboard and filled it with coffee. "I don't know about that, Howard," I heard Sally say. "Maybe later in our relationship..." She left the sentence hanging.

Norma would have cocked her ear at that. I'd never known Sally to play hard to get.

FRENCH LEAVE

"Well." She paused. "I've had the same man for years."

My ears twitched. We weren't talking monogamy here. Her personal Rolodex was filled to capacity.

"Of course, I appreciate the offer, Howard. I'm certain you would do as well if not better, but I would rather wait until we are more…committed, shall we say?"

He must have agreed because the conversation ended with Sally saying she was glad he understood. She left the office and went upstairs.

I was in the kitchen again refilling the mug when she came back down, car keys in hand. She was wearing a plain beige dress. Plain didn't suit her. She loved bright colors, packing her curves into hot pink spandex for the gym, a gold lamé gown for a cocktail party, swaggering out in an orange T-shirt over green toreador pants for a hot date. Beige's new standing in her color scale left me puzzled.

"What?" she asked, catching me staring.

"I didn't think you liked beige."

"I don't but Howard says it's becoming." She cocked an eye at me waiting for a response.

"Well?" she said when I hesitated.

"I'd take a couple of iron pills if I were you. It makes you look anemic."

She left in a huff.

***

Marlene, my neighbor from across the street, watched me from behind her front window as I walked down the driveway to check the mail. We had known each other since we were kids, but had a falling out in the eighth grade over a boy whose name I couldn't even remember. She grew curves early, tough competition for skinny girls who barely filled their A-cup bras. Now married with three kids, she couldn't stand to see me living with a guy handsome enough to appear on TV in *The Bachelor*.

A mammoth SUV coasted to a stop in front of Pete Jensen's house. Another Mustang fan. I checked the mailbox and carried the mail back up the driveway. Ruth ambushed me on the breezeway and followed me to the house in the hope of caging a cup of French roast, the kind Joe favored. Ruth loved it and looked upon our house as the nearest and cheapest Starbucks.

A fold of yellow paper, tucked between the frame and the lock, fell to the ground when I opened the screen door.

Ruth picked it up to look at it. "Doesn't make a bit of sense."

FRENCH LEAVE

I took it from her. The message written across the page was similar to the one Joleen had found a few days earlier. Another giant question mark punctuated words that again meant nothing to me.

Qui sé la femme, blanc?

Blanc again. A stick woman stood hands on hips beside a string of numbers. Corkscrew curls sprang from her balloon head.

"That's you, ain't it?" Ruth said. "Look at that hair."

The hair matched mine and the hands on hips pretty much summed up my personality.

"Ain't 'femme' woman in French?" Ruth went on. "I know that from crossword puzzles."

"It is, now that you mention it."

"What's 'blanc' then? You should know, your dad being half French."

"Which makes me a quarter French, not enough to be a native." He might have taught me the language if he hadn't scooted when I was five, disowned by Cora and fired from his teaching job at the local high school. "It means white."

"White woman?"

"I don't think so," I said, taking a closer look. "There is a comma between white and woman."

I unlocked the door and Ruth scooted to the island to hoist her skinny rump onto one of the stools. She smoothed the scrap of paper with the heel of her hand. "What're those numbers at the bottom? A phone number maybe?"

"Looks like it." I set my purse down on the counter and searched the silverware drawer for the scoop to measure coffee.

"You ought to call it."

I looked over my shoulder. "Why?"

"Whoever left the message is telling you something."

"Then he should say so in English. And if he doesn't speak English, what's the point in calling?"

She sighed. So did I when I opened the box that held the coffee filters and found it empty. Flour and sugar canisters, salt cellars, pepper grinders, Joe's consistent failure to replace what he used drove me crazy. I dropped the box in the recycling bin and ran down to the basement for another. When I came back Ruth was hanging up the phone. "They got an answering machine with a computer voice," she said, trotting back to the island without looking at me. She knew she had done wrong.

"I didn't leave a message," she said in her own defense, raising her voice to be heard over the buzz of the coffee grinder.

I ignored her. "How's Gladys doing?" I asked, scooping coffee grounds into the filter. "I haven't seen her since the garage burned down."

"She got herself a lawyer."

I plugged in the coffee pot and turned around to look at her. "What for?"

"The firemen found traces of accelerant on boxes stacked inside the garage. The insurance company wants an investigation."

Behind me the coffee pot spluttered, diffusing the rich aroma of French roast. "Do they think she's the one who set the fire? Why? It's not like she's in dire need of money. Didn't you tell me she paid cash for her house after selling the old one in Cleveland?"

"I did. But I don't think it's got to do with money. The insurance company's looking into the shooting. They're thinking the men who ran up her driveway might've known her, as well as the man who got away."

I filled two mugs and carried them to the island. "That's a stretch. It's more likely the man in the hat just ran up the nearest driveway. Depending on where he was he could just as easily have run up mine, or yours."

"That's the way I see it," Ruth said.

I replayed the scene in my head: the man looking in our direction, turning on his feet and sprinting up the driveway. But where did he go after that? The cops searched the garage and didn't find him. He left a considerable amount of blood on my porch, so he may have been there a while. Could he have been waiting for the police to leave so he could go to Gladys's?

It was a possibility, but I had trouble connecting the Whistler with the fifty-something black grandmother who cleaned teeth for a living. I supposed they could've known each other back in Cleveland before Gladys moved to Clayton to follow her boss, a dentist who specialized in pediatrics and decided to set up shop in a small town after selling his large Cleveland practice.

What did the Whistler and Gladys have in common? Not age. Gladys was younger. I didn't know about background, but they were poles apart in personality. She was focused and decisive. He appeared to be just the opposite, somewhat goofy, given the wardrobe and happy-go-lucky style.

So why would he come to see her? Did it have to do with drugs? Gladys worked for a dentist, which meant she possibly had access to some. Possibly, but I didn't see her taking advantage of it.

"Sounds like the insurance company is looking for a reason to avoid paying for the garage," I said. "I hope they change their mind."

"Good thing she's got a lawyer," Ruth said, holding out her mug for more coffee.

CHAPTER FOUR

I went out to water the garden after Ruth left. The squeak of the outdoor faucet took me back to summer mornings when Gin rose at dawn to water the tomato plants, which occupied half of the vegetable garden at the back of the lot. She would fill the bucket and carry it down to the garden plot, one shoulder pulled down by the weight, the soles of her sandals slapping her bare heels. I had traipsed behind her barefoot, the dust of the lane as soft as talcum powder between my toes. Water splashed over the rim to puddle on the lane. The smell of wet earth carried me back to the happiness of those days: the satisfaction of being the center of Gin's world, the joy of being loved.

Loud barking jarred me back to the present.

"Hush, Cleo, it's only Claire," Mrs. Paolini told the spaniel jumping against the back fence. The dog was obnoxious. Mrs.

Paolini spoiled it the way she had spoiled her kids, three girls close to my age who currently lived out of state and pretty much ignored her. They bullied me when we were in grade school. "How are you, dear?" their mother asked, as she approached the chain-link fence for a chat. "You haven't worked in your garden lately, but I saw your helpers."

I approached the fence. "What helpers?"

"The two young men I saw on your side of the fence—Somalis?" she asked with a hint of disapproval. She belonged to the anti-refugee crowd.

"I wouldn't think so. When did you see them?"

"Off and on. Maybe they were just taking a shortcut to get to the park."

"That must be it." The park on the next street with basketball courts and a soccer field drew neighborhood kids all through the summer. "Thanks for telling me. I'll ask Ruth to watch for them. I don't like the idea of people on my turf."

***

I was scheduled to work at Sally's the next day. In spite of our combined efforts, *Mischief in Michigan* was going nowhere. The original plot was sound. Felicia, a nineteenth century penniless orphan, had traveled to the wilds of Michigan's Upper Peninsula to work as a governess for the children of a widower, only to discover that her future employer was no widower but a man running a bawdy house in a logging camp. The book had all the elements of the classic bodice ripper: beautiful young girl faces a predator, fights for her virtue and is rescued by a dashing stranger who is handsomely rewarded in the end. But Sally for some reason had failed to give the girl the rebellious nature of her typical heroine and turned her into a spineless idiot. And her suitor's puritan bend—he was a preacher—made the long-awaited fireworks at the end of the book improbable.

We were bound and determined to reverse course and infuse some life into the characters. However, the scheduled meeting never happened. Sally called to cancel.

The morning now stretched in front of me. I had work to do, but nothing that couldn't be put off and I didn't feel like staying home. Grocery shopping and a trip to the hardware store for pre-mixed spackle to fill cracks in the kitchen ceiling took me to lunchtime. At noon I drove to an Italian deli to pick up a sub and took it to Lisa's studio.

My friend Lisa was a potter. We had known each other since

first grade. She rented space in an old brick warehouse, part of the downtown wasteland that stretched along the river. Before the advent of PVC, industrial potteries made drain tiles with the local clay and shipped them by barge across Ohio and to neighboring states. After they closed, the plants were left to decay. Now the century-old buildings overlooking the river attracted artists and artisans drawn by the cheap rent and airy quarters. Lisa shared the warehouse with two sculptors, a weaver, and a man who painted pictures of rose-covered English cottages and seascapes to sell at flea markets.

Lisa was eating lunch when I entered her second-floor studio. The space was cavernous, lit by three large metal-framed windows that took up the length of the outside wall. The potter's wheel stood in the center of the room. Metal shelving lined three sides shouldering a sink on an inside wall and a wooden workbench close to a window. The place was shabby but functional, soothing in its simplicity.

Except for her hands, pink from a recent scrubbing, Lisa was dotted with clay. She sat at the bench facing a plate, one of hers glazed in light yellow with bands of dark blue running along the rim. It held a cheese and veggie wrap neatly cut in half.

"Ugh! Salami," she said when I approached with my Italian sub. "It's not for you."

"I should hope not." Lisa didn't eat meat. She took a small bite of veggie wrap, crunching down on lettuce and carrots. A carrot shred caught in her teeth. "What brings you? I hope you don't stay too long. I'm busy."

"You aren't busy. You're eating."

"I'm busy eating and not in the mood for one of your mini-dramas, Claire. There must be one or you wouldn't be here in the middle of the day. What did Sally do now? Or is it Joe?" Lisa frowned. "No, it can't be Joe because he's gone during the week. So it has to be Sally. Is it the office manager idea? I told you not to go for it."

There was little Lisa and I didn't know about each other. We had been friends since first grade and swore to stay close, all the way through Medicare, bunions and thinning hair. But there were times when I wished she didn't know me so well.

"She planned this, you know," Lisa continued, brushing lettuce shreds off her clay-encrusted front. "She's using the fancy office as a lure. Before you know it, not only will you be answering her mail and making her appointments, but you'll be picking up her dry cleaning and weeding the backyard. The woman's a user. She knew she had you hooked with those built-in bookshelves and the fancy leather chair."

I bit into the sub. The leather chair was new, bought to reel me in. It was impressive, and for a while had me considering wearing a power suit and high heels. As for the dry cleaning, it was right on. I had once dropped a load on my way home and Sally had called the next morning before I left for work asking me to stop by a mini-mart to buy milk for her breakfast.

"I haven't given Sally an answer yet, Lisa. I'm letting her stew."

"Nothing wrong with wanting a leather chair, Claire," Lisa continued as if I hadn't spoken. "But it should be yours and it should be in your own office. There's an empty room on the ground floor right under this studio. It's small but you don't need a big room to work in. Why don't you call the landlord and ask about it? Forget Sally. Get your own place and put the word out that you're available. People in the business are already familiar with your name. Before long you'll make more money than she ever gave you."

"I wish." It wouldn't be the first time I contemplated leaving Sally. The idea was exhilarating, like speeding down a road in a convertible with the top down. It gave me a sense of freedom, of space.

"Well?" Lisa asked, her voice sharp.

The building had a good feel. But I would have to pay rent and sign a lease. "I don't know, Lisa. It's a big step."

"So?"

"The idea of paying rent scares me."

"You have to spend money to make money. It took me a while to make a profit here, but I don't regret it. I tapped into my savings. You can do the same. Didn't your grandmother leave you money?"

"She did, but not a lot. And I have bills to pay. I mortgaged the house when I inherited my half from her."

"Use what you can spare. Think of the office as an investment. It worked for me."

True. But it was a gamble. It had taken her several years to find outlets for her ware. How long would it be before I earned enough to support myself? For the last five years Sally had been my main source of income. "How much is the rent?"

"I'll find out."

When lunch was over, I went home. Ruth must have been

watching for me because she called as soon as I got home. "I saw you pull in. There's a package for you on my front porch."

Package was a misnomer. The thing propped against the wall of her front porch was a bulging three-by-four-feet box sloppily tied with string. "What makes you think it's mine?" I asked, looking at the side that faced me. "There's no label."

"It was dropped at your door. That makes it yours. Plus it's got your address written on the side facing the wall."

I turned the carton around. "Just the address. No name. That's weird. Why did you move it?"

"I was afraid someone would steal it. Cal helped me carry it to the porch, but he's gone to work so it's just you and me now."

We grunted as we lifted the box by the string that bound it. It was heavy. The string cut into our hands so we set the carton down and dragged it across the driveway to the breezeway and on to the kitchen. I opened the door and we slid it inside.

"Do you really think it's mine? My name isn't on it. And the mailman couldn't have delivered this, or any of the carriers. There's no barcode."

"Can't tell you what I don't know," Ruth retorted. "Are you going to open it?"

I thought about it. "No, I'm pretty sure the box isn't mine. But it may be for Joe. He has a buddy who works in a junkyard and gets him parts for the Mazda. It's possible the guy dropped some stuff off thinking Joe was home."

Ruth left in a huff. No doubt she had hoped to see what was inside the box, but oily, messy parts fresh from the junkyard would have sent her scurrying for a pail of soapy water and a brush.

I pushed the box across the hall all the way into the spare room closet, the one that was assigned to Joe. He would deal with it when he came home.

CHAPTER FIVE

While I was gone, Sally had called my home phone to reschedule our meeting. She said she'd see me in the morning.

Lisa called around five. "I just talked to the guy who manages our building. He said a weaver gave a deposit to rent the downstairs workshop I mentioned. But he may have something else for you. I'll keep you posted."

I was disappointed, a sign that the idea of getting my own office was taking hold.

***

The next day, a Thursday, was cleaning day. Norma arrived bright and early pulling her vacuum, a monstrous thing made of spare parts cobbled, I suspected, from industrial machines. It roared like a Tyrannosaurus rex and worked on carpet fibers like a hyena worked on a carcass. Everything Norma used was on steroids. She loved power.

I parked in the back and opened the kitchen door. Norma heard me and looked in from the hallway. "No need to come in. You're going back out. Sal's gone. She says for you to pick up a dress she left at the cleaner. She has a party tonight."

I looked at her across the expanse of recently washed tiles. In blue scrubs with booties on her feet and gloves on her hands she looked like a scrub nurse. Except that the gloves were yellow rubber and big enough to fit an ape, and a bandanna covered her hair instead of a disposable cap.

"That's the second time she's stood me up. Tell her to get her own damn dress." Maybe I could do her nails, too.

Norma took off one glove and nudged her glasses with a large thumb. "OK. I take it the book isn't going well?"

"You got that right. If this keeps going your check may be late."

Norma nodded and went back to work. She didn't look overly concerned, but then she had no reason to be. If Sally ever was short of money—which was unlikely—she would fire me long before letting go of Norma. I doubted Sally knew which end of a vacuum cleaner was up.

Faced with another morning of idleness, I decided to drive to the bookstore where Carmen, the friend who talked me into tutoring Faduma, worked. Curb parking wasn't available so I drove around back to the alley and left the Ford between Carmen's Honda and the shop's white van. Sam, the owner, sat behind the cash register eating Oreos and reading a Sue Grafton. He acknowledged my presence by raising a hefty hand in greeting without lifting his eyes off the page. Sam was equally addicted to Oreos and mysteries. He had read hundreds of books, remembered every author's name, every title. His memory was prodigious. Too bad his brain was the only part of his body he exercised. The rest of his substantial six-foot frame overlapped the padded stool behind the cash register.

Carmen managed the place around him and in spite of him. For the past twenty years Sam had been too busy feeling sorry for himself to do anything constructive. He had never recovered from the humiliation of his wife's fling with the young Hispanic illegal who took care of their yard. The ensuing divorce left him with his business and a vacation home on the Ohio River, while the errant wife, who accused Sam of being emotionally abusive, walked away with half of the couple's savings and the family home.

"Carmen's in the stock room," Sam informed me as I walked past. "She'll be out in a minute."

"OK, thanks." I went to the romance aisle to see if the last of Sally's newly released books was on the shelf. I didn't find it but killed time by checking fellow authors—it didn't hurt to keep up with the competition—and went down the mystery aisle next. Carmen came out of the stock room, keys in hand, just as I headed for the cash register with an Elizabeth George. Carmen was wearing a dark blue linen dress that set off her silver hair.

"And there she is, all dressed up to meet her old foreign biddies for the second time this week," Sam murmured as she made her way to the door. "Leaving me to do all the work."

Carmen stopped. She had good ears. "What work is that, Sam? Unless you mean working your way through a case of Oreos. Did you come for me, Claire?" she asked, turning to address me. "I'm afraid I can't stay."

"That's OK, I'm just shopping."

"Good. How is your Somali student doing?"

"Fine."

Carmen gave a distracted nod and left. A native of Spain but fluent in English, she had spent years after coming to Clayton teaching English to refugees and women like herself who moved to the States after marrying a GI.

Sam took the Elizabeth George out of my hand to ring it up. "Your esteemed boss came by this morning."

"Esteemed" came with a heavy dose of sarcasm. Sam's reverence for Sally equaled the respect he gave his ex-wife. I figured it was because she made more money writing "trash" than he earned selling it.

"She came in company of her latest—a man foolish enough to believe she has a brain. He talked her into buying a set of Shakespeare plays."

"*Shakespeare plays*?" I had never known Sally to read anything other than romances.

"Nicely bound, three hundred bucks' worth. The man did me a favor. But I fear she wasted her money."

"She can afford it."

Sam had a reason to despise women, two reasons really. Not only had his wife fleeced him, but he had lost the bulk of his inheritance years earlier to a woman his father married late in life.

Carmen, the only woman he now tolerated, nurtured his bitterness by listening to his rants and condemning his abusers. She mothered him, as she had mothered her late husband, a chronic complainer.

FRANÇOISE BARTRAM

As I went back to the car I wondered why Carmen hadn't asked me to come to her meeting. I was an honorary member of her group of aging foreign brides, spouses and widows of GIs once stationed at the closed army post. Carmen, whose father was English by birth, had tutored the newcomers until my father, a French teacher at the local high school, took over the job. I was three or four then and I tagged along because at the time I was pretty much tied to his coattails. The women who stayed in the area kept in touch and met for lunch once a month.

Had I been invited to join the Foreign Legion, as I named the group, I would have feasted on quesadillas, chow mein or sauerbraten depending on whose turn it was to host the luncheon. When I was small, the women took turns feeding me. Austrian pastries, chimichangas, rice balls with bits of fish, I ate anything they put into my mouth. After my father left, I didn't see the women for six or seven months, but the feedings started again when at their request, Gin agreed to drop me off whenever they met. The food was great, but I liked the attention even more. Manuela the Salvadoran sat me on her lap and told me stories. Rose the Taiwanese showed me how to use chopsticks and write Chinese characters. Helga the Austrian taught me words in German. There were many others, but those three were my favorites.

Thinking about food made me hungry. I went home. Surprisingly, Joe's company truck was parked at the curb. It was Thursday, early for him to be done with his route. On the street the same SUV I had seen parked beside Pete's house cruised past to park just beyond the Somalis' duplex.

The kitchen smelled of Chinese food. Three cartons stood in line on the counter. I dropped my purse on the floor and rummaged for a fork in the silverware drawer. The first carton held fried rice, the next sesame chicken and the third shrimps with snow peas—my all-time favorite.

"Claire," Joe bellowed from deep inside the house. "I know you're here. Leave the food alone."

The man had ears like a cat. I speared a shrimp and popped it in my mouth. "Quit it!" he said when he came in. "The last time I got shrimps with snow peas you ate all the shrimps. Whose stuff is that?" he asked, holding out a pair of worn jeans in one hand and a faded T-shirt in the other.

I stopped chewing. "I don't know. Where did you get it?"

"In the guest room closet where I keep my stuff." The "stuff" in question included Playboy centerfolds pinned to the walls displaying bosoms big enough to keep the house afloat in a tsunami. "There's a box in there."

"Oh, *that* box! Isn't it car parts for the Mazda?"

"Obviously not."

"I thought one of your car buddies left it for you. You say it's full of clothes?"

"Look for yourself."

I followed him to the guest room. The carton was filled with used clothing, jeans, T-shirts, shoes and coats. Half of the jeans were thirty-four, the others smaller around the waist and shorter in the leg.

"What do you think that's about?" Joe asked holding two pairs of boots, one a size nine, the other a thirteen. "Everything in there comes in two sizes."

"Wardrobe for Junior and Pa?" I quipped, taking out a man's crumpled medium-size coat with frayed cuffs. I shook it to get rid of the wrinkles. Something fell out of the pocket and landed on the floor.

It was a bundle of twenty-dollar bills secured with a rubber band. Money, and lots of it.

CHAPTER SIX

Joe counted $800 in fives, tens and twenties. "The plot thickens."

"But not in a good way."

"Are you sure you don't know who dropped it off?" When I shrugged, he asked, "What about Ruth?"

"She doesn't know either. Cal says the box wasn't there when he read the paper on the porch yesterday morning. Ruth was in the basement canning. She saw it when she came up for lunch."

Joe looked at the money in his hands. "What do you want me to do with it?"

"Put it back where we found it. Maybe whoever left it will realize he left it in the wrong place and come back to claim it."

He handed me the stash. "Sounds like a plan. But if no one claims it in a couple of weeks, it's ours. Come and eat. The food is getting cold."

"I'll be there in a minute." I put the money back in the coat pocket, the clothes in the box, and pulled the flaps down to tape them shut. It wasn't that I didn't trust Joe, but once in a while he felt obligated to bail out his Aunt Lou, a woman who believed the path to Nirvana crossed every bingo hall within a fifty-mile radius of her house. When she ran short she begged her favorite nephew for a loan to tide her over until her next Social Security check. I slid the box inside the closet and hurried back to the kitchen. But it was too late. Joe had eaten all the shrimps.

***

The temperature was close to eighty when I left the next morning. Sally had called to say she would be home for sure. As I went up the freeway ramp the Oldies station interrupted the Beatles for a traffic report. A three-car wreck west of the Woodland Avenue entrance had traffic blocked over two miles. At the top a semi let me in and I slipped between it and a van loaded with kids. We crept at five miles an hour until we reached the bottleneck. I shut off the engine and used my cell phone to let Sally know I was running late.

It was hot. I opened the windows and changed the station to classical. I liked rock, but classical music kept me calm when I was stuck in traffic. Hard telling where I acquired a taste for it. Gin

FRENCH LEAVE

listened to tunes from the fifties; Ruth liked the fiddle; Cora wasn't musical at all and Mirabelle went for whatever was popular.

Heat shimmered on the roof of the van in front of me. The children inside hung out the open side windows making faces at me, ignoring the mother yelling at them to get back in their seats. Adding to the aggravation, gas fumes wafted from the diesel engine of the black Dodge pickup alongside my car. I rolled my window part of the way up as a hint, and the men in the cab wearing identical caps and wraparound glasses turned to look at me.

The van in front of me started moving. I fired the engine and shifted into drive. The line of traffic crawled at ten miles an hour all the way to the wreck site, an SUV lying on its side in the fast lane. Two passenger cars, front ends crumpled, windshields shattered, had plowed furrows into the grass in the median. A single high-heel shoe, a young-woman type of shoe, lay on its side in the grass. There was no sign of the other.

I was still thinking about the wearer's fate when I rolled to a stop in front of Sally's house. A sedan was parked in her driveway, an old one the size of a boat with white sidewalls and polished flanks, the kind sold in the eighties when engines were V8s and gasoline was cheap. I left the Ford at the curb and walked up the driveway.

The sedan was a Chrysler, same color and make as Orville's baby, his first and only car.

"What are you doing here, Claire?" Ruth's star boarder asked as he walked out the front door carrying a carton of files.

"I work here, Orville, as you well know." He looked distracted. "You came to see Sally?"

"Yes, she asked for me."

I was surprised. Even though he and Sally had met at a barbecue I hosted two years back, I didn't think she remembered him. "To do what?"

He blushed, breaking into a little laugh that ended in a squeak. "I work for her too now. She asked me to be her bookkeeper."

"Really?" Orville had retired from bookkeeping two years back, but kept a few clients, partly to supplement his income, partly to feed his addiction to numbers. I didn't know he was taking on new ones. And Sally had a bookkeeper anyway. "What happened to Roger Watkins?"

Orville flexed stork-like legs and shifted the carton in his arms. "He moved to Florida. Sally, Ms. Bloomfield, said he left suddenly and left her in the lurch so she asked me to take over."

A fresh blush washed over Orville's narrow face. He wasn't used to dealing with women like Sally who aimed pheromones at every man within spitting distance. An only child, he had lived with his mother for most of his adult life until her death. A week after the funeral he moved into Ruth's house.

He nodded at me before walking to his car with the carton. He moved in slow motion, every step, every gesture precise. At the car he set the files down on the ground to unlock the car door, opened the door, released the trunk, picked up the files again and carried them around to place the carton exactly in the middle of the trunk. Watching him was rewarding—the choreography flowing like a Bach piece—but exasperating as well. I itched to push the fast-forward button.

He finally got into the Chrysler and left. I turned and went in the house. Sally stood at the foot of the stairs, packed in spandex, every voluptuous curve restrained in shimmering fuchsia. No wonder Orville had lost his head.

She shook her finger at me. "Punctuality, Claire, punctuality! You're late."

"You don't pay me enough for punctuality, Sally. Anyway, I

left a message on your phone telling you I would be late. There was a wreck on the freeway."

"That's no excuse."

"It is for me, especially after you stood me up twice. Orville tells me Roger Watkins moved to Florida. Did he retire?"

Sally rolled her eyes. "The man is a disgrace! He left a message telling me he was moving to Florida and explained that since he couldn't find me home he left all my files in the garage."

"Did he say why he was leaving?"

"No. He didn't bother with an apology either. I immediately thought of Orville."

"That was nice of you, but go easy on him, OK?"

Sally put a hand on her hip. "Meaning what?"

"Meaning you shouldn't pull your 'you Tarzan, me Jane' act on him. Orville eats, sleeps and dreams numbers. That's all he understands. He won't know what to do if you flutter your eyelashes at him."

"Flutter my eyelashes? You make the most absurd statements, Claire. I do no such thing. And I would never, even in my wildest imagination, compare Orville to Tarzan. The man is built like a stick."

I pushed away an image of Orville in a loin cloth, all legs and no butt. "So you ready to work today?"

She frowned. "I was planning on going to the gym."

I had been deluding myself thinking we were going to get the job done. "You stood me up twice already, Sally. Are we going to finish the book or not? I'm sick of fiddling with it and going nowhere."

She clicked her tongue. "And you think I'm not? I worked half the night to make up for my absence yesterday. Take a look at what I've done and tell me what you think."

She scurried out and I didn't see her for the rest of the day. After I listened to the chapters she had left I understood why she made herself scarce. The work she had done during the night was no better than the stuff she'd given me earlier. I debated calling her to complain, but in the end took the path of least resistance and wrote what she had left me. If the editor rejected the book—and this seemed likely—it would be on her.

I quit work in mid-afternoon. Storm clouds were rising to the west. The heat was oppressive. The fleet of trucks and beat-up subcompacts that ferried the hired help to jobs in Sally's upscale neighborhood was gone. Only a black pickup remained, parked at the curb in front of a sprawling Victorian half a block away. It moved away as I got into my car.

By the time I stopped by an Italian deli to buy cold cuts for the weekend, the clouds were overhead, low and menacing, smothering traffic sounds. The squish of melting tar under my heels and the crinkle of the plastic bag swinging from my arm were loud in comparison. The parking lot was empty except for my car and a Dodge pickup with its engine running. The heat from the engine compartment scorched my legs as I went past. Lightning sizzled. The ensuing roll of thunder presaged a downpour.

I ran to the car but the rain held back. The pickup pulled out of the parking lot after I did. A block later I spotted a solitary man standing at the bus stop, hunched against the rising wind. It was Ibrahim, a neighbor of Faduma's who lived in the other side of the duplex with his wife and three young children. The most open-minded of the Somali men, Ibrahim was the one who had persuaded Faduma's bossy brother-in-law to let her learn English.

I slid the car to a stop and Ibrahim scooted to the passenger door. It wasn't the first time I had given him a ride. "Thank you, thank you, teacher," Ibrahim said affably when he opened

FRENCH LEAVE

the door. Like Faduma, he brought music to English, giving his speech a rhythm that made me wish I could tweet a flute or beat a tattoo on a drum in accompaniment. "Weather, not good. Blenty rain soon."

"We'll make it home before the rain. How are you?" I asked as I pulled from the curb.

"Good, good. How are you, teacher?"

"I've been better," I confessed. Ibrahim gave me a puzzled look and I felt bad for confusing him. "I'm OK," I amended. "How is work?" Ibrahim had a job in a downtown dealership washing cars.

"Job OK," he answered. "But after, after." He gestured, waving his hand to indicate, I thought, the passage of time.

"Later. Like next year?" I suggested.

"Yess, yess!" He beamed, glad I understood. "One year, two years maybe," he counted, holding up two fingers. "Better job."

"The same one?"

He shook his head. "Not same here. Old job, Somalia."

I pulled around a slow-moving van filled with senior citizens. "What did you do in Somalia?" I seldom asked Faduma questions about her life back home because reminiscing pained her. But I had no such qualm with Ibrahim. He was happy to talk.

"I have farm Somalia. Lambuzz," he said, adding an extra syllable for the plural.

"You raised lambs in Somalia?"

"Lambuzz, yes!" He gave me a delighted grin. "Now, here too."

I was surprised. To my knowledge no one had tried raising sheep around Clayton. The meat wasn't popular with the locals. I must have looked doubtful because he added, "Sell Somalis Columbus. Many many Somalis Columbus. Sell goatuzz, too."

"That's a great idea." Columbus, with a Somali population second only to Minneapolis, was a ready market for meats that were staples of the Somalis' diet. Ibrahim told me that he planned on hiring two men from the Somali community: a butcher to slaughter according to Muslim law and a truck driver to transport the meat to Columbus in his refrigerated rig. He said he was considering hiring Faduma to help in the office when her English improved. She could sort the mail and answer the phone.

I imagined her joy at having a job, making decisions, having the confidence to trust her own judgment without risking

FRENCH LEAVE

her brother-in-law's disapproval. I was proud of her and said so. Ibrahim nodded.

I dropped him at his house and drove the short distance to mine. Joe was gone. He'd sent a text earlier telling me he had one more client to see before the weekend. I picked up the mail at the curb and walked up the driveway to the kitchen door. A new yellow note hung between the screen and the jamb. No caption this time, just a drawing of the same little man gushing tears.

I raised my head when I heard a male voice in the backyard. The top of a straw hat drifted past the pole beans, closely followed by a ball cap. Two hats, two men.

I loosened my grip on the screen door. It slammed shut with the sharpness of a pistol shot.

The hat came up. Its wearer called out a warning in a foreign language. Two youths, one tall, one short, burst out of the garden like birds flushed out of the bush. Bare-chested and bare-legged, they ran like the wind, their dark skin glistening with sweat. I went after them. They turned the corner of the house and disappeared. Out on the street I heard a male American voice ordering them to stop. The command triggered a volley of rapid-fire words in a foreign tongue. The voices stopped abruptly and a second later car doors slammed, an engine fired. By the time I ran down to the street, it was empty. The wide-brim straw hat lay in the gutter.

I picked it up, turned it over in my hands.

A bolt of lightning, flickering like a bad neon bulb, split the sky. The deafening clap that followed lit a fuse under my feet. I slapped the hat on my head and ran, leaping across the lawn to the front steps. The skies opened. Hail hit the porch roof like machine gun fire. Nearby a dog yelped in pain, and above the rising wind I heard its owner calling in a voice filled with anguish.

The thunderstorm lasted an hour. Faduma called to cancel our lesson. Another storm rolled in two hours later, and another, and another. Thunder played the house like a drum, rattling windows. Rain came in waves, filling gutters that hummed like swarms of bees and spat water in high arcs out of clogged gutters. Lightning jabbed at the blinds. I put a pillow over my head and catnapped during the lulls. Joe woke me up at two when he came in. The roads around Clayton were flooded, he said. He took a chance and drove through water on an underpass, hoping the truck wouldn't stall. He barely made it.

"That wasn't smart," I said, turning away from the overhead

light shining in my eyes. But I was glad he made it home. I burrowed my face in the pillow and didn't stir until seven the next morning.

***

Joe was a hump under the covers. I got out of bed, shut the bedroom door and padded on bare feet to the kitchen to make a pot of coffee. While the coffee brewed, I went to the back porch to look outside. Even though I'd heard and felt the wind throughout the night, I wasn't prepared for the damage it had wrought. The backyard was an alien land, the lawn littered with broken limbs and leaves, the garden flattened. Sodden tomato plants stretched on the ground like algae at low tide, the splayed stems tangled with cucumber vines and felled pole beans.

"…high winds brought down trees," the radio newscast announced, floating out the open door, "and overturned two mobile homes in Melba Park. No injury reported. Motor vehicle accidents across the city caused two fatalities and several injuries. A city bus and a pickup truck collided at Main and Third. The bus driver and two passengers were taken to the hospital and released; the driver of the pickup is still hospitalized. A woman trapped in a car stalled on a flooded underpass was rescued by police. In a separate incident, two men died on Route Four when a pickup skidded off the pavement and crashed into a tree. A passenger in the vehicle was critically injured. Yesterday, the stock market…" I stopped listening.

I ate breakfast then put on cut-offs and a faded cotton shirt. I was reaching for my gardening hat when the doorbell rang. I paused. Who could be foolish enough to ring doorbells at eight on a weekend morning? It rang again, urgently this time. Afraid it would wake Joe, I crossed the foyer and opened the door.

CHAPTER SEVEN

A middle-aged woman stood on the doorstep. She was small all over—from teeny feet in strappy sandals to small well-kept hands gripping the purse strap looped over her shoulder.

"Claire?" she said, looking up at me.

"Yes." I couldn't place her, but the triangular face with widely spaced brown eyes seemed familiar.

She gave me a radiant smile. "But you look so much like your fazzer!"

The accent tipped me off. She was French. I studied her face. We had the same arched brows, the same high cheekbones and straight nose. Stature-wise I was taller but not by much.

Long before I was born, my French paternal grandmother divorced her American husband and moved back to her native country where she remarried and had a daughter.

"Chantal, right?" I sounded unsure of the name. To say I wasn't familiar with my father's side of the family was putting it mildly. We hadn't communicated for over twenty-five years.

She smiled again, but with noticeably less enthusiasm. "Yes."

What possessed her to come looking for me? I glanced at the street. A silver subcompact sat at the curb. It was empty, which meant she had come alone. I didn't particularly want to meet her, but it would have been even more difficult to deal with her *and* her brother—my father. I refused for years to communicate with him.

"Come in."

The invitation was grudging.

I led the way through the foyer to the living room where dust motes danced in the sunlight flowing through the east window. Joe's shoes lay abandoned midway between the door and the couch, and his overnight bag, trailing a shirt sleeve, graced the coffee table.

My father's sister crossed the room and sat down on the couch, barely denting the cushions. She didn't take up much room, but her presence in my space was like a hair on my tongue.

My life was divided in two parts—when my father was

around and when he wasn't. Enough time had passed to make me more comfortable with the latter.

Chantal looked at me with Audrey Hepburn eyes filled with apprehension.

After a longish pause she said, "You are not *contente*, not happy. I am sorry. It is perhaps too early to make a visit."

I dropped into the chair facing the couch. "Later wouldn't have made any difference. Why did you come at all?" Why end an estrangement that suited everyone?

She flinched. "Your fazzer, he asked me. The reason I came—"

I cut her off. "Now that I'm past needing child support, now that I no longer need shoes or an allowance, no longer need to be tucked in or read to before going to sleep?"

"You are thirty, I know," Chantal returned, sounding snippy. Apprehensive didn't make her timid.

"So why come now that I don't need anything?"

Her composure slipped. "We are," she hesitated, "*apparentées*. Related. No?"

"Yes, I know we're related. Thanks for reminding me."

Bernard's sister passed a hand over her head, ruffling short brown hair mixed with gray. "Do not be angry, Claire. Bernard said I come to tell a story, *his* story, not like the one you heard from your mozzer. She is not neutral, no?"

"No, she isn't." Cora didn't do neutral. Once she sank her teeth into a belief she didn't let go.

"Good." Chantal ruffled her hair again. She had made a point. "She *chose* to marry Bernard, did she not? Because she wanted your sister to have his name?"

I shrugged. The announcement came as no surprise. I knew Cora had insisted Bernard adopt Mirabelle.

"Your parents, they were not good together. I do not say they were wrong. Marriage, it is difficult. But your mozzer, she had no right to make him leave his house. He was not a criminal, Claire."

I knew that already. Bernard, my father, had been arrested for escorting Manuela's Salvadoran brother, Eduardo, to Ohio. On the way, Eduardo fought with a man who threatened them with a gun. In the tussle, the other man was shot and died. Eduardo and Bernard called it self-defense, a claim undisputed by police until a witness insisted Eduardo had attacked the elderly man. My father and Eduardo were placed under arrest, but eventually released when the witness recanted.

"When Bernard, he is arrested, your mozzer, she says he is

so bad he cannot live in his own house and cannot see you anymore? It is not right. When Maman hears what happened she is so *bouleversée* she has a stroke."

"Your mother?" I'd never given much thought to my paternal grandmother. How helpless she must have felt after hearing of her son's arrest. "I'm sorry. Did she recover?"

Chantal nodded. "Oui, after Bernard he comes to take care of her."

Out of the corner of my eye I saw Joe emerge from the bathroom naked and pink from the shower. Catching sight of Chantal, he froze and turned slowly around and walked off in the silent soft-footed stride of the Pink Panther. Afraid she would turn to see what had caught my attention, I leaned forward to say, "I am sorry. It had to be hard on her."

"It was difficult," Chantal admitted. "But your mozzer." The z surfaced with a vengeance. "Elle a été si méchante. She was so mean to say he could not see you."

Yes, it was mean. But by scooting to France he pretty much accepted not seeing me. "But he left," I reminded. "Even though the arrest warrant was lifted."

Chantal spread her hands in an eloquent gesture. "He wanted

to be with Maman, of course. And he had no money because he could not work anymore." Bernard had taught high school French in Clayton for ten years. The school board fired him when he was arrested and made no offer to reinstate him after he was cleared of wrongdoing. I suspected Cora may have had something to do with it.

"The judge, when they divorced, he said Bernard could see you. Bernard had Maman with him, and that made him happy, but he didn't have you, Claire, and it made him very sad."

"Why didn't he do something about it then?"

"He did. He asked your mozzer several times if he could see you, but she always said no. You have to understand, Claire. It is not possible for your fazzer to go where he is not wanted."

"But *I* wanted him."

Chantal curled her hands into fists. "But he did not know that! Later, Cora, she wrote to say that she was married. She told Bernard you liked her new husband and that you did not remember your fazzer at all."

Joe, now fully clothed, stood in the hall, hesitant to walk in.

I held my tongue. The claimed close father-daughter relationship with Richard never happened. He was far too reserved to be a dad. His only mark of affection then, one I learned to value, was to always treat Mirabelle and me with the respect he accorded adults.

"And so Bernard let her win."

Chantal's shoulders slumped. "Yes, yes he did."

"And later, when I was grown, why didn't he get in touch?"

"He wrote. Cora, she didn't tell you? He married a woman who is a teacher like him. They separated, but he has the boys."

"The *boys*?"

Chantal recoiled, startled by the sharpness in my voice. "Two sons," she said, her voice guarded. "They live with him."

It never occurred to me that Bernard might remarry. I never thought of him as somebody else's father. He had been mine and mine alone to despise.

Joe came in to stand behind me. The warmth of his hands on my shoulders felt good. Chantal gave me a knowing look.

Joe said, "Hello!"

She smiled back. "Bonjour. I am Chantal, Claire's aunt from France."

"Glad to meet you, Chantal. I'm Joe." He went around me to sit at the far end of the sofa. "Are you here on vacation?"

She hesitated. "Pas exactement. Not a vacation exactly, but a visit. I wanted to see my niece."

"I understand." What sounded normal to him wasn't for me, but even if it hadn't seemed normal, Joe wouldn't have said so. He was unfailingly courteous. "Is this your first trip to the States?"

She shook her head. "It is the second. I came when your grandmother lived here," Chantal said turning to me. "I remember it well."

"You knew her?" I didn't remember Gin ever talking about her.

"I met her when you were four." A smile hovered over her lips. "I remember teaching you words in French: Papa, Maman, tante, oncle, grandmère."

Joe relaxed, resting his long lean body against the sofa cushions. "Well, it's a good thing you speak English, Chantal, because Claire's French hasn't improved a bit since."

I snapped. "Why should it?"

"Oh, but I am glad to speak English. Your fazzer," she said looking at me, "he taught me."

"Is he coming as well?" Joe asked.

This was a question I had been careful not to ask. I dreaded the answer.

CHAPTER EIGHT

"But Bernard, he is here already!" Chantal cried, spreading her hands to express her delight. If she expected me to share it, she was disappointed. "He left before me to visit with friends in Clayton. I hope it is not inconvenient, Claire," she added as an afterthought. "Perhaps we should have asked you."

No perhaps about it. They had my address. Why not write, or call? What was the rush anyway?

The French aunt waited for an answer I didn't give. Joe broke the awkwardness of the moment by getting up. "Coffee anyone? I haven't had mine this morning."

Chantal exhaled a sigh of relief. "Yes, I would very much like to have a cup of coffee."

When he went off to make it I scooted after him.

"Why are you so hard on her?" Joe asked as he started the

coffee grinder, the whir covering his words.

"Would you rather I told the truth? Told her it was inconvenient and to try again in twenty years? She crossed the Atlantic to see someone she hasn't seen in years and she wonders if she should've asked first? I would've said no and she knows it."

I was aware Cora vilified Bernard. I suspected he wasn't as bad as she made out, but that didn't make me eager to see him. All my life I had wondered about his real reason for staying away. Was it because I somehow disappointed him, because I wasn't smart enough or pretty like Mirabelle? The feeling of inadequacy lessened as I grew up, but it never disappeared.

Joe rubbed my shoulder with his left hand while holding the coffee grinder in his right. "Your father screwed up, babe. His mistake, not yours," he said, reading me correctly. "Maybe he's ready for the truth. He's back. Look at it as a chance to set the record straight."

"Is there a hotel near your house?" Chantal asked when we re-entered the living room carrying the coffee pot and a tray with cups and saucers. "I have need of a room until Bernard comes."

Joe paused in the process of pouring coffee. "There's one close by. We'll call to ask if they have a vacancy, but I'd be surprised if they do. There isn't a decent room to be had within twenty miles of Clayton."

"Les hotels, ils sont pleins?" She was surprised. "The hotels, they don't have a room. Why?"

He set the carafe down. "People who came to work in the local shale have taken all of them." He launched into an explanation of how big energy companies had acquired leases to exploit the vast shale deposits in the county, how much the extraction of gas and oil benefited the local economy.

Too much information. Chantal wrinkled her brows. "Perhaps I should go back to Columbus, and wait until Bernard, he comes?"

Joe laughed. "Of course not. There's no need for you to do that, Chantal. We have a spare room."

***

"Of course I offered her the spare room," he later said after Chantal left for a stroll in the backyard, claiming she needed a breath of fresh air. "You can't expect her to stay in Columbus until your father shows up. It's expensive."

"That's her problem. It was up to me to make the offer, Joe. It's my house."

He snorted. "I know it's your house, Claire. You remind me

often enough. But honestly, did you expect her to drive all the way back to Columbus? We don't ask Aunt Lou to stay in a hotel when she comes."

"Your Aunt Lou is a relative, Joe."

"And Chantal isn't? I swear, Claire, you're so alike you could be twins."

"Thanks a lot! The woman's old enough to be my mother. Anyway, she may be my aunt, but she's never acted like one. I never even got one Christmas card from her."

"You don't send Christmas cards either," Joe reminded, his voice muffled as he stepped into the guest room closet to take down his wall display of Playboy centerfolds. "I'm sorry I asked without consulting you. But the deed is done. Accept it. Your aunt cannot be un-invited."

I punched a pillow into shape before slipping a clean case over it. "Don't I know it."

"Good. It's settled then."

The phone rang and I headed to the kitchen to answer it. "Who is that woman in your backyard?" Ruth wanted to know. "She just looked in your shed. Is that Joe's Aunt Lou?"

"Not his aunt. Mine."

"Yours? You only got the one."

"I know."

A pregnant silence followed. "Your dad here, too?" she finally asked.

"Not yet."

She thought some more. "How long is she staying?"

"No word on that." The vacuum cleaner came on in the guest room. "I've got to go, Ruth. We're getting the spare room ready."

"She's staying at your place? What about lunch?"

I sighed. "I hadn't thought about it. I guess we can eat out."

"No, you won't. I'll make fried chicken and potato salad. See you at one."

There were days when Ruth was so aggravating I wanted to slide her in a mailing envelope and ship her to Timbuktu, and days when I couldn't imagine living without her. I thanked her and went back to the business of dusting and general sprucing up. It'd been a while since the room had been done. When we were finished, Joe drove to the supermarket to get a loaf of French bread and a bottle of wine.

Lunch was heavy going. It was clear from the start that the two guests had no fond memories of their first and only encounter. Ruth greeted our guest as "Tchantall" with accents on both syllables, sounding as if she were stomping grapes. Chantal said Ruth looked nice, even though she came in red and sweaty after frying chicken in a hot kitchen.

Joe uncorked the wine. Ruth surprised him by accepting a half glass. Except for Thanksgiving when she took a thimbleful of Asti Spumante with dessert, she never drank. Chantal emptied her glass. She seemed edgy. The wine was enough to promote civility, but didn't loosen tongues. The women each kept a wary eye on one another.

I filled the silence by talking about the weather, bestselling books, the latest movies. Joe didn't help. He was staring at the chicken leg on his plate as if he expected it to jump up and bite him. I understood the reason when I saw Chantal cutting hers with a knife and fork. Ruth, who had fried-chicken etiquette down pat, grabbed a thigh and took a bite.

"I like your plates," Chantal said, breaking the silence.

"My friend Lisa made them." I had bought the set shortly after she first opened her studio. Glazed in burnt orange, the plates each featured a tomato in the center with a garland of leaves running around the rim. Chantal had the Roma; Ruth the Beefsteak; Joe fittingly the Big Boy. My plate had a cluster of grape tomatoes.

Chantal ran a finger around the rim of the plate. "I like the colors very much. Did your friend go to school to learn?"

"She didn't have to. Her mother was a potter."

Joe abandoned his contemplation of the chicken leg to say, "Clayton had potters for years. The local clay made money for the town in its early days."

"Your fazzer, he told me the same," Chantal said to me. She wiped her mouth on her napkin. "He gave me a vase for my wedding. It is from Roseville."

"Roseville was one of the best," Joe agreed. "We had many at one time, but most are gone now."

"C'est dommage. It is too bad. The company where I work, it exports wine and cheese. But we sell pottery also, mostly from Provence."

A wedding present. Her ring finger was bare. Either she didn't believe in wearing a wedding ring or she was divorced—or widowed. It occurred to me that I knew next to nothing about her, not her last name, or where she lived.

"So what's your brother doing these days?" Ruth asked.

Chantal's face brightened. "He teaches French to sans-papiers, the people without papers you call illegals here."

"Did he ever remarry?"

"Yes, he did, but he and his wife are separated now. He works all the time and she did not like that. We have many migrants in France and not enough money to care for them."

"Same here," Ruth said shortly, ending the conversation.

Chantal resumed her morsel-by-morsel feeding. I helped myself to potato salad. The stream of string music coming from the kitchen radio stopped to make room for the news. It was two.

"The wreck of a pickup on Route Four during last night's storm left two dead and a passenger in serious condition. The three victims, one middle-aged male Caucasian and two black males, remain unidentified. The injured man, a young Haitian thought to be in the country illegally, was transported to Good Shepherd Hospital."

Chantal dropped her fork. It fell to the hardwood floor and skittered all the way into the kitchen. She pushed back her chair and got up to retrieve it.

I cleared the table. When I took the plates to the kitchen I found her leaning against the counter staring out the window.

"Are you all right?"

She turned around. "I am a little fatigued."

I served coffee and peach pie for dessert. After lunch Ruth went home and Chantal disappeared into her room to take a nap. I heard her while I was loading the dishwasher, talking, talking, talking, her voice loud enough to pass through two closed doors. "Immédiatement!" she snapped at the end of the soliloquy.

Immediately. It was a good bet she was talking to her brother. No need to rush him on my account.

CHAPTER NINE

After Joe left to run the Mazda through the car wash, I headed for the garden. It wasn't too late to do the work I had intended to do before the French aunt showed up. I stopped by the shed for tools and spare stakes to right the tomato plants that survived the storm. Raymond, Ruth's brother, had built the shed for Gin years ago in a secluded corner of the backyard against the six-foot hedge separating our adjoining properties.

A rank odor met me when I walked inside, a mix of male sweat and unwashed bodies. It was strong enough to make me gag, and I walked back out to clear my nose before going back inside.

The lawn mower had been pushed to the side to make room for a makeshift bed. The old sheets I used to protect seedlings from a late frost lay on the ground, rumpled and stained. Bags of mulch had been used as pillows.

Squatters. I thought about the two men running out of the garden to the street yesterday, their dark skin glistening with sweat. They must have slept in the shed. How long did they stay there? And where did they come from?

The smell was so bad I decided to clean out the shed before starting my garden work. I kicked the bags of mulch out of the way and used the rake to drag the soiled sheets outside—no way was I going to touch them. The clipboard with its pad to record spring plantings had been lying under the heap of sheets. When I picked it up to hang it back on its intended hook I noticed indentations on the top page as if someone had written on another with a heavy hand, pushing hard enough to pierce the paper. Tilting the pad to the light, I saw faint tracings and the outline of a stick man, brother to the one sketched on the notes left at the kitchen door.

The squatters had written them. To say what and in what language? Blanc, femme, those were French words. But the syntax looked wrong. Could it be Creole? Like in Haiti? I pondered the coincidence of Creole-speaking squatters in my shed and the nationality of the young man who survived last night's truck wreck. The radio said he was from Haiti. A second black man in the pickup hadn't survived.

"Claire!"

I stuck my head out. Ruth was standing in the garden. "You coming? There's work to do."

"In a minute."

I slipped on gardening gloves to bundle the soiled sheets into an empty mulch bag and carried the bag to the garage to drop it in the trash can.

"Tchantall sleeping?" Ruth asked when I joined her. She was ripping an old white T-shirt into strips to use as ties. "She looked tired."

"She said she was."

"Did she say anything about your dad?"

"A lot, mostly to explain why he left." I straightened the stake of a disheveled Early Girl and pounded it deeper into the ground. "Did you know he asked to see me after he moved to France?"

Ruth didn't look at me. "Yes."

"And you didn't tell me?"

"Cora didn't want us to. She wanted you to like your stepdad."

"I did from the start. But that wasn't the point. Richard isn't my dad. It was Bernard I wanted."

Ruth finally looked at me. Her face was sad. "I know, hon."

It was hard to think of those days. Cora was so fed up with my crying she took me to Gin's. I had bad dreams every night and woke up sobbing.

At home, the nightmares were worse. Cora would shake me awake and yell at me. I didn't think it was meanness that made her do it, more like panic at not being able to stop me from screaming. My sister Mirabelle was gentler. She took me back to bed and read me stories until I calmed down. Those were the only times I remembered Mirabelle showing me kindness. Mostly she treated me with the contempt of an older sister for a bratty sibling.

It took months for the nightmares to end. The sense of my dad, of what he meant to me, faded with time and I forgot what it was to be the apple of someone's eye. He had cared for me, that much I remembered. Gin, Ruth, and her brother Raymond tried to fill the void. They read to me, taught me games, took me to the park. On summer evenings they played cards out on the porch. I would lie on a cot in Gin's bedroom, the aroma of Raymond's pipe drifting through the open window. Cups clinked on saucers, spoons rang on china. I fell asleep to the murmur of their voices, the soft laughter.

"I always liked your dad," Ruth confided, sitting back on her heels to disentangle pole beans. "Her not so much."

"Chantal, you mean?"

She grunted an affirmative. "Years back when she came, she kind of took you over. Cora didn't care, but your grandma did, I could tell. She didn't complain, but I felt bad for her."

Gin didn't have to worry about the competition. She was my own personal sun, even before Bernard left. I craved her affection.

"Gin was fond of your pa. We didn't know what to think when he was arrested, but even then she never thought badly of him. She was angry when Cora demanded a divorce."

"Did Cora know Richard before Bernard left?"

Ruth hesitated. "I believe so. Your grandma met him when she went to him for her will." She turned her back on me and scuttled to the next tomato plant. "You were your dad's whole world. His eyes would just glow when he saw you. I mean really glow like there was a light back in his head and you were the only switch that could turn it on. It didn't matter how bratty you were or whiny, he always looked at you the same way."

I got up to brush dirt off my shorts. "Tell me more about him. That's assuming, of course, the gag order has been lifted."

Ruth gave me her bird stare, unblinking and dark. "You could've asked."

"By the time I was old enough to ask, I didn't want to know."

"That's what me and your grandma figured. Ray liked him a lot, you know. On account they were both veterans. Your dad had a real hard time in Vietnam. He was a medic."

"No one told me he was in Vietnam."

"He didn't like people mentioning it. He got that PTSD they talk about now. Your dad had a hard time with it. And he didn't have it easy earlier either. Ray knew your Grandpa Palmer. A real hard man, he said, who had nothing good to say about anybody. He called his son 'shrimp' because he was on the short side, and sneered at him for wanting to help people. He took that as a weakness. Still, he didn't object when Bernard stayed with him instead of joining his ma. After the divorce that is. Your granddad wasn't in good health and Bernard worried about him living alone. It wasn't an easy decision for him. He and his ma were close."

"How old was Bernard then?"

"I believe he was in high school. Ray said choosing one parent over the other tore him up. Maybe that's why he didn't fight as hard as he should've to keep you. Maybe he didn't want to force you into making that kind of decision. You have to look at the whole picture, hon, if you want to know what kind of a man he really is. Maybe he didn't always do what you wanted him to, but you can't say he didn't try." Ruth paused. "Ray said he meant well."

A synonym for screw-up.

"He said," Ruth went on, "that your pa was a good-hearted man with two left feet, kind of a cross between Jesus Christ and Moe of the Three Stooges."

Great. I loved him already.

***

"You know tomorrow is the day we go to the family reunion, don't you?" Joe asked as we got ready for bed. We had eaten early, just the two of us. Chantal was a no-show.

"Claire—family reunion?" Joe said again when I didn't respond.

"I heard you. And yes, I forgot." Every August Joe and I drove down to West Virginia to see his relatives. Joe was an only child, but his late mother, the youngest of ten, had provided him with enough cousins to man a squadron. Her siblings had been prolific, and so were their offspring. Relatives in triple digits overwhelmed Joe and he insisted on dragging me along for support.

FRENCH LEAVE

"But you'll have to go solo this year. I can't go, not while Chantal is here."

Joe pulled his polo shirt over his head, his hair crackling as he emerged. "But you've got to come. Aunt Lou is expecting you."

I liked Joe's Aunt Lou. She was the one who scooped him up and raised him after both his parents died in a car crash. A tennis-shoe grandma, she was always on the move, the pockets of her jogging suit bulging with treats for strays, kids or dogs. She shared her meager resources with anyone in need. Her one-woman social service agency also rested on the occasional win at bingo. "I know she's expecting me, Joe. But we have company."

"Chantal could come with us."

"In the Miata?"

"We'll take yours."

"Think of your bunch, Joe, in comfy shorts, running shoes and baseball caps. Picture her next to them in her neat little outfit, not a hair out of place. She'll be as out of place as a truffle on a bologna sandwich. I don't want to deal with that. Either call in sick or drive down by yourself. I don't care."

He flopped down on the bed, landed flat on his back and groaned. I was not swayed. "Cut it out, Joe. There's nothing to be afraid of." Except that people, about two million of them, would crawl over him like ants on a sugar donut. "You'll be fine. If you hadn't given her the guest room, she would've gone back to Columbus and I'd be free to go with you."

He groaned again.

I got into bed. "OK, I admit that was a low blow. But the woman's like an itch I can't scratch. She makes me mean. I keep looking back thinking that if I hadn't opened the door this morning she might've gone away. Or thinking if she'd come last month while we were on vacation she wouldn't have found us."

Joe sat up, punched his pillow and settled into a comfortable position. "But she did. Live with it. Your dad will come, he'll meet you and then they'll go home. It's not as if they can show up whenever they feel like it. It cost them a mint to come see you. You ought to be flattered."

"I'm not."

I drifted to sleep but woke around midnight to the sound of bare feet hitting the hardwood floor. The door to the bathroom squeaked open, squeaked shut; the old-fashioned slide bolt shot home. Thankfully I didn't hear anything else except for a rush of water a few minutes later. After leaving the bathroom, Chantal walked across the foyer. A bar of light appeared under the bedroom door. She was in the kitchen. I heard water running in the sink, the clatter of the kettle on the stove. The refrigerator door opened, closed. I clenched my teeth.

I woke up again around three. The light was still on in the kitchen. Chantal was talking. Her voice was low. On her cell phone or was she making an international call on my landline? The thought made my toes curl. On the other half of the bed, Joe flopped from his side to his back and mumbled in his sleep.

He left around eight. It was nine by the time I stumbled to the kitchen for breakfast. The room was empty, the coffee gone, the day's paper scattered over the island; Chantal, or Joe, had eaten all the bread. Sunday wasn't off to a good start.

After staying up half the night, Chantal slept late. I went to the supermarket for a rotisserie chicken and a tub of potato salad.

At noon I set the table on the porch. The day was cool. "In summer, Maman would set the table out on the terrace," Chantal said as she drifted out an hour later. She walked to the edge of the porch and leaned on the railing to look at the devastation in the backyard. "I live in an apartment now. You are lucky to have a 'jardin,' Claire. Garden?" she asked, looking at me over her shoulder.

"Close, but here we just call it a yard. A garden has things growing in it like vegetables."

She walked back to the table and sat down. I poured wine from the bottle Joe had opened on Saturday and pushed a bowl of tomato salad with onion rings and chopped parsley in her direction. "Do you work in Paris?"

"I do. My office is near my apartment. I walk. When I retire I will move to the country and have a 'garden,' as you say. Maman grew herbs and flowers."

I wrestled a leg from the chicken to put it on my plate. "What was she like?"

"Gentle. She was unhappy here. She said her American husband was a..." Chantal wrinkled her forehead, searching for a word. "A bully, I think you say. He was not a nice man."

My paternal grandparents had met when my grandfather was stationed in an army base outside of Paris. My grandmother worked at a drycleaner near the base. They married before he was transferred back to the US, and she followed him to Ohio when he was discharged. She went back to France after they separated.

"Maman died two years ago. It is sad that she never knew

you," Chantal said, reaching for her wine glass. She had eaten very little.

"You have children?"

"Just one. Alexander is twenty-two." Chantal didn't mention the father.

"What does he do?"

"He is in university studying botany."

"Botany?" Among my school friends, those lucky enough to go to college, most studied business administration. The rest became teachers. "It's an unusual choice."

"His father, he knows about plants. We lived in the country for several years, but we moved to Paris because I needed a job."

After we finished eating I went inside to make a pot of coffee. The local radio station was reporting the news. "...a nurse with some knowledge of French understood the injured Haitian to say that he and his companion were brought to Clayton and dropped at a local house. The patient, who suffered a head injury, only speaks Creole. Police speculated that the aliens either drove or were given a ride in the pickup. Sheriff Gunner says that the crash, while tragic, served to alert the authorities to the possible existence of an underground organization ferrying illegal aliens through the area. He vows to prosecute those involved and possibly charge the owner of the residence being used as a safe house. The sheriff, who ran on an anti-immigration platform, requested the presence of an interpreter to question the alien and determine the location of the safe house. The surviving Haitian will face deportation upon his release from the hospital. The pickup involved in the wreck was reported stolen in Texas. In other news..."

I felt cold. Safe house? The men stayed in my garden shed. *Charge* the owner? I didn't even know the men were there.

Mrs. Paolini had seen them. Had anyone else?

CHAPTER TEN

Chantal slept again until dinner. I had set the table in the kitchen to watch the evening news, hoping to catch an update on the Haitian's condition. She climbed on a stool to sit at the island and propped both elbows on the surface to support her head. Her hair was wild and her eyes heavy with sleep. I poured a glass of wine and slid it in her direction. "You don't look well."

She passed a hand over her face. "I'm worried about your fazzer. He should be coming soon, but I do not hear from him. Il ne répond pas quand je l'appelle. He does not answer his phone. I do not understand why, Claire."

"Maybe he's out of range."

"But he should not be far. His friend Randy, he lives here?"

"Who is Randy?"

"His friend who was in Vietnam with him."

"Do you have his number? He may be able to tell you where Bernard is."

Chantal shook her head. "I do not know it."

"How long ago did Bernard leave?"

"It has been about a week." Chantal took a sip of wine. "I am not sure of the date because I was out of town when he left."

The timer beeped and I turned to take the casserole Ruth had brought earlier out of the oven. She didn't trust me to feed the guest properly. "Where exactly did he intend to go?" I asked as I set the casserole down on a trivet and carried plates, silverware and water glasses to the island.

Chantal fiddled with the table, moving the glasses precisely at twelve o'clock, folding the paper napkins into neat triangles. "I thought it was here."

"Do you know Randy's last name?" I asked as I sat down. "We could look him up."

"No. He is only Randy from Vietnam. That is all I know." She was abrupt.

OK then. I reached for the TV remote. It was time for the news.

"Where's Joe?" Chantal asked when a commercial came on. "I did not see him this morning."

FRENCH LEAVE

"On the road. He's a sales rep for a company that makes agricultural equipment. He won't be back until Friday."

We ate in silence until the commercial ended. A news flash showed a tanker truck overturned in a ditch. A crew in hazmat suits was examining the wreckage. The weather broadcast came next, predicting cooler temperatures for the coming week. After more commercials came sports. I was about to shut off the set when the screen flipped to a young reporter standing in front of the revolving door of the local hospital, looking solemn in a suit and tie. The wind was blowing, flapping his tie and whipping the flags mounted on poles near the entrance. "The condition of the Haitian who was injured in Friday's accident has been downgraded from critical to serious," he said, raising his voice to be heard over the clanking of lanyard clips hitting the metal poles. "The interpreter requested by Sheriff Gunner is due to arrive soon. ICE will take charge of the patient once he is well enough to leave the hospital."

I wondered if the Haitian knew enough to describe me. Did he know my name? Could he tell the interpreter what street I lived on? I couldn't help thinking it would be to my advantage if ICE took him away before Gunner got anything out of him.

"But what is this ICE?" Chantal asked.

"Immigration and Customs Enforcement. It's a law enforcement agency. They'll take charge of him and deport him."

She looked disapproving. "The poor man."

***

The next morning Chantal announced her decision to spend the day touring Clayton. "It has changed, has it not, since I was here last?"

"Some, but not as much as it could've after the economy slowed. Besides the courthouse and the park with a gazebo, there's not much to see. Take a city map with you. There's one in the hall closet. Give me a call if you have a question. I'll be at work until five."

I gave her my cell phone number and a spare key. She was still dawdling over coffee when I left.

It was after ten when I reached Sally's house. She was getting ready to leave, formally dressed in a navy blue blazer and white slacks. In the old days she would've been just getting out of bed.

"You're late," she said, looking at her watch.

"I didn't expect you to be up. Are you going to be long? We need to talk."

FRENCH LEAVE

"What about?"

"The book! What do you think?" I set my laptop on the kitchen table. "What you gave me didn't advance the plot. We're still treading water. Felicia is practically catatonic. She should be fighting off suitors, defending her virtue, but you gave her only one suitor and he's so well behaved he puts me to sleep. Make him something more exciting than a preacher—a surveyor maybe? The Upper Peninsula was still pretty much uncharted at the time. He should be a man at ease in the wilderness, strong enough to kill bears with his bare hands, not one who hardly ever climbs down from the pulpit."

"What's wrong with him being a preacher?" Sally asked.

"Preachers don't make good sex symbols."

"Sex symbols? You make it sound as if I write pornography. The man isn't about passion, but restraint. I see him as more of an advisor and protector than a lover."

"Restraint? You gotta be kidding, Sally! What will you have him do at the end of the book—pat her hand?"

She hesitated. "A bit more than that, perhaps. It will be low-key. Howard says I need to change."

I was surprised. "Howard read your book?"

She laughed. "Certainly not! The man only reads financial reports. But he says I'm wasting my talent writing bodice rippers. He finds them vulgar."

"That's the nature of the beast."

She waved the comment away. "I don't agree. He suggested I try writing something more acceptable, like a novel. Personally, I was thinking memoir. My life, my career would make for interesting reading, don't you think?"

For sure, but we were back to sex and more of it. Why was Howard messing with her? She was happy writing bodice rippers. "Or he could just enjoy your company and let you decide for yourself."

She clicked her tongue. "That wouldn't be right, Claire. Howard has my interests at heart and I trust him. We share everything." She cut her eyes at me. "You and Joe don't appear to have that kind of relationship."

If by that she meant that I did everything Joe told me to do, then no, we didn't.

Sally looked at her watch again. "I'm running late. Go ahead and transcribe what I gave you today. We'll finish our conversation later."

Not likely. Would she still trust Howard's judgment when the editor rejected the book?

She had given me three chapters of fluff. After two hours of painstaking work, the ringing phone came as a respite. I took off the headset and stretched before picking up the receiver.

"Claire?" My mother's clarion voice made me flinch. "Can you come for lunch?"

She wanted something. Cora served on half a dozen boards that raised money for non-profits. Over the last ten years I had bought tickets for the policeman's ball, written checks for school supplies, answered phones to take pledges for the local hospital.

"Possibly. What's up?"

"We need to talk. One o'clock," she said, taking my assent for granted.

The invitation came at an opportune moment. After listening to Chantal's assessment of her brother, I was curious to hear Cora's opinion. It would be negative, but I thought I knew my mother well enough to separate facts from lies.

***

At one we sat down in her kitchen for a lunch that consisted of a scoop of cottage cheese and canned peaches served on a china plate. Cora was forever dieting. But I expected dessert to be better. She had a sweet tooth.

I dropped Bernard's name as she popped almond croissants into the oven. She closed the oven door and turned around to look at me. I expected wariness or anger on her face but saw neither.

"He's the reason I asked you to come."

"Why?"

"He called a while back to let me know he was coming. Is he here?"

"He called you?"

She nodded. "I thought it was decent of him to give me advance notice."

While I digested the news, I watched her measure ground coffee into a French press and fill it with boiling water from the special faucet on the sink. "His sister came ahead. She told me he asked to see me after the divorce, but you wouldn't let him."

Cora turned to take the croissants out of the oven. "She said that?" Deftly she slid them on a plate.

"You didn't tell me."

FRENCH LEAVE

"No." She loaded a tray with demitasses, spoons and the sugar bowl, and carried it to the sunroom. I followed with the croissants. "It wasn't an easy decision, Claire."

"Maybe, but I had a right to know." I sat on the couch while she busied herself pouring coffee. I took a sip. Cora couldn't cook but she made outstanding coffee.

"Actually, no. I don't think you did. You don't know your father the way I do, Claire. He showed poor judgment time and time again. He would feel sorry for people and spend his time and money to help them out. Some deserved it, some did not. He couldn't say no. And you see where it led him, don't you? He almost ended up in prison and he lost his job. You're like him in many ways, and when you were small you worshipped him. He was neither a good influence, nor a good father. Richard was much better."

"But it was Bernard I wanted."

Cora thinned her lips. "You *always* make things difficult, Claire. Trust me on this. I made the right decision. Your father was never dependable. Time after time he volunteered to help people then he couldn't keep up. We were the casualties. We were the ones he abandoned to embrace others, his mother for one. Didn't he run by going to France?"

Not without a push.

"You do know that he's doing the same thing he did here but on a grander scale?" Cora continued. "My fear always was that he would lure you into one of his schemes before you were old enough to know better. You're mature enough to take care of yourself now. But all the same, don't let him pull the wool over your eyes."

CHAPTER ELEVEN

I didn't go back to Sally's after lunch. She was gone and I preferred working from home anyway. Ruth had let herself in while I was gone and left a platter of sliced ham in the refrigerator along with a bean salad. "It's for Tchantall," she said when I called to thank her. "Last time I saw your aunt she looked like she'd been stomped upon. I figured she needed fed."

"She could've eaten what's left of your casserole. When did you see her?"

"This morning. She was in and out all day and came home with shopping bags."

"She said she was going to drive around town, but I can't imagine what she found in Clayton she couldn't get in Paris. I haven't seen her since I came in."

"She's in her room sleeping. It's that jetlag," Ruth said, sounding as if she knew everything about it. "Don't you go rattling around the place and wake her up. Since you're home early, why don't you walk over to Gladys's? She's been wanting tomatoes for her and that girl."

"What girl?"

"Some girl Lamont met at school who moved into his old room. She was looking for a place to live and he told her she could have it."

"Gladys must be thrilled."

"Not so you'd notice. I know the boy was worried about her living by herself."

"What did Gladys say about having a boarder?"

"Something I can't repeat."

I laughed and went out to pick tomatoes. When I came back I found Chantal standing in the kitchen holding a top with a tag dangling from the sleeve. Ruth was right when she said the aunt looked stomped upon. Her face sagged from eyes to chin.

"You look tired. Still no news of Bernard?"

"No. I cannot understand, Claire. He knows I have arrived here. I have fear that something happened to him."

"Like what?"

FRENCH LEAVE

"A car accident? It is possible he is in a hospital and no one knows who he is. Or perhaps he forgot his medication. For depression," she said in response to my questioning look. "Vietnam, it changed him. I have always taken care of him when he becomes anxious. He could be alone not knowing what to do." She squeezed her eyes shut. "I cannot think about this."

"What about his friend Randy? Wouldn't he have called when Bernard didn't come?"

"I do not think he has my number."

"Maybe you should report him missing." But there was no way of knowing where he was when he went missing. On his way to Ohio or here?

She shook her head. "No, Claire. He does not like the police here after what happened to him. I would rather wait."

"Wait how long?"

"A couple more days. Then we will see." She looked at the top she was holding and the tag dangling from it. "I need to cut this off."

"I'm pretty sure there are scissors in here," I said, opening the drawer where we stored odds and ends. She pawed through the mess until she found a small pair of scissors nesting in a tangle of rubber bands. When she pulled the scissors out the rubber bands followed, along with everything attached to them, and everything cascaded to the floor.

I laughed and got down on my knees to scoop up the junk. Chantal joined me. We put everything back except one of the notes left by the Haitian. I'd forgotten I'd stuck it in there.

Chantal smoothed it out. "You write this?"

"No. It was a message left on the mailbox."

"This is Creole."

"That's what I thought. I don't understand what it says. Can you?"

She frowned. "The orthographe—the spelling—it is not right. And the grammar, it does not exist. But I can guess."

"*Ou té, blanc*," she read, the words sounding like they made sense. "This means, '*Where are you, white man?*'"

"I guessed the white man but not the rest of it. Wait, there was another." I sorted through the junk until I found the note with the drawing of the woman.

"*Qui sé la femme, blanc? 'Who is the woman, white man?'*" Chantal read slowly. She looked up. "The woman is you, yes? When did the notes come?"

"Last week."

Her face was impassive, but something in her eyes, a quickening, suggested the time meant something to her.

I waited for her to share the information, but she just thanked me for the use of the scissors and walked out of the room.

Where are you, white man?

Cora had been afraid Bernard would involve me in one of his schemes. Did he? The Haitians waited for a white man who never showed up, a white man who understood French.

If he was the man who failed to show up, was his sister part of the action? Did she come to take charge of the Haitians?

I didn't know what to think. One thing was for sure. If she had meant to rescue the Haitians she came too late.

I sat at the island staring at the tomatoes I had just picked for Gladys. Cora insisted Bernard was an instigator, Chantal portrayed him as a victim. It seemed Cora was right.

It was four when I walked over to Gladys's house. A girl with a mane of tawny hair and a thin face stuck her head out in answer to my knock.

She looked at me suspiciously. Her eyes were small and set close together. "You must be Claire," she finally said. "I'm Lucie. Gladys said you would come."

"Is she home?"

"Not yet. But she wants to see you. Come in."

Lucie opened the door wider. We crossed a spacious and uncluttered living room where light poured through bare windows to bounce off the highly polished floor. Brightly colored hangings stood out against walls painted a deep tan. The wall hangings were wild. Swirly stitching ran at random across a jumble of overlapping triangles. But despite the contrasting colors, the variety of textures in fabric ranging from burlap to silk, the wild swirls of stitching gave a sense of purpose, of movement. I stopped to study them closer.

"We don't sit in here," Lucie said sharply.

Swallowing a protest, I followed her around a leather seating group floating on the wood floor and down a short hallway to the kitchen—retro with its original white metal cabinets. We went out the screen door and down two steps to the lawn to a cluster of Adirondack chairs shaded by an orange umbrella.

Lucie sat down on the closest. The umbrella's warm tone softened her sharp features. Her eyes were an exact match for her hair, brown with glints of red. Her skin was smooth, dotted with freckles.

She stretched her legs. "This is great. Before I came here, I shared an apartment with a girl who was a total slob. I'm an only child so I'm not used to sharing space." She slid an eye in my direction. "You have siblings?"

I dropped the basket of tomatoes on the grass and sat down in the chair next to hers. "A sister."

"My parents divorced when I was small and neither of them remarried so I'm it. My mom moved from the South up to Cincinnati and took me with her when they split. Are your parents here?"

"My mother is."

"And your dad?"

"He isn't."

She shrugged. "I'm close to mine but I don't get to see him often. And it's too bad because my mom and I *really* don't get along." She sat up, lifted the mass of hair off her neck and let it fall. "She's super controlling."

I sneaked a look at my watch, wondering how long Gladys would be. The girl liked to talk and I was a captive audience.

"She won't let me see my dad, but I'm of age now so she can't stop me. I transferred to Clayton Community College to be with him. He lives here now."

"Is that where you met Lamont?"

"Yes. It worked out perfect. He was worried about his grandma and I wanted to be next to Dad. He needs me. Mom says he's a bad influence but that's not true. He's bad-tempered, but that's because he's unhappy. My mom is a social worker. She goes on and on about how poverty and trauma affect kids later on in life, but she never caught on that it's the reason for his anger. He had a tough childhood. Some women are so dictatorial they shouldn't get married."

"Do you like it here with Gladys?" I asked to change the subject. Did I sound as judgmental when I talked about Cora?

"I do. She didn't want me at first, but she changed her mind."

It seemed more a case of Lamont changing her mind for her, but it wasn't my place to say so. "Why didn't you move in with your dad?"

"He doesn't have room for me. But that's OK. I'm comfortable here. I get to see him whenever I want. I like that." She turned to look at me. "Where's yours? You didn't say."

"Not here."

The non-answer earned me a grin full of opossum teeth. "Secretive, aren't you? He isn't someone you want to talk about. Is there a story behind that?"

I shrugged. "If there was, I don't see that you would be entitled to hear it. But there's no mystery. My parents are divorced and live apart, like yours. He lives far enough away to make communication difficult. I got used to it."

Lucie shook her mane. "Not me. I want to spend as much time with my dad as I can. He's fun to be with. My mom says it's not bad to be poor as long as we have food to eat and a roof over our heads. For her maybe. But Dad likes living well. My parents are poles apart, so different in personality and taste that I wonder why they got together in the first place."

I had the same thought about Cora and Bernard. In their case I suspected the need of one and the nurturing instinct of the other was enough to sustain the relationship until Cora found someone better.

The screen door slammed. "Hey, Claire!" Gladys called out.

I shaded my eyes against the glare of the sun and watched Gladys approach. She was in her work clothes, orange scrubs dotted with pink rabbits, an outfit the tall athletic dental hygienist bore with grace. She had inherited the long limbs and high cheekbones of her African ancestors, but white DNA somewhere along the line had lightened her skin to the color of strong tea. Some gray lightened her closely cropped black hair, but her face was unlined.

Two more strides took her to the empty Adirondack chair. "God! What a day. Two broken teeth, a screamer, a gagger and a mom who breathed down my back the whole time her kid was in the chair. I need space."

Spotting the tomatoes, she plucked one from the basket and bit into it. Juice dripped down her chin. She stopped chewing to frown at Lucie. "Don't you have a class this evening?"

"At six. Why?"

"It's five thirty."

"Just what I need, another kid to keep on schedule," she said after Lucie ran to the house. "I've raised mine already. I don't want to deal with wet towels on the bathroom floor, dirty dishes in the sink, and a girl who thinks nothing about invading my privacy, but is paranoid when it comes to hers. Would you believe she locks the door to her room even to go to the bathroom?"

"Because she's used to a prying mother?"

Gladys grinned. "Did she also tell you about the poor suffering daddy? He sounds like a whiner to me, the kind that demands attention and feeds off everyone's sympathy. Too bad she can't live with him. I'm tempted to throw her out, but I'd run the risk of Lamont being in my face constantly to make sure I'm all right. He's a nagger, that one." She took another bite of the tomato. "So what do you think of Lucie?"

I paused to think. "She has opossum teeth."

Gladys chuckled. "You are mean, Claire. The only thing I like about the girl is her loyalty to her dad. She says he had a traumatic childhood."

"I heard. How so?"

Gladys shrugged. "She didn't say. But it could be a lie. The girl does drama like Walter Cronkite did news. Speaking of drama, there's a good one brewing. Lamont tells me she's running around with a rough-looking guy, twice her age. I would flip if she were my kid. I wonder if Daddy knows."

"Probably doesn't care. And as she pointed out, she's of age. What was it you wanted to tell me?" I asked, tired of talking about Lucie.

Gladys looked at me. "What do you mean?"

"Lucie said you wanted to see me."

"And you fell for it? All I said was that I hoped to be back by the time you came. The kid just wanted to meet you. She's nosy as hell. Now," Gladys said, leaning back in her chair. "Tell me about your long-lost aunt and don't spare the details."

Ruth had been talking. The French aunt was the last person I wanted to talk about, but with Ruth priming the pump I knew I couldn't refuse. Who was nosy now?

CHAPTER TWELVE

The evening news didn't give an update on the Haitian's condition. But the interpreter was expected at noon the next day.

Chantal ate little that evening and said even less. I studied her, wondering what she intended to do. If she came to rescue the Haitians, she wouldn't stay with me long. There was no reason for her to stick around. On the other hand, she might, just to find out what happened to her brother.

So where was he?

She went to bed early without telling me what she intended to do the next day. I left her a note in the morning telling her I would be gone until the afternoon. Sally had left a message requesting my presence.

I found Sally eating breakfast. She sat at the table, cup in hand, a plate with a smear of fried egg in front of her. She was reading the morning paper.

I got myself a cup of coffee and sat across from her. "Did you work last night?"

She looked up from the paper, her eyes unfocused. "No. I didn't get to bed until two."

"I was hoping you had reinvented the preacher."

"No, I've been seriously thinking about Howard's idea to write a real book. You think I should?"

Not unless she wanted to live off her portfolio. For five years, bodice rippers had nicely padded her income. Memoirs were nice, but she could hardly write half a dozen, and her one and only might flop. "I don't know that you *should*, but you're certainly free to give it a try."

She caught the reservation. "You don't think it's a good idea?"

"I'm not saying it's a bad one, Sally. I'm saying you'll be taking a chance. Memoirs aren't as easy to sell as romances. It's a totally different market. You'll also be dealing with a different publisher." I paused before asking, "When do you plan to start?"

"Right away."

FRENCH LEAVE

So she had already made up her mind. "OK. So what happens to *Mischief in Michigan*?"

Sally scraped at the egg smear on her plate, picked up a crust of bread to nibble at the edge. "Howard said I should give it up."

The publisher wouldn't be happy. Sally's contract called for two books a year and this was the second.

"If you do, I hope you honor the work I've done so far." There was no reason why she wouldn't, but the reminder was necessary. I needed the money. "Get your ideas together and call me when you have enough material."

The suggestion fell into a void. The silence lasted so long I knew something was wrong.

"That won't be necessary. To call you, I mean. I won't need your help."

"I see." It was the end of my modest but steady income. "In other words, you're firing me."

She pushed the paper away from her. "Not exactly, Claire. We could say we're parting ways. I'm changing course, that's all."

***

Parting ways. I thought of those words a half hour later as I sat in a fast food booth with a Styrofoam plate of hotcakes in front of me. She made it sound as if the decision was mutual. What happened to her idea of making me office manager?

Howard happened.

As soon as he brought up the idea of writing a "real book" she went for it. Bodice rippers made money, but they weren't literature and I knew she yearned for the respect and admiration the public accorded serious authors. Our five-year partnership was no match for a chance at fame. I should've known not to expect loyalty from her.

Lisa was right. I should have left her when she turned demanding, even if it meant losing a regular paycheck. It was no good looking back, but I couldn't compound the mistake wasting time feeling sorry for myself. It was time to advertise my experience as a serious book editor and coach to draw more authors. The first step was to find office space.

How much money would I need? I was jotting numbers on a paper napkin when my phone rang.

I glanced at it. Sally. I let it ring until it stopped. She didn't leave a message. The cell rang a second time. I turned it off and stuffed it in my pocket.

I got up, dumped my untouched pancakes and left, slowing

at the door to give an elderly couple time to exit. The man was leaning on a cane, the woman on a walker. They smiled sweetly when I held the door for them. The couple cleared the way and made their slow progress to the antique Buick parked in the handicapped space. I went around them and headed for my car.

Two spaces from the Buick, Lucie, Gladys's boarder, sat in the front seat of an SUV facing a man who stood near the passenger door holding two containers of coffee. Tall, with a broad back and thick arms, he was hip in tan chinos, a close-fitting baseball cap and boat shoes.

I scooted past. Lucie was laughing at something the guy said. I reached my car unnoticed.

When I arrived home, Chantal wasn't at the house. Given the sticky state of the kitchen counter, it appeared she had eaten breakfast before leaving. Bread crumbs stuck to a smear of strawberry jam, the coffee pot had been left on, and the morning paper was scattered across the island. She had been in a hurry to leave. I rinsed the dried coffee residue out of the carafe, squared the paper and ran a sponge over the counter. The scene in Sally's kitchen kept running through my head, looping upon itself.

I took the paper to the porch. The Metro section was filled with pictures of uprooted trees, mobile homes off their foundations, downed electric poles. The related article detailed the damage left by Friday's storm. It mentioned that the pickup involved in the wreck that killed two men and injured the Haitian had come from Texas. It had been stolen.

"I thought I saw your car," Ruth said, coming up the porch steps, interrupting my reading. "You taking the day off?"

She was in her usual summer outfit of drawstring pants and a man's shirt with the sleeves rolled up at the elbow. Her little bun of gray hair sprang wisps that straggled down her neck.

I put the paper down. "That wasn't the plan."

"Your boss entertaining someone special, is she?" Ruth knew all about Sally's numerous boyfriends. Not from me—I didn't tattle—but Clayton was small and Sally notorious for her flings. "Well, since you've got nothing better to do," she said before I had time to answer, "you might as well take me to the supermarket."

I obliged. We were quiet during the ride. If Ruth was aware that my mind was elsewhere she didn't let on. By mid-afternoon the morning flap with Sally was losing some of its drama and

I was beginning to doubt her intention to quit writing bodice rippers. It wouldn't last. Howard would probably follow his predecessors out the door. With him gone and money drying up, she would want me back.

And I would...do what? Tell her she was on her own? Insecurity put its thumb on the scale. I loved the idea of being my own boss, but building a business that was profitable was chancy.

It was four when Ruth and I came back. Chantal's car wasn't at the curb. I wondered where she was.

We carried Ruth's groceries to her house and I took what I bought to mine. I was heading back out to park the car in the garage when footsteps rang in the hallway. The kitchen door opened and Chantal came in. She was barefoot and half dressed with her blouse hanging out of her pants. Her hair was wild. She stopped cold when she saw me.

"Mon Dieu!" She exhaled heavily and patted her chest. "Je ne m'attendais pas... I didn't expect to see you here, Claire."

"Neither did I. Where's your car?"

"I put it in the garage."

Joe's weekend car occupied half of the two-car garage. The other half was mine. I would sooner let someone sleep in my bed than give up my parking spot. My face said as much and she rushed to explain, "It is only for a little while, Claire. The steering wheel it gets so hot in the sun."

"I thought you were at work," she said after an awkward silence.

"There was a change of plan so I took Ruth shopping and bought a few things for dinner."

"Dinner!" She greeted the word with enthusiasm, visibly grateful for a chance to change the subject. "Of course! I will cook for you this evening, yes? To thank you for your hospitality." She tucked her blouse into her pants. "What did you buy for this evening?"

"There's no need for you to cook. I was going to cook sausages on the grill."

"It is not about need. I would very much like to make dinner for you." She walked over to the counter and looked to see what I had bought. "Poulet. Chicken is good. Cream, butter."

I didn't like the way she was taking over.

"You were making a blanquette de poulet, yes? Chardonnay," she said before I could respond, pulling out a wine bottle. She frowned at the label. "Do you have shallots?"

"No, just onions."

"I will need shallots."

Dinner sounded like trouble. "For what?"

"I could make poulet aux morilles. Your fazzer likes chicken with morels. I have everything I need except for shallots and the morilles, of course."

"And they are...?"

She was surprised. "Mushrooms, Claire. They are not in season, but the dried ones are good also." She looked at her watch. It was four thirty. "You go to the supermarket now, yes?"

I hesitated. My grilled brats would take no time and I was hungry.

"Yes?" she said again, her eyes pleading.

I gave in. "OK. Give me a list."

CHAPTER THIRTEEN

I found out Clayton was a two-mushroom town. While supermarkets offered sliced and whole, the fungi only came in white mushrooms and portobello. The fancy downtown food store where Cora shopped didn't know what morels were and didn't care to find out. I drove to three different grocery stores in addition to the big chain supermarkets before deciding to call the house for advice. Chantal didn't answer.

I was putting the phone away when it dinged to announce a text message. It was from Sally. *Mischief in Michigan* was back on track. She didn't say why, but my guess was that she had called the editor and found out that bailing out wasn't an option. She asked me to come out at eight the next morning to pick up the transcriber with three new chapters. Howard was due at nine. She wanted me gone by the time he showed up.

In other words, she didn't want him to know she was finishing the book. I missed the old Sally, the queen of blunt who wasn't afraid to speak her mind.

I gave up on the morels and bought a package of button mushrooms. Chantal's rental wasn't parked at the curb when I pulled up to the house. It could be in the garage, still. Or it could be she'd grown tired of waiting and was out chasing morels. Fine. I parked in the driveway and went in.

The kitchen was empty, the package of chicken intact on the counter. "No morels to be had anywhere, Chantal. But I bought white mushrooms. Will they do?" She didn't answer. I walked over to her bedroom, knocked on the door and stuck my head inside. The room was empty. I checked the living room next and even looked on the back porch.

OK. So she had gone out.

My stomach growled. The grilled brats would have been done by now. I opened a sleeve of saltines and turned the TV on to watch the local news.

The same young reporter who earlier covered the Haitian story stood in the same spot in the hospital parking lot. Same suit, same tie, but this time the wind wasn't blowing. "...wearing green scrubs pushed the wheelchair out the main entrance," he said, pointing behind him and the camera panned to the set of revolving doors. "The patient..."

The doorbell rang. Had Chantal forgotten her key? I went to the door.

It wasn't the missing French aunt but a kid collecting money for baseball uniforms. By the time I was done with him the broadcast had ended. Was the Haitian the patient the reporter was about to mention? I flipped through the other local channels hoping to catch the story, but I was too late. The local broadcasts had made way for the national news.

I called Ruth. "Did you catch the news about a patient leaving the hospital?" I asked her. She was washing dishes. I heard water running.

"Don't know, hon. I didn't watch the news tonight. Is it important?"

"Just curious." I thanked her and hung up.

The national news ended and still no Chantal. I put the chicken away. What could be keeping her? I made myself a cheese sandwich and flipped the channel to watch *Jeopardy*.

The three contestants, one man and two women, were looking frazzled. Two were in the red, the third, the champion, had so far won $1,200. He chose the $400 clue in the eighteenth century custom category. "Gallic departure," Alex Trebek said. The contestants didn't move. No one pushed the buzzer.

"What is French Leave?" Trebek said, looking a bit smug. It was easy to look clever when you knew the answer beforehand. "It means unceremonious departure, such as a guest leaving a party without thanking the host," he clarified for the sake of the three contestants and the audience.

French Leave? I laughed out loud. Not only had the French aunt French-left, she had reneged on her promise to cook dinner.

Seriously, had she? I looked at my watch. Seven twenty. How long did it take to buy morels? An eternity if one lived in Clayton, but by this time she should've run out of food stores. Surely she didn't go to Columbus. I went back to the guest room to check it more thoroughly. That's when I realized the closet was empty. Her suitcase was missing.

French Leave for sure. Why did she leave in a tearing hurry? Was it an emergency? Did she, maybe, get word that her brother was ill? In need of help? But if she took the time to pack her suitcase, why didn't she leave me a note? Or call my cell? She had the number.

I checked the phone. There was no message.

I searched the room for a note, didn't find one. But when I looked inside the closet I saw that the cardboard box Ruth found on my doorstep had been searched. And the money, the $800 in cash I had found in the pocket of the old coat, that money was gone.

I went through the whole box. Some of the clothes were missing as well.

Which meant she knew the money and the clothes would be waiting for her before she came. It was proof she made the trip to take care of the Haitians. OK. I understood taking the money. But the clothes? They had no value. It could no longer be for the Haitians. They were no longer her concern.

I sat on the bed to think. She clearly hadn't expected me back so early and had sent me on a frivolous errand to get me out of the way. To do what?

What did she need to do right then and not earlier in the day? I didn't get back until the middle of the afternoon.

I walked to the kitchen to make another cheese sandwich and ate it standing up. Eating didn't stir up my little gray cells. Coffee, "the think drink," didn't help either. I didn't know whether to be mad or relieved. I was a bit of both, angry because she had lied to me, but glad to know she and her brother were out of my hair. At nine I went back out to put the Ford in the garage.

I was in bed by ten. It took me hours to go to sleep, and even then I catnapped, alert for the sound of a key in the lock. But it never came.

***

As instructed, I was at Sally's house by eight. Punctuality didn't help. Howard's Mercedes was parked in the driveway. I drove past and went to a fast-food restaurant for breakfast. At this hour it was filled with harried customers on their way to work, served by a harried morning crew. A cloud of frustration and general dissatisfaction hung over the place, polluting the comforting aroma of coffee and hot fat. I ordered coffee and a sausage biscuit and took the tray to the dining area. In the first booth on my right, I ran into Lisa facing a stack of pancakes.

I slid my tray on the table and sat across from her. She didn't seem happy to see me. "Why are you here? It's not in your neighborhood."

She tore open the package of syrup. "I could ask you the same question."

I removed the lid from my coffee and studied her. Lisa never was fastidious about her clothes, but this morning she looked downright shabby, sporting a T-shirt with a hole on one shoulder, and stains down the front.

I observed the bad attitude and the crappy outfit with great interest. Did they mean trouble at home? I'd been hoping for some time that she would break up with her newest live-in, the creepiest of all her short-lived and usually creepy boyfriends. With a hatchet face, thin lips and sandy hair that straggled down his neck, Steve wasn't even close to good-looking. He was also a know-it-all. I knew him all too well. He was and had been Joe's best bud for years.

I put aside my speculation over Lisa's bad mood to tell her I had decided to follow her advice to rent office space.

She was surprised. "Really? I expected you to chicken out."

"I appreciate your faith in me."

"Like you care! I'll let the manager know you're serious about the room. He said there were one or two possibilities."

We talked rent and the cost of outfitting my future office, of utilities. The discussion lasted long after we finished eating. When we were done, she left to go to her studio and I headed back to Sally's. Howard's car was still in the driveway.

FRENCH LEAVE

I went home. At midmorning on a workday Woodland Avenue was quiet. A sprinkler chirped over a lawn; tunes from a commercial floated out an open window; a basketball thumped somewhere in a backyard. The only jarring note was a black and white parked at the curb in front of Marlene's house with two uniforms inside. Police cars seldom cruised the neighborhood. The last time they paid us a visit was the day the two men had shot at Medicare Dundee. I picked up the day's paper lying on the driveway and went inside to make a pot of coffee. My cell phone rang.

It was Lisa. "Look at the paper."

"Why?"

"Take a look at the front page," she insisted before ending the call.

I shook the paper out of its plastic sleeve. The black-and-white picture on the front page, taken from the high angle of a security camera, showed a short thin female orderly pushing a dark-skinned man in a wheelchair out of the hospital's main entrance. Her upturned face looked directly at the lens. "Do you know this woman?" the caption asked in a bold font.

The doorbell rang. I dropped the paper to look out the window. The two uniforms I had seen earlier were standing on the porch.

140

FRANÇOISE BARTRAM

"Claire Palmer?" the tallest of the men asked when I opened the door. They were older than the patrolman who had canvassed the neighborhood earlier. One was on the short side with a compact middle and wide shoulders. His taller companion had a buzz cut, a square chin and thin lips. Over their heads I saw my neighbor Marlene peering out her front window.

"Yes?"

"We need to ask a few questions," Buzz Cut said.

Marlene stood so close to the pane her breath fogged the glass.

"What about?"

The patrolmen exchanged a look. "Have you seen today's paper?"

"No. I just got home."

The short cop handed me a picture. "Do you know this woman?"

It was an enlarged, clearer copy of the shot featured on the newspaper's front page. The woman had wide-spaced anxious eyes.

"Do you?" he insisted when I was slow to answer.

"Can't say that I do."

"It looks a lot like you."

I noticed that earlier, same triangular face, same sharp chin. "But it's not. The hair is different, for one thing."

"You could've changed the style."

Style was a big word to describe the way I wore my hair. "Mine is longer." I pointed, stretching a strand dangling over my forehead. "When was the picture taken?"

"Yesterday."

"I don't think my hair grew two inches overnight." Buzz Cut thinned his already thin lips to let me know he caught the sarcasm. "What did the woman do?"

"She took a patient out of the hospital at nine thirty yesterday morning. The man is an illegal alien from Haiti, a suspect in the theft of a pickup. Can you tell us where you were at nine thirty?"

"At work."

I would've been better prepared if the doorbell hadn't kept me from watching the news the night before.

"Where's that?"

I told them.

"You say it's a private home," Buzz Cut said. "Can anyone confirm you were at work?"

"My boss. We're writers. She was having breakfast when I came in."

"We'll need her name."

FRANÇOISE BARTRAM

I gave them the information they needed. Before leaving, the short cop held up the picture once again. "Give it another look. Are you sure you don't know who the woman is? You look like her. Could she be a sister, a cousin?"

I shook my head. "My sister is a natural blonde and looks nothing like me and we don't have cousins."

Defeated, the short cop put the picture away and followed his partner down the steps.

Did Marlene see Chantal? The French aunt was at my place for four days, long enough to be seen by the neighbors. Or had someone else noticed I looked like the woman in scrubs and notified the police?

Nice to know I had law-abiding neighbors.

I went back to the kitchen to read the article on the front page. The Haitian hadn't been deemed a flight risk because he had a concussion and was bedridden. A nurse gave the alarm when she noticed his bed was empty. A couple entering the hospital saw a woman wearing scrubs leaving with a patient. They described the orderly as slight in stature and struggling to push the wheelchair out to the parking lot.

The sheriff urged all medical personnel to alert police if a tall dark-skinned man in his mid to late teens, with a head injury and lacerations to the face came in for treatment.

Chantal had taken him while I was at work. Now I understood why she looked flustered when I came home unexpectedly, why she was half dressed and disheveled. She had probably just taken off the scrubs to change into regular clothes. Where was the Haitian then?

God, did Marlene see them when they pulled into the driveway?

No, Marlene couldn't have seen them because Chantal had the smarts to pull the car into the garage. The morning glories clinging to the lattice along the breezeway between the house and the garage would've hidden them. Or did she leave him in the car? No, it would have been too hot in there for a man recovering from serious injuries.

She had planned on leaving him in the house while she changed and packed for both. They should have been gone by the time I was scheduled to come home, but I showed up early. No wonder she was rattled.

Where was the Haitian when I came home? She would've kept him out of sight.

Years ago Gin had hired Ray, Ruth's brother, to close off part of the basement to build a third bedroom. Bedroom was a grand name for a windowless ten-by-ten cubicle with a miniscule bath attached. Gin had the idea of supplementing her income by taking in a boarder as Ruth did a decade later. Gin rented the apartment until her last boarder retired. Like Cal, he was a railroader who bunked there on his one night away from home. I rented the room from her when I landed my first job after high school. Even though it was a relief to be out of Cora's house, I never cared for the place. It was cold in winter, damp in summer and dark year-round.

I went downstairs. Green scrubs lay on the floor near the washer. I remembered Ruth saying Chantal had been out all day while I was working at Sally's, and that she had come home with shopping bags. She had gone out to case the hospital and probably bought scrubs and necessities for the kid before driving home.

In the basement bedroom I found a rumpled sheet on the mattress of the bed that filled half the room.

How could Chantal run the risk of taking the boy away? Flashback to her brother's arrest. She had to know what would happen if she was caught.

FRENCH LEAVE

And if she was, would I be accused of conspiracy? If Buzz Cut and his sidekick did a repeat visit they would do more than stand on the doorstep.

I spent the next hour cleaning. I stripped down the bed in the basement, threw the sheet and pillowcase in the washer along with Chantal's bedding and the scrubs she had worn. I vacuumed and dusted the guest room, folded the blankets and stacked them on the bare mattress. When the laundry was done, I buried the scrubs in a bag destined for a thrift store.

I was carrying the bag out to the car when I saw that Marlene was still standing guard behind her front window, hoping for action.

I pretended not to see, and drove off to get rid of the evidence.

CHAPTER FOURTEEN

I went clear across town to drop the bag at a Goodwill store. The rest of the day passed without further incident. I turned in early, but I was too keyed up to sleep. It was close to dawn when I finally dropped off.

I woke up late and dawdled over breakfast. Ruth called to say she had started her canning the day before to use some of the vegetables we had harvested after the storm. She would be busy for the rest of the week.

"Did Tchantall hear from her brother?"

"She isn't here, Ruth. She had to return home because of an emergency. Something to do with her son."

I was grateful for the storm that kept Ruth too busy to read the paper and see Chantal's picture on the front page. Would she have turned her in? I didn't think so, but she would've been tempted. She had little sympathy for illegal aliens.

I went out to work in the garden until the heat drove me back inside. Sally didn't call to reschedule our meeting.

There was no mention of the Haitian and his rescuer on the noon news. Maybe she knew exactly where to go after taking the man from the hospital. Another safe house? The guy could be in Canada already and Chantal heading back to France.

I was finishing lunch when Sally called to say Howard wouldn't be at her house for the next two days and to come the next morning, the coast was clear.

***

Thursday was cleaning day, but there was no sign of Norma's van when I arrived. I went in the front door, and out of habit glanced at the table in the living room. Sally's boyfriends were, by and large, generous. Over the years she had gotten into the habit of displaying the gifts she received on the coffee table. Traditional offerings of flowers and candy were the norm, but there were unusual ones: a Panama hat from a Cuban doctor, a refugee who did his internship in a nearby hospital; a bolt of red silk, gift of an airline pilot who flew a Far East route; and a magnum of Veuve Clicquot champagne brought by a French diplomat. Where and how she had met those men was a mystery, though I suspected it involved a dating service. Howard wasn't generous. Since meeting him the coffee table showed nothing but Norma's polishing skill.

Sally had left a note in the office asking me to work quietly. The previous day had been trying and she needed her sleep.

At mid-morning a florist delivered a cellophane-wrapped bundle of carnations. I placed the flowers on the coffee table and took a card out of the envelope pinned to the wrapping. It just said "Sorry" in a small, almost illegible hand. It looked like Howard's parsimonious ways extended to apologies.

Sally came down at eleven wrapped from neck to toe in a robe made of red shimmery material. A green ruffled cap kept her hair in place. The Fruit of the Loom guys would have loved her.

She glowered at me when I joined her in the kitchen. "What are you looking at?"

"Your smiling face. Didn't you sleep well?"

She reached inside the cabinet for a mug and slammed the door shut. "No. Is there any coffee left?"

I was pretty sure it wasn't insomnia that made her cranky. Howard's one-word apology hinted at a serious difference of opinion. "There's plenty."

She opened the oven to take out the iron skillet, slammed it on the front burner and walked to the refrigerator for a package of bacon. Without bothering to separate the slices she dumped the lot in the skillet and turned the fire on high. "I will finish that damned book if it kills me. Never mind what people think."

Sally turned, catching me watching her. "What are you waiting for? Go back to work."

"I'm going. When you're done with breakfast, you might want to check the coffee table. The florist made a delivery an hour ago."

She froze. "Was there a card?"

"Yes."

She dropped the fork she was holding and left, red robe swirling. Her mules clattered on the hardwood floor until she reached the living room where the carpet muffled her steps. I heard a crinkle of cellophane then nothing until she went back up the stairs, her feet hitting the steps like a sledgehammer. In Sally's book of manners, repentance was measured in roses, one dozen at a time.

I turned the fire out under the bacon and went back to work. Sally stomped back down half an hour later and blew past the office, slamming the kitchen door on her way out. At lunchtime I went to the kitchen and ran into Norma wearing a canary-colored duster that matched the rubber gloves on her hands. A bandana knotted low on the forehead covered her hair. I paused in the doorway, the toes of my sneakers even with the edge of the tiled floor, wondering if it was safe to walk over to the coffee pot. She shot me a look through small rectangular glasses that narrowed her eyes to slits.

"Sally gone?" She lifted the mop she was leaning on to ram it into the bucket at her feet.

"Yes. She left a while back."

"I thought so. Sit!" she ordered, pointing a yellow finger at the table in the bay window.

Crossing Norma wasn't a good idea. In the right mood she just waited for an excuse to fire .44-caliber bullets out of her Magnum mouth.

After I walked over to the table, she clomped to the counter on thick-soled shoes, took a mug out of the cupboard and filled it with coffee.

"Drink," she ordered, slamming the mug down on the table in front of me. "You don't look like you got all your ducks in a row this morning and I want you to pay attention." She dropped into the chair across from me.

I reached for the mug. "Pay attention to what?"

"What I'm about to tell you. But first, what do you know about that Howard?"

"No more than you do. The man is a blank slate. I don't even know his last name."

"Steele," she said. She took off her glasses to clean them on the corner of her smock. Without the rectangular frames her face rounded out.

"How did you find out?"

"Looked it up in Sal's little book," she said without a flicker of embarrassment. Sally's little book held the names of all her boyfriends, along with numbers to rate their performance. She bragged about it but kept it hidden from prying eyes. Obviously not well enough. I wondered if there was a number beside Howard's name. A zero would be good. Sally's top rating was ten. She once confided she had never rated anyone that high, but was still looking.

"No number," Norma said, reading my mind. "It hasn't happened and I know why. He has other fish to fry, and the other fish is half Sally's age and wears tight pants."

CHAPTER FIFTEEN

"I saw them," Norma insisted, reading doubt on my face. "They were coming out of a restaurant together. He looked relaxed, not with his nose up in the air the way he does with Sally. They walked over to the Mercedes and before they got in she put her arms around him."

"Did he see you?"

"No. He was too busy looking at her." Norma frowned. "I don't get it. Here's a man with the charisma of a stinkbug and he's got two women running after him."

I blinked, still trying to visualize Howard with a young thing. "You aren't planning on telling Sally, are you?"

She rubbed her forehead. "I was considering it."

"Don't. You know how she hates interference. What I don't get is why he's sticking around. They aren't lovers. What does he get out of the relationship?"

"Access to Sal's money?"

"Like she would let him!" Yes, money was the most obvious explanation, but in that case why did he talk her into abandoning bodice rippers? He had to know that even if she succeeded in writing a mainstream novel it wouldn't sell as well as her other books.

"What?" Norma asked, picking up on the hesitation.

"He talked her into switching from bodice rippers to novels. That would lower her income."

Norma guffawed. "Sally, write a novel? I don't see it. Unless you..." She cocked an eye in my direction.

I shook my head. "Out of my league, Norma. I'm out of the picture anyway. As soon as we finish *Mischief in Michigan*, I'm gone."

Norma clapped her yellow hands. "She *fired* you? Damn! That's some news you're giving me. That does it, Claire. We *have* to tell her about the girl."

"She won't believe you."

"She will if I take a picture of them together."

"How are you gonna do that? We know nothing about the man, not where he works, not even where he lives."

"We would if Sally's little book listed addresses."

"But we know it doesn't," I said impatiently.

"But there's always the phone book." Energized, she pushed back her chair and headed to the office, nylon smock rustling. She came back with the residential listings. I knew he wouldn't be in there. The listings were old. After peeling her gloves, she licked her index finger to flip pages. "Steele. Here it is. Anthony, Bruce, Charles." She ran her finger down the column. "Harold, Hugh. Damn! No Howard."

"He always calls from his cell. Maybe he isn't from Clayton."

Crouched over the phone book, Norma peered at me over the rim of her glasses. "His car has Ohio plates."

"Ohio's a big place."

She sucked her teeth. "I just figured he was local. Maybe I should look up the second number in Sally's book. He gave it to her when his cell was out and she couldn't get hold of him. I remember her grousing about it."

"And do what with it?"

Norma straightened up. "If it's a landline number, I can look it up in reverse listings. I should look for the book before Sal gets back."

FRENCH LEAVE

Too late. The kitchen door leading to the outside swung open and Sally blew in like an ill wind. Everything about her—the red face, the frizzy hair flaming around her head, the heaving chest—said she was close to combustion. She had gone halfway through the room when she turned to look at us. "What are you staring at? Go back to work!" She stomped out and a minute later we heard her pound the steps to the second floor.

"Well," Norma said, reaching for her rubber gloves. Her smock rustled. "Ain't Missy in a snit! While she's in her room sulking, I'll check to see if her little book's in the drawer of the hall table." She retrieved her mop bucket and pushed it out of the room, the little wheels squeaking merrily. A minute later, she popped her head back in. "I forgot to ask. Who's the dame on the paper's front page pushing the guy in the wheelchair? She kind of looks like you."

"What makes you think it's not me?"

Norma looked surprised. "Is it? Why would you do that?"

"I didn't. I only asked because some people thought it was me."

"Like you would do something that crazy! You can be an airhead sometimes, Claire, but you aren't stupid."

Good to know.

CHAPTER SIXTEEN

Ruth called after I came home. "You heard from your aunt?"

"No."

"Gladys wanted to meet her. She's invited us for pie and coffee this evening. I'm taking a break from canning. You coming?"

"Sure. Call me when you get ready to leave."

I watched the news during dinner. The broadcast was dominated by a protest at the courthouse. The half-dozen protestors with placards condemning fracking faced a hard-faced sheriff and deputies bristling with hardware. It ended with sports and weather. The only mention made of the Haitian was to assure the public that police were still looking.

Ruth and I walked the few steps to Gladys's house together. "Where's your aunt, Claire?" our hostess asked when she let us in.

"She went back to France."

FRENCH LEAVE

"Too bad. I was looking forward to meeting her. Come on then," she said, stepping to the side to let us in. "Coffee's on."

"Where did you get those quilts?" I asked when we passed the wall hangings. "They're unusual."

She stopped. "Is that a polite way of saying you don't like them?"

"No. Actually, I do."

"I made them when I took a class back in Cleveland."

I stepped closer to study the stitching. "You are really good with a needle, Gladys. Did you follow a pattern?"

"No, I kind of felt my way through. The other students chose traditional designs, but not me. I don't like patterns."

Gin had been a quilter and tried to teach me. I was never good at it, but I knew enough about the craft to appreciate the artistry.

Ruth pointedly didn't join in the conversation and went on to the kitchen. Like Gin she had learned quilting at her mother's knee. Traditional was her game.

The kitchen table was set with cups and saucers, dessert plates and neatly folded paper napkins. The coffee Gladys poured was so dark it looked like tar. "It's got chicory in it," she said when she gave me a cup. "I have it shipped from down south. I order so much of it I'm on a first-name basis with the UPS man."

Ruth frowned at the dark brew. "Where did you learn to drink coffee like that?"

"In New Orleans where I grew up. I lived there until I moved to Cleveland with my old man. Two years later he quit working and skipped out on me and the kids so I divorced him." She muttered something about poor judgment as she cut into the peach pie she had brought to the table.

I took a sip of coffee. It was strong with a hint of bitterness. Ruth dumped milk and sugar in hers after tasting it.

"Why didn't you go back to New Orleans after the divorce?" I asked Gladys.

"No money. Dewayne took our car when he left. I didn't miss him, but I sure could have used that car. If it hadn't been for my mama, I don't know what I would've done. She came and stayed with the kids while I worked days and went to dental school evenings."

"Was it your mother who taught you to bake?" Ruth asked after tasting the pie.

"She sure did." Gladys turned abruptly and walked over to the doorway that led to the living room. She bellowed, "Lucie, you want coffee?" There was no response.

FRENCH LEAVE

"Where's your mother now?" Ruth asked.

"Dead." Gladys's bluntness didn't encourage further questions, but her face softened and she added, "She'd just turned eighty when she passed. Dewayne had found us again and kept coming by demanding money. She had a bad heart. I'm not saying he killed her, but he sure didn't make it easy for her."

"I have no use for the man," Gladys said without heat, more in sadness than anger. "I think I knew it from the start, but I was too young to know better. So when Doc Shoenberg moved his practice here and asked me to come, I went for it. He said I might as well. We'd worked together so long it felt like we were married." Gladys chuckled, the sound coming from deep in her chest.

"You know what you should do about your ex?" Lucie asked, slipping into the room on little cat feet. Barefoot and bare-legged, she wore what had to be the shortest pair of shorts in the universe. A towel was wrapped, turban style, around her head. She flapped a hand at Ruth and me in greeting.

"Here comes the resident fountain of wisdom," Gladys said, the smile slipping from her face.

Lucie ignored the jab. "Where's your aunt, Claire?" she asked, looking around the kitchen as if she expected to find Chantal hiding in a corner.

"She went back to France."

"She didn't stay long. You really should tell the fire investigator about your ex," Lucie said in the same breath, turning back to Gladys. "He threatened you. It's obvious he followed you here."

Gladys reached for the pie dish. "And you know this how…?"

"Lamont told me."

"Did he now?" Gladys slid a pie wedge on a plate. She took a paper napkin from the holder on the table, folded it in half, all the while keeping her eyes down. "Did he say he knew his grandfather was actually here?"

"No, but it stands to reason the man followed you here. Lamont said he had been harassing you for ages." Lucie pulled the towel off her head and ran a hand through her wet hair. The scent of herbal shampoo mingled with the sweetness of the pie.

Gladys pushed the plate in Lucie's direction. "Stands to reason is hardly proof."

Lucie rolled her eyes. "Don't say I didn't warn you. Withholding the truth's as good as lying and the insurance company won't like it." She took the plate Gladys gave her and walked out.

Ruth sniffed at her departing back and mumbled something I didn't catch.

"I wish Lamont would keep his mouth shut," Gladys said sweeping crumbs off the table. "But I don't entirely blame the boy. Dewayne pulled stupid shit all his life. But I'll be damned if I tell the insurance company about him. I want him out of my hair for good."

* * *

"I understand now why Lamont didn't want Gladys living by herself," I said to Ruth as we walked home an hour later. Night was falling. Heat lightning zigzagged across the sky. "He was afraid his grandfather had tracked her down."

"With good reason," Ruth said, slipping her arm through mine. "For all her talk, I believe she's glad to have company. There's safety in numbers."

"Depends on the company," I said, and Ruth chuckled. I thought Gladys would've been just as happy with a guard dog.

We parted ways at the bottom of Ruth's driveway. The night was still. In the east where the cloud cover was thinner stars shone weakly. In the west the sky was solid black. I cut across the lawn to reach the kitchen door. The outdoor thermometer on the breezeway said 87.

I unlocked the door and went in. Though I had lived in the same house for years, going in never failed to make me feel good. I turned my face to the cool air flowing from the air vent. Air conditioning had been my second big expense after getting the kitchen done. I never regretted the cost. I offered to get it installed while Gin was alive but she refused, claiming she had learned to live without it and fans were just as good anyway.

I crossed the kitchen and opened the door that led to the foyer. A stream of warm, humid air smelling of boxwood pushed against my face. I traced it to the master bedroom.

The window was open. A breeze bellied the curtain over the sash, pushing the peppery scent of the shrubs that grew along the base of the house into the room. The window had been forced open from the outside, probably with a crowbar. I could see deep indentations on the sill.

Instinctively I looked over my shoulder at the open door that led into the foyer. The fact that the doorway was empty, as was the brightly lit space beyond, didn't reassure me. The house had shifted from familiar to foreign.

I walked over to the door and listened for unfamiliar sounds. The curtain whispered as a breeze swept it over the sill. A floor vent rattled. Outside a car with a thumping radio went past.

My heart beat in my ears. The same car, or another, thumped past again. Kids walking by called to each other and laughed. I went back to the window and lowered the sash, cutting outside sounds.

A comfortable silence, occasionally spiked with familiar indoor sounds, settled over the house. Eventually I felt brave enough to leave the bedroom and search the rest of the house. It was empty. I went down into the basement next. No one was there either. Whoever came in had gone, leaving no trace except for a wisp of fragrance, a green smell sharper than the boxwood's.

Nothing was missing, nothing was in disarray.

I would have felt better if something had been taken, the flatscreen TV or spare change or the gold watch Cora had given me for my high school graduation, anything to make sense of the break-in. But the intruder had floated in and out like a ghost.

A French ghost? But surely by now Chantal had left the state, the country even.

I locked the window before I went to bed and rammed a ruler between the lower sash and the window frame. A bit late but it made me feel better.

***

Norma called the next morning as I was getting ready for work. She said, "I've been thinking..."

I put the phone on speaker and set it on the dresser so I could run a brush through my hair. The mirror wasn't kind. I had bed hair and red-rimmed eyes. "What about?"

"Howard's other number, the one Sally used when his cell was out. We need it."

"No, we don't, Norma. Sally can take care of herself." At the moment I didn't really care what was happening to her. "Let it go."

"Damned if I will! The man is a liar."

"So what? He'll go away eventually. They all do."

"He won't if he's after her money. How are we going to stop him when we don't know the first thing about him, where he lives or what he does for a living? If the number in Sally's book turns out to be a landline number, we could at least find out where he lives. It's a start and that's where you come in, Claire. You can get it."

"What's wrong with you doing it?"

"Because I'm not due at Sal's until next Thursday."

I winced as the brush hit a tangle. "So what? We'll wait."

FRENCH LEAVE

"We can't afford to wait, Claire! Don't you care what happens to her? She's your friend."

"She isn't acting like it. But that's beside the point. Howard is Sally's problem to solve, not mine."

"What do you mean he's not *your* problem? He got you fired, didn't he? And if she quits writing, I'll have to fire myself. Not that I'd miss the money, but she's one of my first people and I'd like to keep her. I'm not asking much, Claire. All you have to do is look in the book and write the number down. How hard is that?"

"I'm not going to search the house for it."

"You won't have to, not if she left it in the hall table. *Please*, Claire?"

I averted my eyes from my reflection in the mirror. My hair looked as tired as I felt. "I'll think about it."

***

I could hear Sally talking to someone on the upstairs phone when I arrived. I made enough noise to let her know I was in the house. She had sworn she would finish *Mischief in Michigan* if it killed her. She was killing the book instead, giving me stuff that was so bad I was ashamed to transcribe it. But what did I care? My name wouldn't be on the cover.

Upstairs, Sally kept talking. Time for a quick look at the hall table and her little book with Howard's second number. The drawer where Sally occasionally stored it was half open. I could see the edge of the book. It was bright red with her initials embossed in gold. I slid the drawer out farther.

Why was I doing this?

It wasn't as if getting the number was for her own good, no matter what Norma claimed. There was no excuse for invading her privacy.

But I reached for the book anyway.

The list of boyfriends was in chronological order. Howard would be last. I flipped through intending to go straight to the last page, but a familiar name caught my eye: Stanley Harris. He was the airline pilot who flew the Far East route. Sally groaned with lust every time he showed up at the door in his uniform. My eyes slid past phone numbers for both home and work, to a single digit, circled in red no less. Sally had awarded him a nine. Out of ten? Travel sure enlightened a man. I scolded myself for looking when I had vowed not to and started flipping through the book again.

A board creaked upstairs. I froze. "Oh, *Howard*!" Sally said. She sounded annoyed.

FRENCH LEAVE

I went back to flipping pages and dislodged a ticket stub slipped between two pages. It was for a performance of Cirque du Soleil in Columbus. Sally had gone there two years back with Mortimer Paulson, a man who owned a company that manufactured and packaged health food for hikers and campers. He claimed he ate nothing but the food made by his company. Mort wasn't the most handsome guy Sally ever dated, and he wasn't the fittest, but he was by far the nicest. He would stop by the office to give me packages of trail mix whenever he came to the house. She hadn't kept him around for long.

Footsteps shook the floorboards. Sally was off the phone.

I snapped the book shut and slid it inside the drawer. "Has the mail run yet?" she asked, leaning over the banister.

I looked up. "I was just going out to check."

"Good." She headed back to her room and I went out the front door, wishing she'd stayed on the phone a minute longer.

***

I was in the kitchen eating a sandwich when she came down two hours later wearing a light gray jacket over a long-ish skirt. "What?" she said when I stopped chewing to stare at her outfit.

"What's the matter with you? Beige, gray, you dress like a church lady now. You need color, Sally."

"Howard doesn't like bright colors."

On her, maybe. But according to Norma the other woman wore tight pants.

"I'd better hurry or I'll be late," she said, heading for the door. "He's busy, but he promised to take me to lunch."

"Fast lunch, fast food?"

She paused, her hand on the doorknob. "I don't eat fast food, Claire. You know that. Howard is taking me to The Champagne Room."

The Champagne Room was the best restaurant in town.

But it only served dinner.

I finished my sandwich at leisure and drank a second cup of coffee, killing time to make sure she was gone before going back to the hall table for the red notebook. But it was gone.

***

I was in the office when Sally whooshed in barely an hour later like a meteor through space. Fast food, like I said. I leaned back in my chair and yelled, "You got fries with that?"

She holed up in her room for the rest of the afternoon. I left at four to go to Cora and Richard's house with two jars of Ruth's prized corn relish.

As I expected, Cora wasn't home. It was her afternoon to volunteer in her charity shop. I always delivered the relish when she wasn't around because I knew she didn't like the fact that Richard enjoyed something Ruth made. For years the two women had been rivals for Gin's attention, up until the time she died.

Richard smiled when he let me in, his homely face lighting with childish pleasure. "I always look forward to this moment," he said, taking the jars out of my hands. "Ruth's relish is as precious to me as a bottle of fine wine. Come to the office. I'll make tea."

His office was the only room in the house that reflected his taste. It was more library than workplace with bookshelves on three walls, ancient club chairs, a worn kilim and warm lighting. Richard left to make the tea. Had he been a woman I would have followed him to the kitchen, but he was a solitary man who functioned better alone, so I sat down and picked up an issue of the local paper that sat on top of a stack of reading material on a side table. The front page showed Sheriff Gunner at a news conference as he vowed to find the safe house that had sheltered the Haitians.

Richard walked in carrying a tray with a teapot and two china cups. "I was surprised to hear there was such a thing as a safe house in Clayton. I had no idea there was a need for them."

I didn't consider a tool shed a safe house, but I kept the thought to myself. "I'm not sure it's true, Richard. Gunner's conclusion is based on the ramblings of someone suffering from a concussion. It doesn't make it a fact. The man is so eager to prove his point he isn't beyond stretching facts. And unfortunately some people believe him."

Richard smiled as he poured tea into a cup. "You're talking about your mother. I know she cannot suffer anyone thinking differently than she does. Her insistence is annoying, yes, but she is passionate about her beliefs. I admire her for it."

I took the cup he was offering. "I don't fault her for having opinions, Richard. I resent her for not respecting mine. And over the years I admit I got into the habit of automatically siding with whatever cause she rejects. I understand in part why she's so dead set against immigration. The numbers are scary: half a million refugees from one country, a quarter million from another. Thinking about everything the government has to do to feed those people, to help them learn the language, teach them a skill is mind-boggling. Yet the system works. By the second generation, they are productive. I am in awe of Faduma for believing in the future after the life she had in Somalia. She is so dynamic. Most immigrants want to succeed. It's not right to throw them in the same bag as drug dealers and gang members."

Richard filled a cup for himself, sat down across from me and placed the cup and saucer on the low table at his elbow. I settled back in my chair and looked at him, a thin graying man with a level gaze. Cora was lucky to have him. Ruth thought she married him for his money, but I didn't agree. I believed Cora was drawn to his integrity, his steadfastness. The marriage wouldn't have lasted this long without mutual respect and affection.

"Some people aren't interested in them as individuals, they just see them as numbers. It was good what you did for that young woman, Claire. Learning English is essential for newcomers."

"The Foreign Legion taught me as much long before I met Faduma."

"Ah, yes, your group of foreign wives. But I believe you might have helped the Somalis regardless, Claire. You're your father's daughter after all." The comparison was fair, but I balked at the idea. Reading my face Richard said gently, "He wasn't the villain many made him out to be. I know he was arrested, but at the time he was just one of many who defied the law. Church members, politicians, housewives, thousands formed the sanctuary movement to stop the government from deporting Central American refugees."

It was the first time Richard had ever mentioned Bernard in my presence. "As an attorney, are you telling me you approve of what he did?"

"I don't, of course. But I know that like your mother he had passion. I admire passion in others because I never had it."

True, Richard was cautious to the point of being stuffy. But that was precisely what I liked about him. When we were kids he gave no demonstration of affection, but he was there for us, steady and calm, and dependable, something Bernard never was. "Passion isn't a good thing to have if you can't control it, Richard. From what I heard it always ruled Bernard. You said lots of people joined the sanctuary movement. Was he very active in the movement?"

I'd always been curious about the extent of his involvement.

"I know he helped one man. I can't tell you if he helped others. I knew both your grandmother and Cora at the time of the arrest, but I never had direct contact with him."

FRENCH LEAVE

"That was at the time of the Contras flap, wasn't it? When the Reagan administration was accused of funding right-wing guerillas in Nicaragua?"

"It was. They were also accused of providing training and arms to other right-wing states. The Reagan White House feared Central American refugees had leftist views and preferred to keep them out of the country. The Salvadoran's sister is one of your foreign wives, isn't she? Did she ever hear from him?"

"No. She believes he was killed when he went back. Bernard lost little in comparison. He had a hard time but at least he didn't go to prison."

"Why the sudden interest in your father's case, Claire? It's been years since he left."

I looked at him. "Didn't Cora tell you?"

"Tell me what?"

"Bernard is coming back."

Richard's face went still. He hadn't known.

CHAPTER SEVENTEEN

On the way back to the house, I came to a stop alongside a Cadillac at a red light, a tan-colored sedan with rusted fenders and a peeling vinyl top. It was the same style and color as the vehicle Watkins, Sally's ex-bookkeeper, drove, so full of junk I sometimes wondered if he lived in his car.

I looked at the driver's bald head, the double chin and the unlit stogie between clenched teeth. It was Watkins.

But according to Orville the man had moved to Florida.

I called Watkins when I got home.

He answered after the first ring. "What's up, Claire? You know I don't work for your boss anymore, don't you?"

"I heard. But I thought you moved to Florida."

"Yeah, well." Watkins paused before saying, "I changed my mind."

"You don't sound happy about it. Will you ask for your job back?"

"Ah, well, no. I don't think I can do that." He paused again. I waited him out, knowing he would fill the silence. We talked often when he worked for Sally. Unlike Orville, Watkins was on the lazy side and disorganized. I bailed him out numerous times making copies and searching files for lost information. "It's decent of you to call, Claire. As opposed to Sally, you've always been nice to me. She was hard to please."

"Is that why you quit?"

"There's that, but that's not the main reason. Thing is," he hesitated, "I was offered money to quit."

The admission took me by surprise. "Why?"

"You aren't going to believe this. It was some guy who said he was from Homeland Security."

"You're right. I don't believe it."

"It sounds far out, I know. He told me they were investigating her for funneling money into some kind of underground organization, he didn't say which, and they wanted one of their guys on the job instead. It didn't sound right and I hesitated, but he got kind of nasty and suggested I didn't want to quit because I was involved along with her. So I took the money and ran."

Roger was a fool. If Homeland Security considered him a suspect, they would hardly give the show away by telling him they were investigating his boss. "That's crazy, Roger. Sally doesn't fund anyone except herself. Besides, if she was funneling money to some group, wouldn't you have known it?"

"If it involved big amounts, yes."

"And did she?"

"No. Over the years she regularly gave to local charities, but never in huge amounts. It was all above board."

"You've been had, Roger. Somebody just wanted to scare you and it wasn't Homeland Security. Did you ask to see the guy's credentials, or did you call their office to make sure he was legit?"

"Neither, but I know I should have. I see that now. Sally was furious with me for quitting and I was relieved to walk away from the whole mess. Plus the guy scared me. He was big and never once took off his sunglasses while he talked. It was intimidating." Roger Watkins didn't have the physique to stand up to a big guy. "I heard Orville got the job. You think he could be the one behind this?"

"Orville?" The thought of Orville hiring someone to beat Watkins to a pulp made me laugh. "No, he's too principled to

FRENCH LEAVE

resort to arm twisting, and he has other clients anyway. He only took Sally on because she asked."

"Well, OK. Someone else then. I know a few of my clients didn't appreciate what I did for them."

Because he was sloppy? It could also be that he screwed up Sally's books, and not knowing what to do, simply walked away. The story about Homeland Security could be a pack of lies.

We talked a bit more before I ended the conversation. A few minutes later, I heard the rumble of Joe's company truck. Was it Friday already? He came in looking tired and hot.

"Man, what a week! Got anything to eat?"

Someday he would come in the door, say it was good to be home and he was glad to see me. He probably was, but I wished he said it before asking to be fed.

He went off to take a shower and change clothes. Ruth was still canning and not taking guests, so I rooted in the refrigerator to see about dinner. Mushrooms, cream, shallots, chicken breasts. I had almost all the ingredients for Chantal's chicken dish.

I was chopping mushrooms when Joe came back. "Where's your aunt? I see the spare bedroom is empty."

"She left."

"Already? She didn't stay long. Did she decide her brother wasn't coming?"

I searched the onion bin for shallots, wondering what to tell him. Then I reproached myself for hesitating. Unlike Ruth, he could be trusted not to call the law. "I don't know. She didn't say."

"What do you mean? Didn't you ask her why she left?"

"I didn't have the chance to ask her anything, Joe. She skipped out while I was gone." I took the shallots to the cutting board.

"You can't be serious."

"I am." I told him about the squatters in the shed, the Haitian's kidnapping and Chantal's involvement.

He laughed. "It sounds like something out of Sally's books. Come on, Claire! Tell the truth. Did you send her packing because you didn't want her around?"

I dropped the knife and went to the living room to get the paper with Chantal's picture on the front page. His mouth dropped when he saw it.

I went on to tell him about the cops' visit, the evidence left in the basement bedroom and my dash to get rid of the evidence.

"And you haven't heard from her since?"

"Nothing from her or the cops, and nothing from Bernard

either. I'm hoping Chantal dumped the kid on somebody else and went back to France. There's been nothing more on the news about finding the man or locating the safe house. I tell you, Joe. Every time I think about the Haitians living in the shed I sweat bullets. What's with Chantal and Bernard anyway? I could just kill them for thinking it was fine to pick my house, *my house*, for their own use." Talking to Joe made me feel better, but reliving the moment the police came to the house while the green scrubs were in plain view made me weak at the knee. What if, what if? What if they had come with a warrant, what if they'd asked to search the house, what if I'd said yes? I picked up the knife and chopped the shallots to mush.

Joe took the knife out of my hand. "Cool it, OK? It's not your aunt on the chopping board. Leave the food alone for a bit and go sit down." He pushed me to one of the kitchen stools, went to the fridge and poured a glass of Chardonnay.

Funny how I kept my head, but the minute I admitted being scared I folded. I sipped the wine while Joe put the vegetables and the meat in the refrigerator. "You aren't cooking tonight. Aunt Lou hit it big at bingo and gave me fifty bucks. I was planning on us eating out tomorrow, but we might as well do it now."

"I can't. Tonight is Faduma's lesson."

"Call her and cancel."

I didn't have to cancel. When I called, her brother-in-law said she was out of town.

The meal ticket had a price. Joe insisted I change from my work jeans into something fancier. He looked on with approval when I came out sashaying on high-heel sandals. The fancy footwear went with skinny black jeans and the stretchy black-and-white top Joe gave me for my birthday. I didn't like wearing clothes that weren't me, but the free meal was worth the sacrifice.

Joe's favorite restaurant was a steak house just north of the freeway called the B & B for beef and beer, a sprawling one-story log building with a big front porch and a row of rocking chairs stretching on either side of the entrance.

Inside, the main source of light came from pillar candles burning on every table and the flames rising from the open grill. The place was dark, so it took us a while to realize that the people in front of us waiting to be seated were Steve and Lisa. No surprise finding Steve there. He loved the B & B. Lisa was another matter. She was a vegetarian.

I looked at her. She was wearing a burnt orange top over a

long skirt in a dark purple and orange print, a vast improvement over the messy T-shirt she had on the last time I saw her. Dangling gold loops brushed her tanned cheeks accentuating her gypsy looks. Her dark curls, not as rebellious as mine, had been brushed into submission.

"What are you doing in a steak house, Lisa?"

"It's *somebody's* birthday," she said, flashing a dark look at Steve, the kind that guaranteed retaliation. "And *somebody* insisted on coming here in spite of the fact there's no vegetarian menu." She turned her attention on me. "Glued-on pants. Really, Claire? Are you planning on ordering from the children's menu?"

"No need. They stretch," I said, ignoring the criticism. When Lisa was in a bad mood, everyone was a target. "You aren't the only one whose arm's being twisted. The fancy outfit is my exchange for eating out. Joe has fifty bucks burning a hole in his pocket."

"Four?" the hostess asked, holding menus. We followed her swinging hips as she wove a path between tables packed with diners. The smell of sizzling meat grew as we approached the grill. Lisa made a face. She pointedly slid a lit candle close to her plate as we sat down. The flame sizzled, fanning vanilla. The gesture was lost on Steve who was deep in conversation with Joe.

The waitress came. Steve and Joe ordered T-bones. I opted for the rib steak. Lisa asked for fish. She wasn't a strict vegetarian—she just refused to eat anything that bled. The waitress, a thin blonde with rings of mascara around both eyes and lipstick so dark it looked black, checked to see no one was listening before bending over Lisa. "Honey, this is a steak place," she whispered. "The fish is frozen and comes in slabs like shingles. You know what I'm saying?"

Lisa set her lips. "Fish," she insisted. The waitress shrugged and walked away. Steve pretended he hadn't heard the exchange and leaned across to talk to Joe. My black-and-white top clung like a second skin. I pulled it away from my body and hummed a tune to lighten the atmosphere. I was hungry.

Conversation lagged until the food arrived. I heaped a mound of fries to shield my rare steak from Lisa's gaze and sneaked a look at her plate. The slab of fish looked like Styrofoam with grill marks. Lisa poked it with her fork. When it didn't give, she pushed it aside and carried a forkful of rice pilaf to her mouth. Next to the rice, the green beans sautéed with garlic and sprinkled with fresh parsley looked appetizing. She chewed, swallowed, nodded and reached to tear off a hunk of sourdough bread from the loaf the waitress had left on the table.

Crisis averted. But it wasn't a comfortable meal. Steve talked to Joe exclusively, Lisa to me. During stretches of silence, I looked around. The restaurant was full. It was mostly couples, but there were large groups as well, a few with men only, oil workers celebrating the weekend; another was a family, two generations celebrating a birthday. A waitress had brought a cake to the table.

"Wow, take a look at that!" Steve said as he reached for his beer. He pointed his chin at a large group sitting in the back of the room. "The boss is eating with the mayor."

Steve was the head mechanic at a dealership selling foreign cars, including a few high-end ones. Ted Bundant, the owner, had been shrewd enough to figure out there was enough money in Clayton to make the business profitable.

In the flicker of candles I recognized Violet Stumpfelt, the first woman ever elected to lead Clayton. Even though I didn't know that much about her, she got my vote because she was a woman and seemed confident enough to deal with the clutch of old men who dominated the city council.

The diners at her side were all men. I had met two at Cora's fundraisings. One was a banker, the other the owner of a regional chain of hardware stores. Sam from the bookstore was there as well, sitting next to a man who turned out to be my stepfather. In turn, Richard sat beside Steve's boss. The last diner, a dark-haired man with his back to us, had Violet's full attention.

"I wonder what the meeting is about," Steve mused.

Our waitress returned with two more beers, one for Joe and one for Steve, and the dessert menu. Lisa ordered apple pie and ice cream. Knowing Joe's fifty bucks wouldn't cover dessert, I asked for coffee.

The waitress had just refilled my cup when the mayor's party broke up. The dark-haired man got up and headed our way. I immediately recognized the broomstick figure of Sally's boyfriend. He didn't look any better up close than at a distance. His whole face, from frowning lines to a thin puckered mouth, registered disapproval. When he came abreast of our table and saw me, he gave me a look that scorched my eyebrows.

"Friend of yours?" Lisa quipped after he left. She was laughing.

"Obviously not."

"I doubt that guy has any friends," Steve said, reaching for the bill the waitress had placed on the table. "He is a total pain in the ass. But he's a friend of the boss so we have to be nice."

"You service his car?" Joe asked.

"The one he drives, yes, but it's not his. The boss loaned him a demonstrator and instead of being grateful he acts like he deserves better."

"*Loaned him*? Are you saying he drives the car for free?"

"That or close to it. If he pays I'm guessing it's minimal. I heard the boss and him go way back, like when they were kids. Bundant is from somewhere south. He treats the guy like he feels sorry for him."

Steve turned to look at me. "You know him, Claire?"

I nodded. "Kind of. He's Sally's new boyfriend. I caught a glimpse of him once when he came to her house."

But he never saw me. Or did he?

CHAPTER EIGHTEEN

The answering machine was blinking when we got home, showing two messages, one from Sally, the other from Norma. Sally wanted to let me know that a policeman had come to the house to confirm that I had been at her house Monday morning. "What's that about?" she asked. She didn't answer when I called to explain.

The second, from Norma, was brief and to the point. "Did you get Howard's number?"

"The book wasn't in the hall table," I said when I reached her.

"Did you even look?"

"*Yes*, Norma. Her cell phone was in there, but the book was gone." At least, the second time I looked.

"She took it upstairs then. She likes it close at hand."

"I saw him. Howard, I mean," I said to change the subject.

"Where? Was he with the girlfriend?"

"No, he was in a restaurant with a bunch of people. Steve, the head mechanic at Luxury Motors, says he knows Howard. He heard he and Bundant were buddies when they were kids somewhere down south, and he says Bundant now lets him use the Mercedes."

"I figured that. Someone at the BMV checked the license plate for me."

"Isn't that illegal?"

"So what? I told you before, cleaning ladies can do just about anything. What else did you find out?"

Didn't sound right to me, but then Norma pretty much made her own laws. One thing was for sure. If I ever had enough money to hire a housekeeper, I would let the house go dirty or clean it myself. "One more thing. Bundant, Howard and a handful of local land owners were eating dinner with the mayor this evening. I have no idea what that was about, but I can find out. My stepfather was there."

"Good idea. But that doesn't get you off the hook, Claire. We still need that number."

***

Half an hour later, Joe and I climbed into bed in silence.

We had argued most of the way home. Joe was mad at Lisa for giving Steve the cold shoulder on his birthday. I blamed Steve for insisting on going to a restaurant that didn't offer vegetarian fare.

I killed the light and the sheets rustled as he rolled over to face the wall. A minute passed. They rustled again when he flopped over on his back. "You've never liked Steve."

I plumped my pillow. "That's true. It's not only his looks, Joe. It's also the fact he always has to be right."

"He isn't like that!"

"Maybe not with you, but I've seen the way he puts Lisa down. He just doesn't like women."

"And you don't like men!"

The accusation caught me off guard. "I don't?" It was true I tended to judge them harshly, but I couldn't say I disliked them. I was very fond of Richard, and I liked Orville even if he was fussy. And I remembered looking up to a couple of my male high school teachers. Joe also mattered a great deal to me. *Mattered?* That didn't sound right. Anyway, I didn't believe I disliked men. I just approached them warily. "I have nothing against men, Joe. But I find it hard to trust them." It was so much easier to blurt

FRENCH LEAVE

the truth in the dark. "But you shouldn't take it personally. I felt that way long before I met you. Blame Bernard."

Joe rustled the sheets again. "Oh, for God's sake, Claire! How long are you going to whine on about that? The man's been gone for years. Get over it. Besides, you weren't the only one to grow up without your dad. Mine didn't stick around either."

"He didn't exactly have a choice, Joe. He died."

"Of course he had a choice!" Joe's voice vibrated with anger. "He could've chosen not to get in the car knowing he was too drunk to drive. I wouldn't have minded so much if he'd been the only one to die. But my mom was with him. I lost her too that day."

If Bernard and Cora had died in a car accident, Gin would have adopted me. I quickly drew the curtain on that fantasy, out of guilt mostly, because so help me the idea was appealing. "I've tried to understand why Bernard did what he did, Joe. Chantal said it wasn't his fault. She may be right, but I can't change my mind overnight. So, yeah, I still resent him for leaving and I suspect I'll always expect the men I know to take a hike. But that doesn't mean I dislike them."

"You expect me to leave?" Joe asked the question quietly. The hurt in his voice made me wish I hadn't been so candid.

"I didn't say that." Was I afraid he would get tired of me? At times, yes. When I'd been a witch, or when I saw him looking at another woman. Was I glad we lived together? I thought about what I liked about him. Joe was smart; he was funny. He could be compassionate and caring. He had far better control over his emotions than I did, and didn't mind acting as ballast when my temper got the best of me. Yeah, that part was all right. But he was also secretive to the point of paranoia. He never talked about his work and rarely called when he was on the road. He said he wanted privacy. It wasn't as if I didn't leave him space. Also, he was selfish when it came to money. He spent his own freely and used mine when he ran out. I resented that. He turned needy when he was depressed or lonely, and strung behind me like a stream of toilet paper stuck to my shoe.

"Well?" he asked with an edge to his voice.

"We both have trust issues, Joe. And it's true that sometimes I expect you to pick up and go," I admitted. "The fear is in me. It has nothing to do with you personally. Most days, I like the thought of you and me together. I know I'm difficult to live with. But let's face it, you aren't easy either. Sometimes you turn inward and hold me at arm's length. You don't say why. I never know if it's because of something I did or if it's an Aunt Lou issue, or problems at work. Frankly, I have trouble dealing with that."

"I left once," Joe reminded in a quiet voice, skirting the issue of his refusal to communicate. "Were you glad when I came back?"

Early in our relationship, Joe had packed his bag and left after an argument over household expenses. He stayed gone for two weeks. My heart had leapt every time the phone rang or I heard a car pull in the driveway. When I finally decided he was gone for good, he showed up. Yes, I was glad to see him, even if I wanted to blast him for running out on me.

I turned on my side. His profile was a sharp cutout in the darkness. "I let you in, didn't I? And since we are on the subject of money, I might as well remind you the gas bill is due."

He laughed. "You never give up, do you? OK. I promise to do better in the future."

As long as Aunt Lou didn't run short; as long as the Mazda didn't need a set of tires, or his cell phone bill didn't break the bank. Heard it all before and would hear it again. But I was glad we made up.

CHAPTER NINETEEN

The following week started on a positive note. *Mischief in Michigan* was moving forward, not in the right direction, but we were reaching the end. The sooner we sent it to the publisher the better. Sally would pay me for my work and I would be free to concentrate on expanding my business.

One morning on my way to work I found Ibrahim at the bus stop. He pulled the door open when I stopped for him and slid inside. "Thank you, thank you, teacher. Good to see you."

"It's good to see you too, Ibrahim. How is work?"

"Good, good." He fussed with his seatbelt until it clicked shut. "Boss give more money."

"You got a raise? Congratulations!"

"Raise?" He repeated the word slowly then moved his lips to say it once more, but silently this time. "New word," he said, beaming. "Yes, yes. More money for Ibrahim. Raise!"

"You'll have to celebrate." It took the best part of two blocks to explain celebrate. When I stopped at the dealership where he worked he asked me to write raise and celebrate on a piece of paper. New words were like new shoes to him. They had to be broken in, used over and over until they became comfortable. He took the paper I handed him, folded it in half and slipped it in his shirt pocket.

"Hold on," I said as he reached for the door handle. "I wanted to ask you something about Faduma. When I called her house, her brother-in-law said she was gone. Gone where?"

"She go Columbus."

"For how long?"

"She go help friend. Friend sick. Many, many children, family." He gestured with both hands. "Cooking. Make clothes. She help."

"When will she be back?"

He raised his eyebrows at my insistence. "Faduma, no husband, no children. She help," he repeated, sharply for him.

Was that how he defined her, still? "But I thought you were going to give her a job keeping books and answering the phone at the farm when you get started."

He glared at me. "She want, yes. But first, she help."

The blood went to my head. Didn't she have a choice? Wouldn't it be fair to ask what *she* wanted? "Didn't anyone *ask* if she minded going? In this country, Ibrahim, women have choices."

As soon as I spoke, I knew I had made a mistake. His face shut down. Had he had the words, he would have told me to mind my own business. Maybe not. He was a courteous man. As it was, he walked away without a word.

∗∗∗

Half an hour later, sitting at Sally's fancy desk, the phone rang.

"Sal home?" Norma asked.

"As far as I know."

"You going to get that number?"

A hand fell on my shoulder. I jumped. "Is that for me?" Sally asked.

"No." I turned to look at her. Her face was puffy, her eyes unfocused. After working late into the night, she slept like the dead, sometimes not even waking to the roar of Norma's monster vacuum.

I hung up on Norma. "I got your message about a cop asking about me. What did you tell him?"

She blinked, waiting for her brain to engage. "Oh, that! Yes,

FRENCH LEAVE

he wanted to know if you were here last week. I checked the date he mentioned and confirmed that you were. What was that about? He wouldn't say."

"Didn't you see the paper with the picture of a woman in scrubs leaving the hospital with a patient in a wheelchair?"

Sally pondered this and shook her head. "I don't think so."

"Well, the patient was under arrest and for some reason the police thought I was the woman who took him. She looked to be my height and had brown hair like mine."

She snorted. "Is that all? I don't know why they singled you out. There are hundreds of women like you." She patted her own copper-colored lustrous hair in a silent but eloquent gesture. "Anyway, I told him you were with me. Now, I'll be going out this morning. Don't forget to check caller ID. if the phone rings. I don't want Howard to know you're here working. OK?" She went back upstairs.

An hour later she stopped by the office again, dressed in a burnt orange tunic over white capris.

"I'm going out. I need a break after working all weekend."

The phone rang. "She gone?" Norma asked.

"Who is it?" Sally demanded, reaching for the phone.

FRANÇOISE BARTRAM

"Norma," I said loudly, hoping Norma would hear. I offered Sally the handset but she waved it away.

"Take a message. I'm leaving."

"Where are you going?" I yelled as she left the room. She didn't answer.

"Where is she going?" Norma asked.

"She didn't say. She's wearing happy clothes so I don't think she's meeting Howard."

"Never mind the wardrobe! Does she look like she'll be gone a while?"

"Hard to tell."

"You'll have to take your chances. Here is what I want you to do: Look in the hall table. If Sal's little book isn't there, go upstairs."

"No!" I was sharp. "I told you, Norma. That's off-limits. And I don't see the point of looking for another number. If Howard isn't local, he doesn't have a landline."

"But he does. I told you he gave Sally a second number when she insisted she wanted to make sure she could reach him. It may be his apartment number, or a hotel's. It could even be Flirty Girl's if he stays at her place. No, not that. He wouldn't have given it to Sal. Don't be such a drag-ass, Claire! Get that number so I can check it."

FRENCH LEAVE

"It could be unlisted."

"It won't stop me, I have ways. *Please* look for Sal's little book. If it's not downstairs, it will be upstairs in the drawer of her nightstand, the one on the right when you face the bed. Now, quit stalling and go. I'll call back in five minutes." The line went dead.

I didn't care what Norma wanted. The second floor was off-limits. On the other hand, the foyer was public space. I got up and went to look in the hall table. The book wasn't there.

The phone started ringing. Had it been five minutes already? The ringing stopped, the answering machine clicked on and Norma's voice blared across the hall. "You'd better not be sitting at your desk ignoring me, Claire. If you don't do what I say, I'll tell the whole world about the time you screwed up the computer and lost half the book you guys were working on, and how you had to pay a tech to retrieve it before she found out."

What Norma promised, Norma delivered. The woman was lower than a plumber's pants.

I ran upstairs. Four doors opened onto a spacious landing. I tried to remember the layout from the time Sally gave me a house tour. The room on the left was the guest bedroom; the guest bath beside it. Sally's writing room faced the top of the stairs. Her bedroom was to the right. From where I stood I could see an expanse of pink carpet and part of a bedpost.

Downstairs, the office phone rang again. Norma was persistent. I crossed the landing to Sally's bedroom. The room, moist from her morning shower, was filled with the scent of her perfume. Blankets and sheets had tumbled off the bed, clothes littered the floor, underwear topmost.

Averting my eyes, I walked around the clutter to reach the nightstand. On the marble top, a bottle of aspirin vied for space with a lamp, two paperbacks and a silver frame with a black-and-white photo that showed a solemn-looking man beside a preteen girl in tight braids and a frumpy dress. She didn't look happy.

I put the picture back on the nightstand and opened the top drawer. The red leather notebook lay topmost. I flipped through it until I found the number I needed. Only then did I realize I didn't have a pen.

I rooted through the drawer in the hope of finding one. It was full of junk, a comb, hair clips, several pairs of earrings, rubber bands, ribbons, a purse-size package of tissues, but no pens, no pencils, not even an old sale receipt to write on. At the back I came across a tube of lipstick.

FRENCH LEAVE

How long had I been upstairs? I hadn't thought of looking at my watch when Sally left. I uncapped the tube of lipstick and twisted the bottom. A glob of coral mush came up. Not much to write with, but I didn't intend to copy *War and Peace*.

When I finally slid the drawer shut, I had orange numbers scrawled up and down my forearm. I left the bedroom at a fast trot, keeping my arm away from my body. As I reached the top of the stairs, I heard the back door click shut. I froze, one foot on the landing, the other on the first step.

Heels clattered across the kitchen tiles. The sound changed as Sally stepped on the hallway's hardwood floor. My hand gripped the banister. The steps slowed as she approached what had to be the office door. In a second she would discover I wasn't where I was supposed to be. I backed away from the stairs.

"Claire?" Sally called. Her footsteps became muffled. She had stepped into the carpeted living room.

I crossed the landing in one bound and opened the door to the guest room. No one had been inside since Norma cleaned it last. Its pristine carpet showed a pattern of vacuum tracks. Unless I could fly, footprints would give me away.

"Claire?" Sally called again. "Where are you?"

I retraced my steps across the landing. The door to the room she called her writing den was locked, and unless I managed to pour myself down the drain, one look told me the guest bath wouldn't hide a cockroach. I went back to Sally's bedroom. "Claire?" she said a third time, her voice sharp. Silently, I slid the closet door open, slipped inside and slid it back in place. The closet was about two feet deep. Clothes hung in tight rows. I plunged into waves of slippery satin, cool silk and clingy double knit. The perfume released by my thrashing tickled my nose. I pinched it between two fingers to keep from sneezing.

When I reached the far end of the closet I plastered myself against the wall. Sally came into the room. "Where is that damn girl?" she asked, her voice muffled by the layers of clothes that separated us. She stomped around for a while. I could feel the vibrations against the small of my back. Without warning, the closet door closest to me slid open with such force it slammed against the frame. Hangers rattled as Sally shoved garments aside. "Now what?" she snapped as the phone started ringing. She turned away to answer it. "What do you want, Norma?"

I knew Norma would call back.

"You want to talk to Claire? That makes two of us. I don't

FRENCH LEAVE

know where she is. She isn't in the office or anywhere downstairs. She isn't upstairs either. And she didn't go home. Her car is out front." Sally paused before saying, "What?" I leaned forward to listen, poking my head past a long dress shrouded in plastic. The hanger slid on the rod with a small squeak. I held my breath. Sally was silent. I couldn't tell if she was listening to Norma or to the sounds emerging from her closet.

"The park?" she said irritably. "What park? Oh, the one at the end of the street."

I breathed a small sigh of relief. She hadn't heard me. It was hot in the closet. I wiped sweat off my face.

"She sometimes eats lunch in the park? I never knew her to do that. Besides, it's only eleven. OK, OK, I believe you, Norma. Yes, I'll tell her you called. I gotta go now. I need to pee." The handset clattered back on the cradle and the floor shook as Sally stomped to the bathroom.

I edged along the wall to the front of the closet and got out. The door to the master bath was partially open, the toilet out of sight. I tiptoed past the bed, past the bathroom door, all the way to the landing. The toilet flushed as I reached the stairs. The lid clattered shut. I jumped on the banister and rode sidesaddle to the ground floor. I landed with barely a thump and slipped out the front door.

Outside a breeze fanned my face, caressed my sweaty arms. The orange numbers on my forearm were starting to blur.

I walked over to the car and rummaged in the glove compartment for a piece of paper on which to write the number I had risked so much to get. The last digit was smudged. I couldn't tell if it was a six or an eight. Norma would have to try both. I rubbed my arm with a tissue to erase the lipstick. It left an orange streak.

I went back to the house.

Sally was in the kitchen propped up against the counter eating cottage cheese out of the container with a pickle fork. She must have forgotten to run the dishwasher.

She looked up when she heard me. "Where have you been?"

Norma's excuse of brown bagging in the park sounded good until I remembered that my lunch, yogurt and a ham sandwich, were in plain sight in the refrigerator. "Out chasing a cat from your flower beds."

Sally had declared war on the neighbors' cats for loitering in her heavily mulched impatiens.

The cat news failed to draw her attention. She was too busy looking at the orange streak on my left arm. "What's wrong with your arm?"

I faked surprise. "Oh my! Could it be poison ivy? I thought I saw a clump in your flower bed, but I wasn't sure that's what it was."

"Poison ivy?" Sally edged away, sliding her rump along the counter. "Do you know what that stuff does to me? The last time I came in contact with it, my eyes swelled shut. Don't you dare come near. Better yet, go home. I don't want you touching anything in this house, you understand? Get out of here! Go!"

"OK, OK!"

It took me five minutes to go out the door, including two to erase Norma's message from the answering machine.

CHAPTER TWENTY

Norma called that evening, giving me all day to wallow in resentment and relive the humiliation of being trapped in Sally's closet.

"Where were you earlier, Claire? Sally said she couldn't find you."

"Hiding in her bedroom closet, no thanks to you! She came back before I had the chance to get back down."

Norma was unmoved. "Good thing you're little. You couldn't fit a silk chemise in there."

"Not funny, Norma. If she'd caught me, it would've been your fault."

"But she didn't, so get over it—did you get that number?"

I pictured myself in a hospital bed, drugged to the eyeballs, one leg in traction after falling down Sally's stairs, and Norma leaning over me to ask, "Did you get that number?"

FRENCH LEAVE

"Yes. And don't ever try to talk me into doing something that stupid again. The last digit was smudged because I used a lipstick to write it down on my arm. I couldn't tell if it was a six or an eight. You'll have to try both."

"You wrote in *lipstick*?"

"I didn't have anything to write with."

Norma laughed. "Just like you to think of that. Lipstick!" She was still laughing when she hung up.

***

I transcribed two more chapters the next morning. Norma called at ten. She was at work. I could hear a washer churning in the background and the hum of a dryer.

"I checked the two numbers in reverse listings," she said. "I eliminated the first. It belongs to a nursing home. The other is for a payphone at the mall."

"A *payphone*?"

"That's what I said. Sally asks for a phone number and he gives her a dud. I'm not sure the phone even works. It's in one of the side aisles where most of the stores are closed."

"The man's hiding something."

"You *think*? So, what's next?"

"For me, nothing. I'm done."

"You're giving up? Come on, Claire! You and Sally been friends for years. Where's your loyalty?"

"Where was hers when she showed me the door?"

Norma fell quiet. "I get your point. OK, let me rephrase the question. What do you think I should do next?"

"Short of finding where Flirty Girl lives, I would call hotels, starting with the priciest. He has to be staying somewhere."

"Sounds like a plan. Have you talked to your stepfather?"

"Not yet."

I would, eventually, when I got over the closet incident. What happened was as much my fault as it was Norma's. I had let her manipulate me. Refusing to do what she asked made me feel in charge.

I would make the call when I felt like it.

***

In the end I didn't have to do anything. Richard called me two days later. "Claire? I apologize for calling during your workday, but I'd rather not wait until evening when your mother will be home. I don't want her to hear our conversation."

My antenna went up. "What about?"

"I wanted to remind you that her birthday is coming up. Have you bought her present?"

I relaxed. "No, I haven't." I always waited until the last moment. Cora expected presents with a wow factor and I hated to part with the money.

"Good. Then I suggest we take her to The Champagne Room for dinner. You know how she loves the place."

Cora loved the place, not for the food, which was excellent, but because it was *the* place to be. "That's an idea." I didn't say it was a good one. The cost of half of Cora's dinner in addition to my own would set me back further than perfume or a scarf I could have bought on sale. "Is Mirabelle coming as well?" We could split the cost three ways.

"Your sister will be there," Richard said firmly. Mirabelle hated to spend what little money she had on other people. She was probably planning on sending Cora a card, sealing the envelope with a smiley face to make it special. "I'll make the reservations," Richard continued. "And I'll give you a call to confirm." His voice dipped indicating the close of the conversation.

I stopped him. "Just a minute, Richard. I want to ask you something."

I got up and closed the office door. "Do you know Howard Steele?"

The question was met by total silence. "Steele?" I said again.

"I heard you the first time, Claire. Why do you ask?"

"I saw him with the mayor at the B and B last Saturday. He happens to be Sally's new boyfriend. She seriously likes him and I wanted to know what you thought of the man."

Static crackled on the line again. This time I waited Richard out.

"I only just met him," Richard cautioned. "He's a friend of Todd Bundant, the car dealer. Steele is a partner in a small oil company involved in horizontal drilling. He came here to buy leases. Todd Bundant thought he would do him a favor by inviting local landowners to meet him."

"Including you?"

"Yes. I checked his company. They're small in the oil business and the future of the company is in doubt. Shareholders are concerned over high debt."

"So he's shady."

Richard coughed. "It's difficult to say, but it would be prudent to let your friend know that the man may not be on solid financial ground."

Richard ended the call and I got up to open the office door. Sally was on her way out packed in spandex.

"Who was that on the phone, Claire? I heard you talking."

"My stepfather. He called to remind me that Cora's birthday is coming up."

"I thought it might be Orville. I left a message on his answering machine earlier this morning asking him to call me, but I haven't heard from him."

"He may have taken Ruth to the store. Does he have your cell phone number?"

"Yes. I'm taking the phone with me. I need to talk to him, Claire. It's important. Make that clear when he calls."

But he hadn't when she returned an hour later. I looked at my watch. It was lunchtime. "Strange he hasn't returned your call. He's always so punctual. Are you sure he didn't leave a message on your cell phone?"

"Yes. I checked. Call him again, won't you? I'll go upstairs to change. Tell him to come to the house."

The phone rang just as I reached for it. I withdrew my hand after checking the number.

"Howard," I said.

FRANÇOISE BARTRAM

Sally made a shooing gesture in my direction and said, "Take a break."

Just as well, I was hungry. "No, not yet," I heard her say as I walked out. "I told you I'd let you know."

Orville still hadn't called an hour later. I left a message on his work phone and called Ruth's house as well. She didn't answer. They had to be out shopping.

I clocked out at five. As soon as I got home, I crossed over to Ruth's side to knock on her door. Cal opened it.

"I see you got my message," he said.

"What message?"

"The one I left on your work phone ten minutes ago."

He had never called me at work before. "I was already gone. What's up?"

"I need a ride downtown to pick up Orville's car. Ruth said you would do it."

Orville never loaned his car. And if he ever considered doing it, it wouldn't be to someone with dirty boots and a lead foot. "Why is the car downtown and why isn't he driving it?" Having a conversation with Cal was like working a puzzle with half the pieces missing.

FRENCH LEAVE

"Didn't Ruth tell you?"

"No, I haven't heard from her."

"Orv got run over when he was crossing the street downtown. Ruth asked me to pick up his car."

"Is he hurt?"

"Yeah, he's in intensive care. Ruth wants the car brought home. Thing is, I've got to go to work." He had on blue work pants and shirt, and the safety shoes he wore on the job. "I could take it to the yard and drive it home when I get back. But I'll need a ride downtown."

I knew why Ruth was concerned. Orville cherished his Chrysler. "Sure, I'll take you. How did it happen?" I asked as we headed out.

"He had the light as he crossed the street but the driver didn't stop. Nice wheels," he said as he settled in the Ford's passenger seat. "How fast does it go?"

"It's a four-cylinder automatic, Cal. You figure it out." I backed out of the driveway. "So the driver was at fault?"

"Looks like it. He skipped. No witness except a guy from the computer store across the street. He got a glimpse of the car after Orville was hit."

I knew the store. Orville had taken me there to buy my laptop.

"You going to the hospital after you drop me off?" Cal asked as I slowed to make the turn on Third Street where Orville had left the car.

I parked behind the Chrysler. "Yes. Ruth will need a ride home."

"Not the way she was talking earlier. She's thinking of spending the night." He opened the passenger door and jumped out. I watched him walk over to Orville's car, a small square man with a compact middle and short legs. SpongeBob in blue. He got into the Chrysler, gunned the engine and disappeared in a haze of smoke.

CHAPTER TWENTY-ONE

I found Ruth in the waiting room that served the ICU. She huddled in an orange vinyl chair under an air-conditioning vent, arms crossed over her chest. The duster she wore for housework was too thin to keep her warm.

I guessed the thin dress wasn't her only reason for feeling cold. ICU was uncomfortable territory for her. Gin and her brother had both died there. In both cases she stayed at their bedside until the very end, fighting for every breath they took. When they breathed their last she acted as if she thought there was a trick to keeping them alive and blamed herself for not knowing it.

She sat up when I called her name, and for a moment stared at me without recognition. "Claire," she finally said, uncrossing her arms. "Have you seen him?"

FRANÇOISE BARTRAM

"No, I just got here. I drove Cal downtown so he could pick up the Chrysler. He took it to work. How's Orville?"

She hesitated. "A bit better. He didn't look so good this morning, but he's fidgeting and the nurse says it's a good sign. Come see."

She led the way. Orville, strung with wires and tubes, was hooked to machines that beeped and blinked. His right leg was in a cast, his head bandaged. If he was breathing, I couldn't see it. Thin eyelids, stubble on his chin, hair sprouting from his nose. It wasn't fair to look at him when he couldn't look back.

I backed away and bumped into a nurse coming in. She cocked an eye in my direction. "Are you a relative?"

"His niece," Ruth said quickly.

"How's he doing?" I asked before the woman demanded proof of kinship.

"Better. So you're still here," the nurse said, turning to Ruth. "Go home. You've been here all day. We'll call if your brother comes to."

Ruth started to argue, but I turned her around and pushed her out of the cubicle. "Good idea."

"Your *brother*?" I said as we headed for the elevator.

"Who else?"

FRENCH LEAVE

"And she bought it?"

"She didn't argue. He gave me power of attorney. He's got nobody else."

We entered the elevator. Ruth would miss Orville terribly if he died. She had spent her whole life taking care of people. Orville needed her. Cal didn't, and I didn't need her enough. I always thought she would have been happier raising a large family, but she took care of her brother instead. I didn't know why. Ray could take care of himself.

I took her home to freshen up and change clothes. Then we went out to eat.

***

The hospital called the next morning. Orville was awake. He had been moved out of ICU to a regular room. I dropped Ruth off before going to work and I came back in the late afternoon to take her home. When I came in they were arguing. "I *never* cross the street against the light," he was saying, squinting up at her as she stood beside the bed. He didn't have his glasses on.

"I don't disbelieve you, Orville. I'm just saying you can't possibly remember for sure. People don't, you know, after a bump on the head."

He coughed once, his way of stressing a difference of opinion. "You aren't listening to me. I didn't say I remembered. I'm saying I *always* look before crossing a street. I *always* cross when the light is in my favor and I *never* jaywalk. Therefore whoever hit me was in the wrong."

"Now, hon, you can't be a hundred percent sure."

"But I am." He shifted the squint to me. "Is that you, Claire? Tell me, do you see me crossing the street against the light?"

Orville wore rules like a straightjacket. They guided his every move from the time he got up until he went to bed at night. Crossing against the light meant defying them. "Frankly, no."

"There!" he said, leaning back. "And Ronald will say the same. He probably saw the whole thing."

Ruth frowned. "Ronald who?"

"Ronald Biscuit, my friend who owns the computer store. That's where I was going when the car hit me." Ronald Biscuit. The name suited the man. He had a white plump face and a doughy body. "Is the word of a friend good enough for you?" Orville asked her, challenging her with a look that was too fuzzy to have much impact. "Or will you 'disbelieve' him as well?"

"Depends on what he has to say."

FRENCH LEAVE

I took her away before she could aggravate him further. We ate dinner in a neighborhood restaurant and later went to a supermarket for groceries. We didn't get back until dark. The answering machine was flashing when I came home, showing two messages. I hit the play button and got nothing but white noise for each call, the first at seven, the second at eight thirty. I went straight to bed after taking a shower. The chirp of the cell phone on the nightstand woke me an hour later. I turned on the light and looked at the number. It was local, not one that I knew, but I answered anyway.

"Claire?" a woman said. The line was buzzing with background noises, music, beeps from a cash register, a jumble of voices. "Are you there?"

No one said my name the way Chantal did.

Not her again! I pushed my head deep down into the pillow. The number on the screen was local. She hadn't left. *She hadn't left!*

So much for feeling safe, for thinking she was smart enough to get away before the law found her.

"What do you want?" My throat was so tight I had to force the words out.

She didn't respond. The only sound on the line was the rustle of her breath against background noises. The music, tinny and repetitive, sounded Middle Eastern. "I'm sorry," she finally said, her voice low.

"Sorry doesn't cut it. Is the kid still with you?"

"Yes."

"For God's sake!" The words exploded out of my mouth. I squeezed my eyes shut and dug my head deeper into the pillow. I so wanted out of this mess.

"I took him away for you," Chantal said with an edge to her voice. "I did it for *you*, Claire."

My eyes popped open. "For me? Oh please!"

"The interpreter. He was coming, was he not? André, he cannot talk to him. He would say things about you, maybe where you live and what you look like. We had to run."

"Not far enough! Why didn't you trust me, Chantal? You could have told me what was going on. At least I would've been forewarned. You lied when you said Bernard wanted to see me. And I hate that, I really do." I heard her intake of breath and added before she could say anything, "Don't tell me again you're sorry. I'm not buying it."

She said it anyway. "Well, I *am* sorry. Your fazzer really wants to see you. That is not a lie. And I did not tell you about the men because I could not be sure you would not tell the police."

"I was tempted, believe me. But you're on their radar anyway." Remembering the cops at the door, the green scrubs abandoned in the basement made me shiver. I saw myself in handcuffs. The image haunted me. "Tell me what made you come all the way from France to help that man. Did you know him?"

"No. But he needed help, that is all."

Chantal's simplistic answer made me want to throw the phone at the wall. "From you specifically? From your brother? Aren't there people here who could have done the same for him?"

"I cannot answer your question, Claire, because I do not know the answer. Things went wrong and now André and I need your help."

I sat up. "Forget it! I don't want to be within a mile of you, Chantal. Your face has been all over the news."

"I know. But I can wear a hat, yes? And sunglasses. And we will meet somewhere safe, and without André. Please, Claire! If I do not get help, I cannot stay where I am and where will I go?"

I hesitated. She was a loose cannon. Knowing where she was

and what she was planning would be better than letting her fend for herself and getting caught. "I see your point."

She breathed a barely audible thank you. She thanked me again a few seconds later in a stronger voice and added, "I was very afraid you would say no."

"Frankly, I wish I had. Where can we meet that won't draw attention?"

"Do you know where Gardiner Park is?"

"Yes." Gardiner Park, named for a former mayor, stretched west of downtown in an area of defunct strip malls, cheap motels and rundown apartment buildings.

"I will be on the bench near the swings at eleven tomorrow. Be careful when you come, Claire. No one must know where you are going. Those people, they are watching and they know where you live."

"What people?" I asked, alarmed. But it was too late. She had already hung up.

**

The next day was a Norma day. Sally was still asleep when I came in.

I was surprised Sally hadn't called to ask if I had located Orville. She had been so anxious to talk to him. She wouldn't know about his accident even if the hit-and-run made the news. She seldom watched TV.

I made a pot of coffee and carried a cup to the office. I didn't look forward to working. She was rushing the book and the closer she came to the end, the worse the writing was. But what did I care? As I kept reminding myself, she'd asked me to stay until the book was done. She didn't say to make sure it sold.

At ten fifteen, I logged out. Norma was running late, Sally still incommunicado. I wrote her a note before leaving, telling her Orville had been hit by a car and was in the hospital. It was ten fifty when I pulled up outside a convenience store just south of Gardiner Park. I had taken a circular route from Sally's house to make sure no one was on my tail. Everything looked normal.

The door was propped open with a cement block, and a handwritten sign in the window said the air conditioner wasn't working. A public phone hung on the outside wall beside the shop entrance, probably the one Chantal had used the day before. The same kind of music played softly. In addition to the usual display of snacks, of canned and bottled beverages, the shelves were stocked with packages of cracked wheat and couscous, jars of olives and peppers, bagged spices. The smell of curry and cumin floated through the air. The clerk, a fiftyish man of Middle Eastern origin, handed me change for a large coffee without sparing me a glance. Invisible was good. After walking to the park entrance I took the lid off my coffee and used the pause to scan the parking lot. It held three cars beside my own, but Chantal's rental wasn't one of them.

I followed the paved trail leading to the playground and stopped beside a clump of oaks overlooking the swings. The bench Chantal had mentioned was empty. Three young mothers stood nearby watching kids at play.

At eleven I saw her entering the park in the opposite direction of the mini-mart. She was wearing white shorts, a light-blue top and white running shoes. No purse. Oversized sunglasses and a baseball cap obscured the upper part of her face. She jogged toward a patch of rough grass where a group of boys played soccer. After circling the soccer field twice, she jogged back to the playground and slowed as she approached the bench. She stopped beside it and sat down. The kids were playing, the mothers talking. No one paid her any attention. I circled the clump of oaks, walked over to the bench and sat down next to her.

The oversized glasses swung in my direction. We didn't speak. A pulse beat on her neck. "You were careful, yes?" she asked after a minute of silence.

"Yes. Traffic was light. It would've been easy to spot a tail. I know the sheriff's looking for you. Who else are you afraid of?"

She took a deep breath. "I do not know. André said two white men with a gun took him away in a truck. His friend, too. He said the men knew where they were staying."

"My house." I said what she had not. "Was it you who told the Haitians they could stay there?"

The glasses swung in my direction again. "But no!" I couldn't see her eyes, but the tone of her voice told me she was angry. "I came to take them far away from you, Claire."

"It was Bernard who told me to do it. He called me at home," she added in a calmer voice. "And he said there would be money to help me. I was to take them to a hotel and wait for instructions."

"From whom?"

Chantal pushed the sunglasses up the bridge of her nose. "Him. He is the 'white man' of the notes." She heaved a sigh before saying, "I thought he was done with that kind of thing.

He didn't say why he was doing this, just that I needed to come quickly."

"Didn't you ask questions?"

"No. I did not understand him very well. His voice, it was funny. Very weak. But he did not call again, at home or here, and I am very worried."

"So you think something happened to him?"

"Yes."

"Did you call him back?"

"Yes, I told you so, but the call, it goes to voicemail. I do not know what to do, Claire."

Chantal took her cap off to run her hand through her hair. She had lightened it to gray since I saw her last. It aged her.

"Who dropped the Haitians at my house—Bernard?"

"No. It was American men, André said, who did not speak French. They took the boys to a centre commercial, a mall, I think you say, near Clayton. There they waited for hours. André asked questions their driver did not understand. The man made several calls on his portable phone. At nightfall he drove them to your house, gave them a piece of paper with a number on it and said a white man would come for them. At least that was what

André understood. When two men came, he did not know they were the wrong people."

"Where is André now?"

"In a motel near here. It is not a good place. They rent rooms by the hour. But that is all I could find. André is very afraid of the men who took them. One is dead, but the other, the one who drove, he ran away. He could come back."

"If the Haitian's in danger, it might be better to take him back to the hospital, Chantal. He was safe there."

She yanked off her sunglasses. "*Safe*? He is just a boy, Claire, barely sixteen as was his cousin. He will be put in jail."

"It's better than ending up dead."

Chantal put her glasses back on. "Do not ask me to do this. I am not taking him back."

"Fine! Then what do you want from me? I can't work miracles."

"I do not want a miracle. I want money."

"For the motel? How much longer can you afford to stay?"

Chantal's chin trembled. "Until tomorrow."

"*Tomorrow*?" I never had a lot of ready cash, and with unemployment looming I couldn't afford to squander what I had. "That's really short notice. Joe may be able to help, but he won't be home for another day and there's no guarantee he'll have money to spare. Really, Chantal! Didn't Bernard have a backup plan in case something went wrong? He should've given you an emergency contact."

Chantal took her glasses off again. "But he did, Claire!" She looked at me in earnest, her eyes wide. "I argued with your fazz-er because I did not want to do this. I worried it would not go well so he said that I could tell you, but only then. He said you knew someone who could help, who would know what to do."

CHAPTER
TWENTY-TWO

"*Me?*" The exclamation caught the attention of the mothers standing near the swings. I lowered my voice. "How could he possibly think I would? For goodness' sake, Chantal, I haven't seen the man for years. And back then I was a kid. The most time I spent with him was at night when he read me to sleep." Out of the blue came the cadence of his voice reading Mother Goose as I lay in bed. I saw him hunched over the book, bathed in the soft glow of the bedside lamp. His glasses were low on his nose, and once in a while he looked at me over the lenses, his eyes twinkling.

"That is what he said, Claire," she insisted. "So it must be true. He said you would know someone who could help. Think!"

I was too angry to think. The man had asked his sister to bail him out by doing something he was unable or unwilling to do, and now he wanted the same of me. What could I do anyway? I supposed I could volunteer to drive the Haitian to the border, but then what? It wasn't like trapping a groundhog and releasing it in a field somewhere. The kid needed a place to go.

"You must, Claire! Your fazzer, he said you would know."

Her insistence infuriated me. But I knew she was desperate. "I really don't, Chantal, but let's forget about what he said for now. The important thing is for you to stay put. I'll get enough cash to pay for your room for a couple more days and I'll drop off the money later. Where are you staying?"

"At the Motel Petunia on the other side of the park."

"I've heard of it. It has a reputation." No wonder she was able to get a room. The place had a high turnover.

She nodded. "It is scary, particularly at night, with people coming and going, but I do not go out at night. The manager, he does not care what we do because I give him a lot of money and I clean the room so no one sees André."

I hoped the cops didn't decide to raid the place while she was there.

We stayed on the bench until the mothers scooped up their kids and left. Only then did Chantal decide it was safe for her to leave. I drove to an ATM on the way home to get enough money to cover the cost of the motel room for a couple more nights.

Ruth called my cell just after I got home. "Are you still at work?"

Phone in hand, I slipped off my shoes and padded across the tiled floor to the refrigerator for a can of soda. "I'm off. It's a slow day. You need something?"

"I do. I'm at the hospital. They say Orville might be well enough to be discharged as early as tomorrow. He'll need a special bed, the one in his room being so big and all." Against his landlady's advice, Orville had bought a double bed to replace the twin size he had used for years. The new sleeping arrangement, cheek to jowl with a computer desk, filled his small room to capacity and would make navigation impossible for a man with a cast. "So I want you to call to have one delivered." She gave me the number of a place that rented medical equipment. "Ron who lives two streets over said they were pretty quick to send a bed over when his mom broke her hip last fall." Personal recommendations mattered to Ruth, even if, as I suspected, she barely knew

Ron two streets over, much less his mother. "Also he'll need a ride home. I'll let you know when he's ready."

When I called the medical supply place, the clerk told me that we would need a prescription from Orville's doctor before we could have the bed delivered—unless he wanted to pay for it up front. I decided he could and asked for the bed to be delivered in the morning. I called Ruth's landline and left the information on her answering machine.

I popped the tab off the soda can. Chantal's words rang in my head. *Your father said you would know someone who could help.*

I'd been too angry to think clearly when Chantal quoted him. But now that I had time to focus I realized I did know of someone, a bunch of someones: Carmen and her crew. Apart from the fact their sympathy for immigrants made them the perfect teammates for the planned rescue, they were the only people Bernard and I knew together.

And they were devoted to him.

OK. Knowing what he meant was an important first step, but it didn't get me that much closer to securing a safe place for Chantal and the Haitian. The kid was a wanted man. If I asked the group for help, would the women agree to take responsibility for his welfare or would they play dumb? I had known them for a long time, but would they trust me with information that could get them arrested?

I doubted Carmen would. She had great admiration for my father. The fact that I didn't share her views drove a wedge between us. She wasn't as affectionate with me as the other women were.

I decided to bypass her and approach Manuela instead.

But she wasn't home. The grandson who picked up the phone said she had gone out and wouldn't be back until evening. I called Helga next, but struck out there as well. No one answered.

Rose, another of Carmen's lieutenants, had just moved to a condo. I had an address for her but no phone number. It wouldn't have done me any good to call anyway, because it was close to impossible to communicate with her on the phone. She could read English, she understood it. Speaking was another matter. The words were indistinct, as if she had gravel in her mouth.

I noticed that the Foreign Legion women with children who spoke their native language at home seldom developed good English skills. The ones who didn't were more likely to be fluent. In Rose's household everyone spoke Chinese.

So I was back to Carmen. I could've waited till the next day to talk to Manuela, but I wasn't sure how long Chantal would be safe at the Petunia Motel. The place was a magnet for drug addicts and prostitutes, and every passing day took her closer to the eventuality of a police raid.

So I called the bookstore. Sam answered and told Carmen to pick up the phone. He sounded testy. I figured I had caught them in the middle of an argument, one of many that filled their day. "This is not a good time, Claire," Carmen said when she came on the line.

"I won't keep you. Can we meet later? I need to ask you something."

"I don't know about later. As I said, I'm busy. What is it about?"

"Something personal, a family matter."

"Really?" I could tell she was intrigued. A family matter was likely to mean the paternal side since no one in the group had met Cora. Busy or not, I figured Carmen wouldn't miss a chance to discuss Bernard. It had to be important because I never talked about him. "All right. I'm leaving shortly to meet the group at Rose's new place. Do you have her new address?"

"Yes, I do."

"Meet me there. I suppose we can give you a few minutes."

FRENCH LEAVE

"OK. Thanks."

She broke the connection and I hung up in turn. I was looking up Rose's address when the phone rang. It was a blocked number.

"Claire?" a man asked.

"Yes. Who is this?"

"Sam. Listen, I know you just called. Are you going to Carmen's meeting?"

"I am. Why do you ask?"

"She left, but she forgot to take a book for one of her old biddies. I swear, nowadays she spends more time with that group than she does at work. Would you mind swinging by to pick it up?"

"I don't know, Sam. I don't have much time."

"It won't take you long. I don't know why Carmen bothers to run a library for that bunch. I can't believe any of those women read English."

I knew for a fact that most of them did, but I didn't bother correcting him. He wouldn't have listened. I agreed to pick up the book. The detour would only take ten minutes.

***

FRANÇOISE BARTRAM

A parking space opened in front of the bookstore just as I arrived. I slipped between a pickup and a subcompact, ignoring the red flag on the meter before running inside. "I appreciate you doing this, Claire," Sam said as he handed me a manila envelope. The look on his face had nothing to do with gratitude. It only showed condescendence. "It was good of you to take the time. Tell Carmen to enjoy her afternoon of leisure while I do what she's paid to do."

I took the book and left. His bitterness was wearing. Carmen excused it by pointing out that he had been abandoned by every-one he had tried to love—father, stepmother and wife. She once said tearfully that he told her the only person he trusted was the friend he made in boot camp.

Why not her? He had no reason to question her loyalty. May-be he did because he didn't trust women.

I left him to stew over Carmen's imagined abuse and reached the car as the meter maid started crossing the street in my direc-tion. I waved at her and drove off.

Rose lived in a new development, in the end unit of a row of brick townhouses trimmed in white. Multiple rows spread over several acres separated by well-trimmed lawns and bright flow-

FRENCH LEAVE

er beds. She opened the door before I had a chance to knock and briefly enveloped me in a hug, her arms stretching to reach my shoulders.

She was shorter than me, a miniature adult, slim and graceful with finely drawn features and dark liquid eyes. Though her skin was unlined, her black hair was heavily streaked with gray. I figured she was at least five years beyond Medicare, the same age as most of the group's original members.

She gave me her secret closed-mouth smile before leading me to a patio where the women sat around a table under the shelter of a striped umbrella. The usual get-togethers saw as many as fourteen, but that day only local members were in attendance. Rose sat down at the head of the oval table with Carmen on her right, Helga on her left. Manuela, lesser in importance and feeling it, glowered at the far end, flanked on one side by Estelle, a newish member from the United Kingdom, and on the other side by Esmeralda and Corazon, two Filipino women in their sixties who joined the group after Bernard left. Estelle had come to Clayton with her engineer husband who worked for a big energy outfit.

Usually when I came the women fussed over me, patted me, hugged me, told me I was too thin, too pale, asked if I ate properly, took my vitamins. This time they stayed put. They were quiet, another indication something was amiss. The meetings were usually loud with good-natured exchanges in broken English and spontaneous bursts of laughter.

The designated hostess always fed the members before the meeting started, but this time I was surprised to see that the table was bare. My stomach grumbled loudly and Manuela caught my eye, her round brown face splitting in an impish grin. She knew I had hoped to be fed.

Carmen politely ignored the gastric rumble. "Before we start, Claire, I want to tell you that I caught Sam eavesdropping on my phone calls this morning. So be careful what you say next time you talk to me."

Why would that come as a surprise? "I'm pretty sure he listened when I called earlier because he knew I was coming to the meeting. Forget it, Carmen. It's just Sam being Sam. The man is rude."

She gave me a dark look out of half-lidded eyes, her way of telling me I was there on sufferance, not to deliver criticism. She was right of course, but Sam was a brat and I couldn't understand why she was patient with him yet found fault with everyone else.

I took a seat between Esmeralda and Corazon and extended

the manila envelope I picked up at the bookstore. "Speaking of Sam, he asked me to give you this."

She reached for the envelope and turned it over in her hands. "What is it?"

"A book he said you meant to take. He called as I was leaving and asked me to come by to pick it up."

Carmen frowned. "I don't remember needing to bring a book." But she undid the clasp and pulled out a paperback titled *The Mystery of the Vanishing Clerk*. "Oh, that man!" She threw the book across the table. "He's intolerable. Vanishing clerk, indeed! He knew where I was going." She blew an explosive breath. "Really! I don't know how much longer I can put up with the man."

We heard the comment often enough to know it was just talk. No one said anything. She reached for the book, slipped it back in the envelope and said reproachfully, "He used you, Claire."

So it was my fault. "I can see that. I gather he's unhappy because he says you spend too much time with the group."

Corazon made a small sound of distress. She put her hand on my arm. "A causa de mì."

In the course of my years with the group I had acquired some Spanish, enough to know that "a causa de mì" translated as "because of me." I had barely glanced at Corazon when I came in, but now that we were sitting close I noticed that she had dark circles under her eyes and projected an unusual feel of sadness.

She reached for my hand and whispered, "Luisa." The sound of her daughter's name released a flood of tears. She got up and ran crying into the house. Esmeralda followed in haste.

A year ago we had given a party to celebrate Luisa's remission from breast cancer. During her illness we'd taken turns cooking meals, shopping for groceries and babysitting her children to make her life easier after chemo left her too weak to function. Luisa was my age.

"The cancer came back?" I asked, wondering why no one had thought to tell me.

Carmen sighed. "It did. We kept quiet because Corazon asked us to. Luisa is enrolled in a new study so there's hope, but it's no guarantee she'll make it and Corazon is taking it hard."

I started to ask details about the study but she waved my question aside. "Later, Claire. This meeting is all about Luisa and we don't have that much time to spare. Now, you mentioned a family matter. Is this about your father?"

"Yes." I hesitated, not sure how to introduce the subject of

Chantal and the Haitian. I didn't want to spook them. "Do you know he has a sister?" Safer to approach at an angle.

Manuela nodded. "Sì, Chiquita. Little woman like you. She come when you were little."

"So it's about your aunt, not your father?" Carmen sounded disappointed. "We don't know her well. It's been years since we saw her."

"Actually, it's about Bernard and Chantal both. She's here."

Manuela sat up. "Ha! I *say* that woman look like little Claire. I *say* she come and—"

"Callate!" Carmen ordered. She slammed the flat of her hand down on the table with such fury everybody jumped.

Manuela glared. "Noooo, I no shut up. You not my boss!"

"In this group I am!"

Manuela narrowed her eyes to slits. Even though the two women shared a language and a religion, they had never been close. Too different in personality maybe. Manuela was impulsive and boisterous; Carmen, poised and keenly aware of decorum. I had seen the way Carmen responded to Manuela's rapid-fire Spanish with her more precise and elegant speech, her face stiff with disapproval. Once during a heated discussion she had called Manuela a "mestiza," the name clearly meant as an insult, and Manuela had never forgiven her.

The "mestiza" now let loose a flow of Spanish which Carmen answered in kind. The volume rose. Estelle covered her ears. Rose's face, usually impassive, creased in concern and Helga squared her jaw. She pushed back her chair and rose, unfolding her substantial frame until her crown of white hair brushed the underside of the umbrella.

"I sink now we listen to little Claire," she said, raising her voice over the exchange. Her accent was thick. It happened when she was upset.

I looked from Helga to Carmen, hesitant to challenge Carmen's authority, but she seemed more startled than angry. At least she'd stopped shouting.

"Do you happen to know where Bernard is?" I said, taking advantage of the lull. "Chantal is looking for him. She said they agreed to come and see me. They didn't leave at the same time, but she expected him to be here when she flew in. Only he never showed and he isn't answering her calls. She's out of her mind worrying about him."

I ran my eyes around the group, studying the women's reac-

FRENCH LEAVE

tions. Estelle didn't seem concerned, but then she'd never met Bernard. Manuela's mouth parted as if she were about to say something but thought better of it. Helga's face was wooden. Rose said nothing, but then she seldom spoke.

Carmen coughed. "I wouldn't take Chantal too seriously, Claire. From what I hear your aunt can be a drama queen. There may be a good explanation for your father's delayed arrival. Chantal could have the date wrong."

"Possibly, but she said she called him repeatedly and never got a response."

"He travels all the time. He could be out of range."

"That long? From what she said, it's unusual for him not to keep in touch."

Manuela leaned forward. "But tu tia, Chiquita..." She hesitated. "She's at tu casa, yes? With—"

Rose cut her off. "I make tea," she said decisively, rising from her chair in a fluid move, and turned to Estelle. "You come."

I was surprised at Rose's abrupt demand, but Estelle didn't seem to mind. She rose without fuss.

"Good idea!" Carmen enthused. "Can we have something to eat as well? I didn't eat lunch."

"Shortbread?" Estelle offered. As the newest member she curried favors by supplying the group with home-baked cakes and cookies. She didn't need to earn her keep, but no one objected. She was an outstanding baker. "I also brought a jam roll."

"Come." Rose turned to go and Estelle followed her into the house.

"You know Chantal has the Haitian, don't you?" I asked the rest of the women when the sliding patio door clicked shut.

Manuela gave Carmen a look of defiance. "Sì. We saw her, Chiquita."

Helga raised a large hand in protest. "Chust on television and we were wonderink—"

Carmen cut in. "We noticed the resemblance, that's all. But it was so extraordinary to think your aunt had crossed the Atlantic to rescue a young man she didn't know that we decided we were mistaken."

"You weren't mistaken. Did you know Bernard was responsible for the Haitians? Something kept him back so he asked her to come instead. He told her he would join her as soon as he could, but that never happened and now she's stuck in a sleazy motel taking care of the kid. You know the sheriff is looking for her, right? Her money's running out. She can't afford to give up her room. I'm on my way to give her some cash, but it's a temporary fix."

The screen door started to slide open. Estelle was coming back with a plate of shortbread. Helga looked at me. "You go now," she said. It was an order. "We go after Corazon and tea, and bring money. OK?"

"Fine with me." I pulled a business card out of my purse, wrote the motel address on the back, and gave it to her. "See you there."

CHAPTER
TWENTY-THREE

Outside, a growling of lawn mowers harmonized with the roar of leaf blowers. A small army of landscapers in brown uniforms were tending to the lawns and flower beds facing the street. I walked over to the car, nodding at a young Latino blowing cut grass off the sidewalk. He didn't meet my eye and pushed past, hiding within the roar of his machine. I did my best to ignore him, thinking he looked like a man in dire need of the services of the Foreign Legion.

The women never admitted to knowing Bernard was coming but, as far as I was concerned, they admitted it by agreeing to bail Chantal out. Which meant she was off my hands. I breathed deeply of air that smelled of gasoline fumes and cut grass. I was free.

Or close to it. I still had to drive out to the motel and wait for Helga and the others to show up.

I started the car and headed for the exit. A white SUV came close behind, one of the big boxy ones that towered over subcompacts and the like. I found they often had impatient drivers, and this one didn't disappoint. The SUV pulled behind me as I made a left turn, barely missing a car heading in the opposite direction.

Traffic was heavy. Road construction narrowed the street to one lane. It took much longer than expected to reach the Petunia Motel, a frame structure painted a garish pink with bright yellow trim. Chantal's room was the one farthest from the office, adjacent to the straggly line of shrubs that separated the motel parking from a check-cashing place. I pulled the Ford into the space facing her unit, dropped the car keys in my pocket and stepped onto the cement strip that ran along the front of the building. I heard a car pull into the parking lot as I neared the door. I started to turn around to see who it was, but the drape covering the front window moved, distracting me.

It took a minute for Chantal to open the door. She looked stressed. Her hair was straggly, her eyes were red-rimmed. Her face relaxed marginally when she saw me.

"Claire."

"Bernard was right," I said when she stepped aside to let me in. "I found the people we were looking for."

I thought she would be glad to hear it, but instead her eyes widened in alarm. Next thing I knew I was lying face down on a gritty carpet. My head ached, red-hot pain pulsating at the top and streaming down the sides. When I moved the pain got worse, so I lay still and tried to figure out what happened.

Chantal had stepped aside to let me in. Did I stumble, fall and hit my head? If so, why wasn't she helping me? Where was she? I cautiously turned my head and saw chair legs, the corner of a bed and a length of blue blanket trailing to the ground. No Chantal. I probably would've stayed still longer if I hadn't heard a scream. It stopped as suddenly as it started.

Was that her? I forced myself to move, rolling over to my side, then to my knees. The room swam when I got up, but I made it to the door.

My eyes had trouble focusing. A shape was moving across the parking lot. I blinked and the shape morphed into a man carrying Chantal. Her head of gray hair dangled over his shoulder. One arm hung down his back.

FRENCH LEAVE

He was moving at a fast clip toward an SUV parked behind my car. A *white* SUV. The engine was running. Once there he thrust her into the back seat, slammed the door and vaulted into the driver's seat.

I croaked out a protest but it was too late, the big SUV was leaving. It sped out of the parking lot, tires squealing. That SUV had to be the one that followed me out when I left Rose's parking lot. Chantal told me to be careful but I didn't listen.

But why take *her*? It was the Haitian they were after.

The Haitian. I turned around to look inside the room. A boy with a bandaged head, the bandage stark white against his dark skin, was lying in the far bed staring at me, eyes wide with fear.

What was I going to do with him?

I stepped out and pulled the door half shut behind me. No need to alarm him further. I pulled my phone out and texted Helga to let her know what had happened. The Haitian was theirs to rescue. I was going after Chantal.

How long had it been since the SUV left? Two, three minutes?

I went to the car and took a sip of water from the bottle I kept between the seats, hoping to clear my head. The fog was lifting. I started the car and headed in the direction the SUV had taken.

248

FRANÇOISE BARTRAM

The lights stayed in my favor until I ran into a bottleneck. A crocodile of cars bearing the purple flags of a funeral procession was rolling across a nearby intersection, herded by the strident whistle of a motorcycle cop. After what seemed an eternity he thundered to the front of the line, and one by one cars started moving. The UPS truck in front of me rumbled forward. I gave it space, hoping to catch sight of the cars ahead of it, but it was too tall. When it changed lanes I saw what I had hoped to see—the top of a white SUV rising above smaller vehicles.

There was a good chance it was the one I was looking for. If so I needed to be careful. The man who took Chantal—he was likely the reason I ended up on the floor—knew my car. The Ford was six years old, silver gray, with no discernible features. Aging gray subcompacts were legion. Maybe I wouldn't catch his attention.

But the guy was sure to spot my top, a blue-and-white striped T-shirt, distinctive even at a glance. I fell back. A panel truck swung in front of me. It made a good screen, but it blocked my view. At the next stop light I took the time to inventory the clutter on my back seat. In the tumble of reusable grocery bags, spare umbrellas and last winter's crop of ice scrapers I found a white zip-up hoodie and one of Joe's baseball caps. The long-sleeve hoodie was a bit warm for the day, but it concealed the striped top, and the cap did a good job of keeping my springy hair in one place. A pair of dark glasses completed the disguise. The guy might recognize me at close range, but at a distance I'd be fine.

The panel truck turned off three blocks later. The SUV was still in sight, five cars ahead. The car in front of me, a VW, made a right turn, leaving a small pickup, a minivan and two sedans in my lane, one of them silver gray.

The van turned, so did the pickup. A big eighties-style Chevy sedan took their place. I was now close enough to see through the SUV's back window. A passenger sat in the rear, slight in shape and wearing a cap. A woman, I thought, but taller than Chantal.

The distance between the SUV and the Ford increased and decreased depending on traffic. It thinned as the street narrowed from four lanes down to two. We were approaching an older neighborhood of houses once imposing, but now in disrepair. Peeling paint, crumbling porches, weedy lots. The only car left in front of me, a four-door Chevy with faded blue paint, pulled over to the curb. I fell back. The SUV's brake lights flashed as the vehicle made a sharp right. I kept on driving, slowing to look as I went past. The SUV was backing up a narrow drive leading to what looked like a one-car garage. I kept going, finally pulling into a parking place in front of a full-size Dodge van with rusted fenders.

I waited five minutes before shutting off the engine. The street was deserted. I got out of the car and followed the sidewalk back to where the SUV had turned. The corner house was a big two-story frame with a porch along its width. Two windows flanked the front door. One was obscured by faded drapes that didn't quite meet in the middle. The other was covered by cardboard three quarters of the way up. Three mailboxes beside the front door indicated multiple tenants. The SUV was parked beyond the porch. It was a white Cadillac Escalade with Texas license plates and a dented front bumper. The vehicle was empty.

I meandered past. The garage's opening had been framed in. A mailbox flanked the narrow door that led inside the structure. Someone lived there. Overgrown shrubs and towering trees swathed in ivy darkened the backyard. Light spilled from behind a tall arborvitae crowding the single window on the far side.

I moved on. The next house was better kept. A privacy fence surrounded the property within six feet of the sidewalk as if to distance itself from its shabby neighbor. A curtain twitched as I went past. A hundred yards up the street a mailbox stood at the curb. I walked up to it, opened the chute, and pretended to drop a letter inside. The curtain twitched again as I retraced my steps. Once out of sight, I slipped between the privacy fence and a Japanese honeysuckle and crouched in its shadow. No one noticed my presence except the mosquitoes. I moved deeper into the backyard to approach the garage at an angle and stopped near the window in the shadow of the arborvitae. The bottom sash, raised by a couple of inches, spewed musty air that mingled with the sharp smell of ivy. The tilt of the blind offered a truncated view of the room with half a sofa, a corner of a dinette table and an overstuffed chair with soiled armrests. A woman, or girl, I assumed to be the SUV passenger, sat at the dinette. Only her legs were visible, skinny legs ending in pink sparkly running shoes. And yes! My heart skipped a beat. There was Chantal, the upper part of her stretched on a sofa. Her left cheek was red and puffy, her eye swelling shut. She'd been hit and she wasn't moving.

The man sat in the overstuffed chair with his back to me, the overhead light reflecting off his shaved head. "What makes you so sure she'll talk?" he said.

The sparkly shoes jiggled. "Trust me. She will."

"I still think it was a bad idea to take her. She may not know."

FRANÇOISE BARTRAM

"Of course she knows! She's in it up to her neck. I have no doubt she'll tell us what we want if we promise to take her back to the motel. She's worried about the Haitian and she isn't about to turn us in after what she did, is she?" The girl's voice sounded familiar, but I couldn't place it.

"So you say," the man in the chair said. He stood up and stretched. He was tall, with Popeye shoulders and a narrow waist.

"I do say." The girl sounded annoyed. "It was the right thing to do. You don't understand how hard this whole thing has been on Dad. He's waited years for this."

"It's kinda personal for me, too. I loved that old man."

"What do you mean, *personal*?" The girl was contemptuous. "You're doing it for money. Dad paid you."

"Yeah, well, I need the money. And it's not the first time I've helped your dad. We go way back. You never knew your granddad, but I did. He meant a lot to me."

The girl snorted. "I sure hope you *helped* Dad better in the past." She moved away from the window. I heard water running. "If you and your cohort had done what you were supposed to do, everything would be over by now. But no, you had to pull out a damn gun. Dad was really upset about that."

"You weren't there, were you? The guy swung around just before going inside the garage. I thought he had a gun. What could I do?"

Popeye was talking about Medicare Dundee! So much for Cal thinking the shooters were bail bond agents.

"And you didn't have to take those boys either," Sparkly Girl added. "That wasn't the plan."

The man turned to look at her and I saw his face. I didn't recognize him as one of the men who had run past Ruth's porch, but I hadn't had the chance to get a good look either.

"Don't you think I know that?" He was angry. "We just wanted to talk to them, find out what they knew. But they started yelling and carrying on so we stuffed them in the pickup. We would've taken them back if we hadn't crashed."

Popeye passed a hand over his shaved head. "I feel bad about Hank dying like that. But what's done is done." He straightened up. "Anyway, I'm not the only one who screwed up. You dropped the ball, too."

"Oh, for God's sake!" I heard a crash followed by the sound of breaking glass. "Damn it! I just broke a glass. How many times do I have to tell you? There was no way I could watch the place twenty-four-seven."

"Maybe not, but you're the one who insisted on being on the spot. You didn't even catch on about the aunt until she'd been in the house for a couple of days, and you didn't know she was the one who snatched the kid from the hospital until I told you. You made no effort to see what was going on."

"No effort, *really*? Didn't I go and check the place out after the hospital snatch to try and figure out where they'd gone? Going in was a breeze. The window wasn't even locked. But it was scary. There was no guarantee the place was empty."

"No one asked you to go in. It was too late."

I barely heard what Popeye said. The girl was the one who broke into my house? I clenched my fists, hating the thought of her roaming through my house.

"I almost got caught when I torched the garage," Popeye went on. "The kid whose room you took drove up just as I was getting started. All that because you insisted on living there, but I was the one who went out on a limb."

Torched the garage? To scare Lamont into thinking his grandfather was involved?

"Oh, quit your bellyaching!" the girl snapped. And just like that I placed the voice. "Dad thought it was a good idea for me to be there, and after that Lamont begged me to move in. What matters now is getting the aunt to tell us where he's hiding."

"*If* she knows. And what if she tells us he went back to France?"

"He can't be. Not as long as the Haitian needs his help."

It was Bernard they wanted.

I remembered Medicare Dundee walking down the sidewalk, looking as if he didn't have a care in the world. He left his blood on my back porch. Why didn't he knock? Why didn't he ask for shelter? Was he afraid I would turn him away?

The thought hit me like a punch to the gut, that he thought I was mean enough to do it.

Miss Sparkly Shoes came back to the dinette and sat down facing the window. Tawny hair, a narrow mouth full of sharp teeth. It was Lucie.

CHAPTER TWENTY-FOUR

Who was Lucie's father and what could he possibly have against Bernard? The great drama in Bernard's life was the shooting death of the Texas farmer. Lucie's father must be a relative.

"You hit her too hard," Lucie said, bending over Chantal. "She's still out."

Popeye shrugged. "Not hard enough to hurt her. She'll come out of it."

She already had. I had seen her flinch when Lucie broke the glass.

"When? I hope it's soon. Dad will want to know."

"We'll just have to wait." He got up. "Are you hungry? I could get a pizza."

FRENCH LEAVE

Lucie straightened abruptly. She turned around to look at him. "How can you think of food at a time like this?"

"Easy. I told you. I'm hungry."

She walked back over to the table and sat down. Her mouth was set. "Forget it! No way are you leaving me alone with her."

Popeye laughed. "You're afraid of an old woman who's knocked out cold? You have a gun."

"No, *you* have a gun."

"I can leave it with you."

"I don't want it. That's the one thing Mom and I agree on. Guns are bad. Never mind," Lucie said, getting up. "You stay. I'll go. Give me the keys," she said, holding out her hand.

Popeye didn't move. "Nope. The SUV is mine."

Lucie cocked her head at him. Her tawny eyes, the same color as her hair, narrowed to slits. "Dad used it and he said I could use it."

"I say you can't."

Her mouth tightened. "You aren't the boss."

"When it comes to the car I am. You want pepperoni?"

She studied him, maybe weighing the possibility of taking the keys from him. Eventually she gave in. "OK, you can go, but take her back to the bedroom and tie her up. I'm not taking any chances."

The fact they didn't get along was a point in Chantal's favor, but it was the only one I could think of. I had no idea what to do next. Popeye was leaving, but he wouldn't be gone long.

I could call the police. But Chantal would end up in jail. On the other hand, I had to think about what Popeye and Lucie would do to her once they realized she didn't know where her brother was.

I shifted my weight from one foot to the other, careful not to rustle the ivy that covered the ground. My back was stiff, mosquitoes were eating me alive. But my problems were nothing compared to the ones Chantal was facing.

She didn't move when Popeye wrapped duct tape around her hands and feet. He taped her mouth as well. They carried her to the room at the back of the structure, Lucie holding her legs and complaining about the weight, Popeye agreeing that the French broad wasn't as light as she looked.

He left a minute later.

Lucie stretched out on the couch and flipped through her phone.

FRENCH LEAVE

How could I get rid of her? Knock on the door and attack her? I didn't think I was strong enough to overpower her.

Lucie frowned as she poked at her phone. Her foot jiggled. Patience didn't seem to be one of her strong points. She was accustomed to getting her way. She also had trust issues. She obviously didn't trust Popeye, and I remembered Gladys saying she was secretive to the point of paranoia, how she locked her bedroom door whenever she left. Why? Was she hiding something in there—drugs? It was always drugs these days.

The possibility gave me an idea.

I turned from the window, pulled out my cell phone and walked back to the shelter of the Japanese honeysuckle to call Ruth.

"You!" she said when she heard my voice. The "you" carried enough loathing to make me duck even though she was nowhere near. "Where have you been? Not that it matters now because it's too late."

"Too late for what?"

"To drive Orville home."

He had been the last thing on my mind. "I'm sorry. I forgot he was being discharged today. Bring him back in a cab if he's ready. I'm good for it."

"Didn't I just say you were too late? We got him home already."

"Oh, well. I would've been there if I could. But something came up."

She snapped, "More important than Orville?"

"I'm not about to answer that. Look, I'll explain later. Could you give me Gladys's cell number? I need to talk to her."

"You don't need her number. She's right here. And the reason she's here is because she's the one who brought him home." Ruth slammed the receiver down on the counter and called Gladys. A minute later her smoky voice came on the line.

"I hesitate associating with you, Claire. If Ruth had her way she'd be measuring you for a rope right now. You want something?"

"I do. Do you have Lucie's cell phone number?"

"Sure. You want it?" She was surprised.

"No, I don't. Listen, you need to call her. I'm afraid she's in trouble."

"What kind of trouble?"

"Remember the older guy Lamont said Lucie was running around with? I've just seen him and I can tell you he's bad news. They're together right now and he's trying to talk her into some seriously bad stuff."

FRENCH LEAVE

"What kind of bad stuff?"

"I'm not sure. I only caught a word here and there." I was making stuff up as I went. "They happened to be in a booth at McDonald's and I was sitting near enough to hear them. They were arguing. It sounded like he wanted her to do something that involved drugs."

"Drugs! Are you sure?"

"Pretty sure. You need to stop her before she does something stupid."

"How in the world am I gonna do that, Claire? I ain't her mama."

"I've been thinking." That was no lie. My brain was working overtime. "You could tell her that your house was broken into, that someone got into her room and you're about to call the police. If there's something in there she doesn't want found, she'll rush home."

Gladys wasn't convinced. "Are you sure she's in trouble?"

"The guy is a skinhead, Gladys, and he's twice Lucie's age. Think drugs. Do you want her stashing some at your house?"

"Lord, Claire! You're scaring me. OK." She hung up.

I pocketed my phone and walked back to the window, careful to approach it from the side so Lucie wouldn't see me.

She was standing beside the sofa, the phone pressed to her ear. "No, no! Don't call the police, Gladys! Let me check my room first, OK? Give me ten minutes." She ended the call, scrolled down the screen to make another. "Get your ass back here now!" she shouted. "I need the car. Gladys just called and said the house was broken into. I have to get to my room and make sure everything is OK before she calls the cops."

"No, it *can't* wait!" she argued after a pause. "I've got a bag of pills and some pot in the nightstand drawer. If whoever broke in didn't find them the cops will. And I left my laptop in the room. It has some pretty incriminating emails about what we're doing here. I need to go over pronto."

Lucie stopped to listen. She started shaking her head from side to side, sending her hair flying. "No, *I'll* take the car. You need to stay here. What? Oh, fine! Just drop me off then."

A horn tooted five minutes later. Lucie ran out. I heard the Escalade tires crunch on the gravel driveway. The engine accelerated, then the sound faded into silence. I hugged the wall of the garage, crept out to the street to look around the corner. The SUV was gone.

CHAPTER
TWENTY-FIVE

I ran through the backyard along the wall of the garage and turned the corner. There was just one window at the back of the structure. The sash's wooden frame was silvery with age. Dry putty around the glass barely held the panes in place, but the window was locked in place. I plucked a good-size rock from the long-defunct flower bed running along the back wall and threw it at the bottom pane. The sound of breaking glass drew squawks from a flock of grackles roosting in a nearby tree. They rose in a great beating of wings.

I removed the biggest shards of glass still clinging to the frame and took off the zip-front hoodie to protect my arm from those remaining. Reaching inside I unlocked the window, lifted the sash and climbed inside.

Chantal lay on a bare soiled mattress. Her eyes widened when she saw me. She mumbled something under the strip of tape that covered her mouth.

She flinched when I pulled it off. "Leave!" she begged in an anguished whisper. "The people there," she said, jerking her chin at the room behind us. "They are very bad."

"They left," I replied in a normal tone of voice. "But they won't be gone long. We have to hurry."

"How did you..."

I shook my head. "I'll tell you later."

I tried to loosen the tape from around her wrists. But there were layers of it, all stuck together.

"I'll get a knife," I said to calm her when she fought the bonds. I walked into the next room. The kitchen/living room combination smelled of backed-up drains and rotten food. Flies buzzed around an overfilled trashcan, the sink was filled with dirty dishes and the carpet crunched under foot. I found a serrated knife soaking in greasy water.

It took precious minutes to cut through the layers, but finally she was free. She rolled to the edge of the mattress and almost fell when she got up. We walked out of the bedroom and through the living room at an agonizingly slow pace.

FRENCH LEAVE

How long would it take Popeye to drop Lucie off? He would be in a hurry to come back. I forced myself to relax. Gladys's house was some distance away. They were probably just getting there.

The street was empty when I opened the front door to check. So far so good. Walking from the garage to the car turned out to be the most frightening experience of my life. Knowing we would be vulnerable in the open, I tried to talk Chantal into waiting in the backyard while I retrieved the car. But she refused and I didn't press her.

We went at a snail's pace, hoping we wouldn't run into anyone. Chantal was a sight. Not only was one side of her face swollen, but the tape had left red marks all around her mouth. We met no one. We were turning the corner, within yards of the Focus, when I heard the sound of a car approaching. It was going fast. We were, by then, level with the old Dodge van with the rusted fenders. I jumped off the sidewalk, pulling Chantal after me.

The car turned the corner.

If it was Popeye, how long would it take him to realize she was gone? Not long at all. I grabbed Chantal for the second time and half carried her to the back door of the Focus, popped it open and thrust her inside.

My hands shook as I put the key in the ignition. Where could we go? I didn't know the neighborhood. Popeye, on the other hand, would be familiar with his surroundings, and he had the advantage of a faster car. Speeding away with no destination in mind would be a disaster.

I went up to the next corner and swung right onto a street lined with multi-story apartment buildings. Short driveways led to open parking behind the structures. I took the first one. All the buildings shared a common parking space, partially filled at this time of the day. I drove half the length of the lot and slipped between a pickup and a panel truck. If Popeye drove through the lot we were sitting ducks. If instead he sped by to scout the neighborhood, we would be safe for a while at least.

I took a deep breath and leaned against the headrest. Chantal stirred in the back seat.

"Stay low," I said. "We'll wait here until people drive home from work. It's almost five. The street will be busy then, and we can leave."

"The car. Was it that man?"

"I don't know."

"He wants Bernard, you know."

FRENCH LEAVE

"That's what I heard. Do you know why?"

"Yes. It is that shooting in Texas from many years ago. They talk about it because they think I do not hear."

"You weren't out that long, were you?"

"Just a little," she admitted. "That man, he hit me in the face. But we can't wait, Claire. We need to go to André. He must be scared."

"We can't. That's the first place the guy will check. Remember the contact Bernard said I would know about? I figured out who he meant. Someone is with André already. He's safe." I hoped that was true.

"That is good." Chantal didn't sound convinced. "But I am very worried about your fazzer, Claire. They want to hurt him."

"He managed to get away. He'll come back when it's safe."

"But how will he know? And what if he is hurt?"

"One thing at a time, Chantal," I said to reassure her. "Let's make sure you and André are safe first, OK?"

She didn't respond, and after a while I realized she had fallen asleep.

I spent the next ten minutes looking at a street map I found in the glove box. The street we were on paralleled a main thoroughfare that eventually crossed the freeway. I knew where I was now. But where could I go? I couldn't take Chantal home, obviously. Popeye knew where I lived. I couldn't take her back to the motel. Rose's apartment was out. He had seen it. I had never been to Carmen's house, but I knew where Manuela and Helga lived. Manuela's house was the closest. She lived in what used to be military housing just outside the defunct military post. Her two-bedroom ranch was filled with the grandkids and great-grandkids she babysat while the parents worked. One more body wouldn't matter to her. Plus, she knew how to treat bumps and bruises. Chantal would be in good hands.

The parking lot started filling in. The panel truck next to us backed out, leaving us exposed. I decided it was time to leave. The street was busy enough to assure, if not anonymity, at least safety in numbers. I kept an eye out for white SUVs, but most of the vehicles I saw were pickups and compacts. It was the wrong neighborhood for Cadillacs. Three blocks down, the street crossed another that led to the freeway.

I followed a line of cars up the on-ramp and merged into heavy traffic. Even though I was anxious to get to Manuela's I stuck to the slow lane, staying between two semis. A continuous stream of vehicles sped past on my left. Again, I watched for

FRENCH LEAVE

white SUVs. Two went past in the first five minutes I was on the freeway. Neither was an Escalade. A third appeared in the wake of a panel truck. My heart skipped a beat. It was taller, bulkier than the first two. The driver appeared to be in a hurry.

I told myself that Popeye had no reason to be looking for me on that section of the freeway. We were heading in the opposite direction of my house, and miles from Chantal's motel.

When the SUV came closer I instinctively hunched lower in my seat. The brakes of the semi in front of me flashed. I slowed. Traffic in the fast lane slowed as well as the SUV came alongside. I glanced at it. Behind the tinted window someone moved. It was just a shape, but I sensed that whoever was inside was looking at me. At the same moment I realized I had left the zip-front back at the garage. My striped tee was in plain sight.

I held my breath. Whoever was behind the glass kept looking. The staring match seemed to last forever. Then the semi in front accelerated and traffic in the fast lane picked up. The SUV moved away. I let my breath out. Later, as I exited the freeway, I saw it way ahead, still in the fast lane, still speeding. It must not have been Popeye after all. Maybe whoever was behind the wheel looked at me simply because I was looking that way.

FRANÇOISE BARTRAM

Still, I took a circuitous route to make sure no one was on my tail.

***

"Are you sure you don't mind keeping Chantal here?" I asked Manuela half an hour later. We were sitting in her yellow kitchen sipping inky coffee. Chantal was tucked in bed with an ice bag.

The coffee would do nothing to settle my nerves.

"No, Chiquita. I let her sleep a little bit and I get her up. I tell Helga about her. Helga, she says the boy, he is at her house now. Nobody knows."

By "nobody," I assumed she meant Estelle and the others.

"Did he go with her without any trouble?"

"Sì. He is afraid, but more afraid to be alone, so he go with Helga. Those people, what they want with tu tia?"

"They wanted her to tell them where Bernard's hiding."

"Pobrecito. We not know. Why they want him?"

"Your guess is as good as mine." I didn't want to tell her the people chasing Bernard blamed him for the death of the man her brother had shot. She would hear soon enough.

Her house, warm and welcoming, as uncomplicated as she was, had a calming effect. But my brain was still going full tilt, reliving the morning, presenting me with worse-case scenarios, such as Popeye arriving a few minutes earlier, soon enough to spot us as we turned the corner on the way to the car, or as we left the garage.

"Tia Chantal, she is safe now, Chiquita," Manuela said quietly, studying my face. She placed a plump hand over mine. "You did OK."

"I did." I took a deep breath. The room smelled of sautéed onions and peppers, the vegetables that went into the pupusas she made daily. She had raised her kids on this staple of Salvadoran cuisine, corn tortillas filled with cheese and refried beans, or pork when finances allowed. She had to make do with the meager pay her late husband, a career army man, earned in the early years of his enlistment. Even though the family's income increased as he rose in rank, the menu stayed the same. For Manuela, pupusas were comfort food, an unbreakable link to the country of her childhood.

I checked on Chantal one more time before leaving, walking through rooms that were painted different colors, sky blue, apple green, bright pink. Paintings hung on every available wall. They were all pictures of the Virgin Mary, drawn by Manuela with the lack of perspective that defined the naïve style. In some, she had Mary sumptuously dressed and bejeweled, in others wearing the traditional blue dress. In every one her subject was bathed in light and radiated joy.

Chantal was curled under the comforter. She didn't seem to have moved since I had seen her last. Her breathing was even and deep. She looked so comfortable I wished I could have stretched out in the twin bed beside hers and slipped into the same kind of mindless sleep.

But I didn't have time to sleep. I needed to talk to Gladys.

***

She must have known I was coming because I found her standing on Ruth's porch.

"Girl!" she said as soon as she saw me. "You have a lot of explaining to do. You were right about Lucie's sidekick. He's one bad dude. But you never said he was coming with her."

"He came in?"

"Not when he dropped her off the first time. The second time. He rang the doorbell and just about knocked me down coming in."

I took a quick look at her house and moved deeper into the porch. "Are they still there?"

FRENCH LEAVE

"Lord, no! They scooted off a while back. Him and Lucie first went to her room and I heard them arguing. Then they loaded up her stuff and left. You were right about the drugs. I looked after I called her and I found a big bag of pills. That may have been what the argument was about. So I guess I owe you."

"You coming in?" Ruth asked me, sticking her head out. "Or you about to run off again?"

Running off was tempting, but Gladys quirked an eyebrow at me and I followed her inside. The living room furniture had been pushed to one side to make room for Orville's hospital bed. Four dining room chairs placed around the bed provided seating for visitors. A man with a round face and silver-framed bifocals occupied one of them.

I took the one at the foot of the bed. Orville pointed a beaky nose my way. The left side of his head had been shaved. Black stitches followed the curve of his skull looking like the tracks of a miniature railroad. I averted my eyes, not eager to follow their path. A crocheted afghan covered the cast of his injured leg.

"I would've been home much sooner had you answered your phone, Claire," he said in the prissy voice he used to point out the faults of us lesser mortals. I liked him much better when he was lying mute in ICU. "Fortunately Gladys gave us a lift."

"You could have called me," the round-faced man said, sounding annoyed. He was short, dressed in a white button-down shirt and black pants, graying hair slicked back from a wide forehead. I remembered him from the time I came to his store to buy a laptop.

"You were at work," Orville reminded. "But I'm glad to have you here now. You can tell Ruth what you saw. She thinks it's my fault I was hit."

"It's not what I saw, Orville," Ronald said, waving a plump hand. "It's what I heard. I never saw you fall. But I have good ears and I'm certain I heard an engine surging *before* that awful thump. That's when I looked out and saw the SUV."

"What does *that* mean?" Ruth challenged. She sat on the other side of the bed, close to the kitchen door.

"It means, to me at least, that the driver was waiting for Orville to step off the curb. The police didn't think so, but they wrote down the description I gave of the vehicle so I'm confident they'll look for it. It should be damaged from the impact."

Ruth mumbled, "Bunch of claptrap." The little bun of gray

FRENCH LEAVE

hair she pinned low on her neck was sliding, a sure sign of agitation. "I wish you'd all quit talking about it."

Ronald Biscuit took the rebuke in stride. "I won't try to change your mind, Ruth, but I'm not given to flights of fancy and I can't ignore what I heard: an engine surge just before the accident. Orville was lucky to survive. The SUV that hit him was big. It's one of the fancy ones with big wheels, lots of chrome and tinted windows."

"An Escalade?" Gladys suggested.

Ronald took time to think. "Possibly. You know cars?"

"No, but I know what an Escalade looks like because my boarder has one. I saw it again today."

"The one involved in the accident was white."

"Same as Lucie's," Gladys said. "And the front was all dented up," she added, sounding thoughtful. "But it couldn't be her. She was in class that day."

Orville became agitated. "The girl was next door. She must know me. Who is she, Gladys?"

"A student in Lamont's class. Her name is Lucie, Lucie Steele. Does the name mean anything to you, Orville?"

CHAPTER TWENTY-SIX

I went home a few minutes later using work as an excuse to explain my getaway. I couldn't sit there impassively while the others discussed the similarities between Lucie's SUV and the vehicle that hit Orville. Gladys kept glancing at me, probably wondering why I didn't join in. I made a quick exit before she decided to ask.

Home felt strange, as if I had been gone for weeks rather than mere hours.

I had totally missed the connection between Howard and Lucie. But how could I have known? They didn't look like they were related. The only things they had in common were an excessive narrow-mindedness and a nasty habit of shoving their opinions down people's throats.

What did Howard want from Bernard anyway? Lucie said he had waited years to see justice done. There was something inflexible about him, a steely resolution to get his way that made me doubt he would leave the task unfinished.

So Bernard's fate was still uncertain. But the fact that Howard was still looking for him suggested Bernard knew he was in danger and was lying low. I just hoped he didn't decide to come back before the field was clear.

There was no way to warn him. Chantal had the vague impression that he had gone to visit his friend "Randy." But the name meant nothing to me. I was too young to remember the people who came to the house to see him. Mirabelle wouldn't know either. She was never close to him. But there was a chance Cora might remember Randy.

I called her. "Have you heard from Bernard since the last time we met?" I asked, broaching the subject with caution. She had been willing to discuss him the last time we met, but that wasn't always the case.

"No. Have you?"

"Not yet, but his sister is here. They agreed to meet at my house. He's running late and she can't get hold of him."

"Just like your father," Cora remarked, unconcerned. "He probably got the date wrong."

"Chantal said he came ahead to see one of his friends, a man named Randy. Does the name mean anything to you?"

"Randy? Of course it does. He and your father met in Vietnam. Randy followed him here when they were discharged and got a job teaching math at the high school. They were good friends."

"Do you know where he lives? Maybe I can get in touch with him."

"I don't have his address, but you should be able to track him down. His last name is Martin. Last I heard he was still in town."

***

Martin was a common name, but after several tries I found a Randall G. Martin that looked promising. The phone rang a long time before a girl answered.

"Dad's been out of town for the past two weeks," she said when I asked to speak to Randy. "I'm not sure when he'll be back. Is it important?"

I explained that I was trying to get in touch with my father, Bernard Palmer, a longtime friend of her dad. "Do you know if they're together?"

FRENCH LEAVE

The girl was apologetic. "I wouldn't know. I just came back from vacation. Before I left, Dad told me he was going down to our cabin in the hills to patch the roof. I haven't heard from him since, but I didn't expect to. There's no cell phone service down there."

"I see. If he gets in touch would you ask him to call me?" I gave her my number.

"Sure thing."

If Randy had been gone for two weeks, he would have left shortly before or shortly after Bernard got shot. How long did it take to patch a roof? He should have been back by now.

Norma called as I was putting together a cheese and tomato sandwich for my dinner.

"Sal read your note about Orville. She called the hospital to ask how he was doing, but they wouldn't tell her anything."

"He's doing better, Norma. The hospital discharged him. Is she home?"

"I'm not sure. She took off around four like her butt was on fire. Your note really upset her. It's not like she's close to the guy."

"She's known him for years, Norma. He's my neighbor."

"So? It's not like he's the kind of guy that puts a glint in her eye. Anyway, call her. She needs to know he's OK."

FRANÇOISE BARTRAM

But Sally didn't answer her landline or her cell phone.

I sat at the island to eat. The kitchen window suddenly turned dark and the wind rose, whipping the small lilac bush that stood at the corner of the house. Drops of rain slid down the glass, slowly at first, then with increasing speed.

Why should the news of Orville's accident upset Sally? Norma was right. Sally knew him, but it wasn't like there was any kind of emotional attachment between the two, not on her part anyway.

Did the fact that she had lost two bookkeepers in quick succession raise her suspicion? Watkins had just walked away, but Orville's possible violent removal was another matter. Was she heading to the hospital to see Orville when she left "like her butt was on fire," as Norma said, to find out what happened?

Norma was right. I had to let her know.

I took my purse, wrapped myself in Joe's poncho, a tent-like garment guaranteed to keep the wearer dry in a hurricane, and ran out to brave the elements. The wind whipped it like a sail.

A Mercedes with high beams was just pulling into Sally's driveway when I approached her house. The lights went out and the driver's door opened. I stopped the Ford two houses down

FRENCH LEAVE

and shut off the engine. Howard got out. He was talking on the phone. I rolled the driver's window down but I was too far away to hear what he was saying. Rain spit at me.

Sally came out on the porch. "About time you showed up." The wind carried the words to where I was parked. Her voice was high and angry. "What kept you?"

He looked up and reluctantly put the phone away, saying something I didn't catch.

"Too busy to send a text? Or answer my calls?" She didn't wait for a reply but marched back inside the house. After a pause, Howard climbed the porch steps and followed her. The living room window remained dark, which told me they had gone through the house all the way to the kitchen. I locked the Ford and followed the line of shrubs that separated her driveway from the neighbor's and walked all the way to the backyard. Years ago when Sally had the kitchen remodeled, she insisted on keeping the old-fashioned fan that pulled cooking odors through an opening in the outside wall. The metal housing acted as a mini megaphone. I stood under the dripping eaves to listen.

Sally was talking. "…kept insisting I get rid of Watkins. He quit. I hire Orville over your objection and he meets with an accident. Would you care to explain this?"

I hunched inside Joe's slicker. Rain dripped on the hood in a version of Chinese water torture. "I never said you had to get rid of either man, Sally. I suggested that, with my knowledge of finances, I would do the job better and for free. It sounded perfectly logical to me."

Sally wasn't buying it. "You're telling me it's mere coincidence that two men who worked as my bookkeepers left in short order, the first abruptly and seemingly without reason, the other when he was injured in a hit-skip, and all this shortly after you offered to do my books?"

She had connected the dots. It wasn't surprising. When it came to protecting her money, Sally was shrewd. Right then I would've given a month's pay to be able to see Howard's face.

He laughed. "You think I got rid of your bookkeepers to get the job? Dear, dear Sally! But I shouldn't be surprised. Your books are all about drama."

"*My* books are all about drama? I'll take that as a compliment. Earlier you said they were vulgar. But we aren't talking drama here, are we? We're talking greed. You wanted the bookkeeper job to see how much I have. I'm guessing Watkins was paid off, but you knew from the way I described Orville that he wasn't the kind of man who would be so easily persuaded."

Silence followed Sally's accusation. A full minute passed before Howard gave his signature dry cough. "I'm not sure how to respond to this, Sally. It hurts to know you think so badly of me. I have no need of your money. I'm a wealthy man."

"Are you? You drive a Mercedes and wear fancy shoes, but you eat on the cheap. That doesn't say wealthy to me."

"Eating on the cheap doesn't mean I'm destitute. Shale oil is big business. I eat at fast food restaurants for the convenience. I have no time to dawdle over meals."

"So you say. But you're evading my question. Did you or did you not have anything to do with Orville's accident? A yes or no will do."

A tinny jazzy tune came through the vent, repeating itself. "Hallo?" Howard said.

Sally heaved a sigh. The interruption was taking the steam out of the argument.

"You did *what*?" The fan housing amplified Howard's exclamation. I'd never heard him raise his voice before. "And she's gone?" The caller must've answered in the affirmative because Howard groaned. "Oh, God!"

I leaned closer to the fan. "Because of the break-in? What break-in? You mean it happened at the same time? What the hell did you do, Lu—" he stopped before blurting her name.

I didn't hear anything until he said sharply, "No! Not her. Leave her alone. She's the bait. Look, I don't like the way things are turning out. Call our contact, tell him you're heading for our meeting place and go home from there. Yes," Howard insisted. "You're done. I'll announce the next step when I see you. It will be soon, tomorrow at the latest."

Was I the bait?

"Are you done?" Sally snapped when Howard ended the call.

"Trouble at work," he said calmly. "I told you earlier. I'm busy."

Busy arranging for a kidnapping? Maybe not. He had been surprised at the news. But I wondered where the meeting place was.

"Never mind business," Sally said. "We were having a serious conversation before the interruption. Did you or did you not have anything to do with Orville's accident? I want an answer."

Howard cleared his throat. "I don't believe you deserve

one, Sally. If you believe that I'm dishonest and capable of violence, it's clear you don't trust me. And what's a relationship without trust?"

"Trust goes both ways, Howard. You scrutinized my life but you insisted on keeping yours totally private. I know nothing about you. Have you been married? Do you have children? You never said. I don't even know how long you'll be in town and where you'll go when you leave. You call that trust?"

"I'm a private person, Sally. A relationship needs time to mature. But discussing the future of our relationship is useless at this point."

"Spare me the drama and answer the damn question, Howard," Sally snapped. "Did you or did you not try to harm Orville? Damn it! I want an answer."

"But would you believe it?"

"Yes. Just tell me I'm wrong, Howard. That's all I want to hear."

"Too late, my dear. The only thing you'll hear from me is goodbye."

Howard's footsteps came next, loud on the tiled floor. The front door slammed. Minutes later an engine fired. The tires whispered on the wet asphalt as the Mercedes pulled away.

FRANÇOISE BARTRAM

Silence spread. As it thickened, every small sound took on space—the plop of rain on the hood of the slicker, the murmur of water in the gutter, a rustle of leaves. And yet another sound emerged from the kitchen vent: Sally was sobbing.

CHAPTER
TWENTY-SEVEN

I drove home a few minutes later.

I understood the tears. Sally wasn't used to being dumped. Personally I enjoyed Howard's dramatic goodbye. Not for the panache. I just wanted him gone from her life. But without her I wondered how he would keep an eye on me. I would have to be careful.

I was in bed and fast asleep when Ruth called at eleven. "I've been watching the news," she said, not apologizing for the late hour. "The police think they've identified the car that knocked Orville down. Some woman who lives on Chapel called to say she'd seen one like it. She said it belonged to a man who rented a room in the house next to hers."

It would be the neighbor who twitched the curtain as I went past. "Did they find him?"

"No, he got away, but the woman gave the police the license number. She wrote it down after she caught him speeding. She said he was reckless. Maybe they'll catch him."

I hoped they would so I could stop looking over my shoulder. The guy scared me. I figured it would be months before the sight of a white Escalade no longer made my heart jump out of my chest.

***

Orville was watching TV when I came by to see him the next day. He had on an old pair of glasses with rounds lenses and a black frame that made him look dorkier than usual.

"Claire!" His face lit up when he saw me. "Did you watch the morning news? They say the SUV that hit me was stolen in Texas."

It took a few seconds for the announcement to sink in. "The SUV was stolen?"

"That's what I said. And a reporter just called to ask if they could interview me," he said, his eyes bright with anticipation. "I told her I would."

The aroma of baking cookies drifted by. Ruth was busy in the kitchen. Sally had sent a fruit basket and a get-well card, Orville

FRENCH LEAVE

said, blushing with pleasure. A couple of his longtime clients had called to wish him well, and Ronald was coming by to see him. He was enjoying his minute of fame.

I had hoped to hear from Manuela with an update about Chantal, but she didn't call. It was Friday, a day that usually found her knee-deep in grandkids. Helga didn't answer her phone so I drove to the bookstore to see Carmen.

I parked around back. Carmen's Honda was the only vehicle in the space reserved for employees. The shop van was missing.

"Where is Sam?" I asked Carmen when I joined her behind the counter. She was swamped. A line of customers snaked all the way to the entrance.

"He drove to his cabin down south to check for wind damage after a storm."

I picked up two books she had just scanned and slipped them into a plastic sleeve with the store logo. "Was it bad?"

"I don't know. He can't get a signal down there. If it is, he'll be there for a while. He usually does all the repair work himself."

The man who was buying the novels chuckled. "Hard to believe Sam can do more with his hands than hold a book," he remarked as he paid.

Carmen gave him a dark look. "Sam is an excellent carpenter," she said stiffly. "He and his father built that cabin together."

"I'm sure. He's a good fisherman, too," the man hastened to say, picking up on the disapproval. "He can spend hours sitting on a riverbank."

Sam was good at sitting, period.

After the customer left I asked Carmen how our "friend" was doing. "Fine," she said shortly. "Come to Rose's after dinner this evening and I'll tell you," she said as the next customer approached the counter.

I went back to the car and headed to Sally's, wondering if she was getting over being dumped. Of course, she wouldn't admit it. Easier to say *she* ended the relationship.

The Cadillac was in the garage, the kitchen pristine from Norma's last scrubbing, the house silent.

I thought maybe I should let her sleep. It wasn't that late. But something about the house's stillness bothered me. I looked up at the ceiling for inspiration and finally walked to the bottom of the stairs to call her name. She didn't answer, and after several attempts to rouse her, I climbed to the second floor.

Her room was empty. The bed hadn't been slept in since Norma made it. I checked every bedroom on the second floor, went back down to search the first. She wasn't there.

But the car was in the garage. I called her cell phone. It went to voicemail.

Where could she have gone? Not to any of the neighbors. She hardly knew them.

I went out to the garage. Sally and the Cadillac were inseparable. Except for the times she went out of town or the car was in the shop, they were never apart. I entered the garage and felt the hood. It was warm. She had driven up, parked and left again. On foot? Sally never walked if she could ride.

The Cadillac was dusty. Mud and grass littered the driver's floormat. I opened the rear door to check the back seat and found her purse on the floor.

I looked inside. It held her wallet, a bulging cosmetics bag, her cell phone, a package of tissues, a comb, a brush, a small appointment book and a change purse. Her credit cards were in her wallet as well as eighty dollars in cash.

Women didn't leave their purses behind, not willingly.

Someone had used the Cadillac recently. Not Sally. The driver's seat was pushed back all the way.

I returned the purse to the back seat and stood beside the car, not sure what to do next. Alert the police or call around first to try and locate her? She had few close friends, but an army of ex-boyfriends. I was thinking of calling the one she was with before Howard when my phone rang.

Norma.

She asked if I knew where Sally was.

"No, and I'm worried about her, Norma. Her car's in the garage and the house is empty. I have no idea where she could be."

"Shit!" she said explosively. "Then it must be true. I just got a call about her."

"What about? Was it from a hospital?" She could've had a fall or suffered a seizure, and someone drove her to the emergency room. That would explain the empty house and the purse left behind. "Is she OK?"

"I'm not sure. Some guy called to tell me she spent the night in a park down by the Ohio River. He found her when he went out for his morning jog."

"*What?* That makes no sense. Did you talk to her?"

"No, the man said she had nothing but the clothes on her back, no phone, no credit card, no money. He didn't have his cell so he ran home to call for help. She gave him my number—she couldn't remember yours—and said for him to tell me she wanted you to pick her up. When he asked her what happened, she clammed up."

"Who is this guy?" I was thinking about Popeye. "Did he tell you his name?"

"He gave his name as Jake Sattherwaite. Sounds posh to me. He has a voice like a bass drum and uses big words. If he's a crook, he comes with a degree."

A voice like a bass drum not only left Howard out—Norma would've recognized his voice—but Popeye as well. I remembered his voice more like tenor. "Did Sattherwaite offer to call the police?"

"He did, and she went ballistic. You know how she feels about drawing attention."

Sally didn't always use good sense in her choice of boyfriends. She liked men with a wild streak. Her reputation suffered after two of her relationships ended badly enough to require a police presence. She had kept a low profile ever since.

"You going?" Norma asked anxiously. "I'd go with you, but I'm out in the boondocks. It would take me half an hour, maybe more, to get to you."

The excuse sounded fabricated and I figured she either found the situation too risky or she just didn't want to take time off work. Probably the latter. Norma liked to keep to her schedule.

I wondered why Sally asked to have me pick her up. Did she make the request, or did someone else make it to get at me? It could be a scam. Popeye and Lucie probably wouldn't have minded getting their hands on me.

"If I go alone I'm going to need some sort of backup, Norma," I said. "Make sure you keep your phone handy. I'll call when I get there, and I'll keep you on the line until I'm absolutely sure Sally and I are safe. OK?"

Norma said she would and gave me directions. But in spite of her assurance I worried all the way down. How did Sally and her cherished Cadillac part ways? She never loaned it to anyone. Maybe it was hijacked, and whoever took it dumped it to keep her from reporting the theft. But if that was the case, it would be miles away now, not in her garage.

Or was it Howard who hijacked the car with her inside in an attempt to extort money from her? He was spiteful enough to leave her stranded if she turned him down.

FRENCH LEAVE

I couldn't figure Jake Sattherwaite's role in all this, whether he was a Good Samaritan or a participant, but I would soon find out. After getting off the interstate I stopped in a mini-mart to buy two large coffees and a box of donuts.

A wooden billboard at the park entrance displayed a map highlighting the hiking trails and the gravel road that crossed it. The picnic grounds were at the end of a foot path that branched off the main road. I drove down until I saw an arrow directing visitors to the grounds, and parked in a paved area alongside a silver BMW, the only car there. It probably belonged to Sattherwaite. I left the path to approach the area from another angle, weaving through a clump of cedars that overlooked the grounds, hoping to see Sally and her rescuer before they saw me.

What was a Jake like? I only knew of one, Joe's uncle, a laid-back farmer at ease in his Carhartts. A Jake with a BMW was bound to be different. It made him posh as Norma said, but not necessarily nice. For all I knew he could be a moneyed serial killer who had disposed of Sally and was now waiting to pounce on his next victim.

An open-sided shed with a shingled roof stood in the center

of a grassy area flanked by four charcoal grills on metal poles. A cement path led from the shed to a row of outhouses. The shed held four picnic tables. Sally was sitting at the closest facing me. She was wrapped in a blanket.

I was too far to see her face clearly. The man sitting across from her was talking. A breeze carried the deep rumble of his voice. I took the cell phone out of my purse and brought up Norma's number. She answered immediately. I kept the phone to my ear as I left the cover of the trees.

It took me the best part of a minute to walk down the short slope and across the grassy area to the picnic table, plenty of time for the guy to assess me. I watched him back. Silver hair and vivid blue eyes against a golfer's tan. Posh, as Norma said. It wasn't only the designer clothes that defined him, but also an air of inborn confidence.

"Looks good so far," I told her. "Stand by. I'll call you back in about thirty minutes or so."

The man got up when I came near. "Jake," he said, extending his hand. His grip was strong, his smile welcoming.

I shook it. "Claire. I'm Sally's ride."

Sally peered at me from inside her cocoon of blanket, looking

FRENCH LEAVE

as vulnerable as a baby bird fallen from the nest. After a night spent outdoors, her hair fanned out in a mass of frizzes. Streaks of mascara ran down her cheeks.

"I brought you coffee," I said to hide my dismay. Hard to believe I was looking at the same woman who posed for the author picture on her book jackets, eyes crinkling in a come-hither look, her chin lifted in challenge.

Those eyes now flickered at the mention of coffee and she propped one hand on the table to push herself upright.

Jake Sattherwaite rounded the picnic table to give her a hand. "I would've brought you some, had you asked, Sally." He sounded defensive. "But it would've taken time to make it and I wanted to get back to you as soon as possible. She refused to go home with me," he said, turning to address me. "She even refused to sit in the car until you came. It's clear someone frightened her badly. I wish she'd let me call the police."

"No police," Sally stressed in a surprisingly strong voice. She shook him off and marched on, unassisted. I didn't know if it was anger that put a spring in her step or the thought of coffee waiting for her in my car.

When we reached the parking lot, Sattherwaite cast a dubious look at the aging Focus parked beside his shiny BMW, but he didn't object when Sally made a beeline for the Ford.

"You have my number," he reminded as she opened the passenger door. "Call me when you get home. I want to make sure you're all right."

She took the time to thank him for his help before settling in the passenger seat, but I could tell she couldn't wait to leave. I glanced at the rearview mirror as we drove away. Sattherwaite stood beside his BMW, eyes trained on the Focus. He was still looking when I turned the corner.

I called Norma to let her know we were on our way. Sally drank her coffee in silence and ate a couple of donuts while I was on the phone. She kept Jake's blanket pulled around her. It was a cozy throw made of fine tan wool with narrow red bands woven at either end, the kind people drape on the back of the sofa for cold evenings.

"What happened?" I asked after she finished her coffee.

She sank deeper into her nest of blanket. "I don't want to talk about it."

Just like her to be obstructive. "My car, my rules," I said firmly. "You asked for me. I came even though I had no idea what I was walking into. Something happened to scare you out of your wits and I want to know what it is."

She flipped a corner of the blanket away from her face and turned to look in my direction. "Howard happened, that's what."

"I thought he might be involved. What did he do?"

"He tricked me into driving out of town and then he dumped me at the park."

"Tricked you how?"

"By lying to me. We broke up yesterday after a big argument. An hour later he called to apologize, and like a fool I thought he meant it. He told me he knew of a romantic inn near the Ohio River and suggested we spend the night there. I said OK. We took the Cadillac because his car was in the garage, or so he said. On the way down he talked about his work and asked if I would be interested in investing money in his business, that it would be a good investment. He didn't seem upset when I said no. We stopped at the park to use the toilets. When I came back the car was gone."

Her voice gave out then and she had to compose herself before going on. "I couldn't believe it," she said after a pause. "At first I thought it was a joke. But he didn't come back. There I was without my phone, without money or credit cards. I didn't even have an ID."

"You'd left your purse in the car?"

"Yes, it's usually on the passenger seat, but he was sitting there so I put it in the back. I saw no need to take it. You think he would've stopped me from taking it if I tried?" There was fear in her voice. "You think he would've hit me?"

"Possibly."

She scrunched down. "The more I think about the situation, the scarier it gets."

"You must've felt terribly vulnerable in the dark."

"I was, yes, but actually I was glad it was dark when he came back."

I took my eyes off the road for a split second to look at her. "*He came back?*"

"Yes, and he wasn't alone. When I saw headlights in the parking lot, I hid behind some trees because I had no way of knowing who was coming. Two men started down the path. I knew right away one of them was Howard because he called my name. He said for me to come out, that it was just a joke. The other man didn't say anything. He stayed close to the trees as if he didn't want to be seen. Howard called again and walked over to where the toilets were to check every one of them. That's when I walked farther into the woods and I didn't move until they left."

"The man meant to hurt you. What do you intend to do about it?" I asked.

She gave me the same answer she gave Sattherwaite. "Nothing! What would I gain by calling the police? He'll deny he did anything wrong. Unless I tell them he stole the car, they'll have nothing on him."

"You can't even say that. The Cadillac is back in your garage."

She drew her breath in sharply. "See? I would end up looking like a fool again. I was right, no police!"

She leaned back in her seat and pulled a corner of the blanket over her face. I left her alone and she slept until we reached her house.

CHAPTER
TWENTY-EIGHT

Sally refused to leave the car until I made sure Howard wasn't waiting for her inside the house. When I sounded the all clear she bolted into the kitchen and hunched at the table, still wrapped in her blanket.

She didn't say anything while I made coffee and popped two slices of bread into the toaster. The kitchen filled with a comfortable warm smell. "Does he have a house key?"

"No and he doesn't know the code for the alarm system, but after what he did to me I wouldn't put it past him to have both."

I brought her a mug of coffee and some buttered toast. Her hands were tucked inside the blanket. The phone rang just as she was reaching for the mug. She jumped and coffee spilled over the side. "Who's that?"

I looked at the screen. "It's a blocked number."

"Don't answer!"

We waited for the voicemail to come on. But the caller didn't leave a message. "It's him, Claire. I know it. He's watching me."

"I suppose he could be, but I can't see him sticking around after pulling that trick on you. The man isn't stupid."

"How can he be gone when he brought the car back?" she argued. "He's here. How else would he know to call the moment I got home?"

"We don't know it was him. The call could be a coincidence. But I understand why you don't feel safe here. You could move to a hotel for a couple of days, or stay with a friend."

She hesitated. "No, I'd rather stay home. But I want someone with me." She didn't look in my direction, but I knew she meant me.

"Maybe you can ask Norma," I said firmly. The refusal was petty, but I was tired of her counting on my loyalty after what she had done to me. It was a childish impulse, but there was nothing childish about my determination to stop her from using me.

She didn't insist, and after drinking her coffee she went upstairs to take a shower and change. While she was gone I looked in the refrigerator to see if I could make a hot meal, but apart from a few eggs and a chunk of desiccated cheese there was nothing worth eating.

"You don't have much in the way of food. I could go out and get you something to eat. How about Chinese?" I asked when she came back down in an old robe, her hair wrapped in a towel.

"That would be good. But don't stay gone long. In the meantime I'll call Norma."

***

At the restaurant I ran into Steve, Lisa's boyfriend, who was waiting in line to order take-out. He had come straight from work in his uniform of tan pants and shirt with his name embroidered on the shirt pocket. Buying dinner was an everyday thing for him. Lisa never cooked. She said her job was to make plates, not fill them.

"You buying something for Joe's dinner?" he asked, making an effort at civility. He was no happier to see me than I was to run into him.

I had forgotten it was Friday. Joe would want dinner when he came home. "Actually I'm doing a double run, one for Joe, one for Sally."

FRENCH LEAVE

Steve's eyes flickered at the name. "Is she still seeing Steele?"

I hesitated, loath to discuss Sally's private life with him. Like Lisa, he disapproved of her. "Why do you ask?"

"I was wondering if he's staying with her. The boss has been looking for him."

"He isn't at Sally's house. I just came from there. I think he left town."

Steve looked grave. "That's what Bundant is afraid of. Steele borrowed some money from him. Yesterday he returned the Mercedes, just left it in the lot with the keys inside. The boss is steamed. Would you let me know if Sally hears from him?"

I said I would.

CHAPTER TWENTY-NINE

"I'm glad you brought dinner. I'm starving," Joe said when I came home. "I've been on the road all day." He took the carryout bag out of my hand. "Chinese? Where from?"

"From the usual place. I ran into Steve when I was there."

Joe raised his head sharply. "Steve? My buddy Steve?"

"Yes, your buddy Steve. He was getting dinner."

"You talked to him?" Joe was suspicious. "What did you say?"

"Nothing! For goodness' sake, Joe. I know Steve and I have our differences, but we are civilized. We just talked." I realized I was hard on Steve, but Joe didn't have to make me into Genghis Khan.

"What about?"

"Sally's boyfriend."

Joe was relieved. "Oh well, that's OK. You both hate his guts. What about your aunt, any news?"

FRENCH LEAVE

"Chantal has resurfaced, minus the Haitian. She's at Manuela's."

Joe took possession of the carton that held shrimps with pea pods and sat down. "Why at Manuela's instead of here? Did you pull out the welcome mat?"

"No, I didn't. She's hiding out."

He paused in the process of breaking apart a pair of bamboo chopsticks that came with the food. "From the sheriff?" he asked, looking at me. "I'm glad she isn't here then. I don't know how I would feel about hiding a fugitive."

"It's not the sheriff she's worried about," I said as I took a fork out of the flatware drawer. I never learned to handle chopsticks. Joe popped the top off a can of beer. While we ate I told him about Chantal's ordeal, how I tracked her down.

"Are you crazy? You *tailed* the guy? That was totally stupid, Claire. He had to know what kind of car you were driving."

"He did, but the world is full of Fords, Joe. Mine doesn't exactly stand out. Anyway, I was careful."

Joe skillfully picked up a shrimp with the chopsticks and popped it in his mouth. "I still say you're crazy. If he'd made you, you could be dead and I'd be eating shrimp alone."

I put my fork down. "Would that be an improvement?"

He laughed. "Not if I had to pay for dinner. So what happened to the Haitian?" he asked.

"Carmen took him." I went on to tell him about the Foreign Legion's likely involvement, about Lucie's family ties with Howard, about Howard leaving Sally stranded at the park.

He laughed. "Great stuff for the next book! You have the makings of a bestseller here."

"Really, Joe? The situation Sally was in wasn't the least bit funny. That's all you have to say apart from calling me stupid?"

"Well, you were. Sometimes you're way too impulsive, Claire. You need to think."

The subject of Sally's next book gave me a chance to tell him I wouldn't be the one writing it, but I stayed mum. He would find out soon enough. Anyway, admitting out loud that I'd lost my job was still beyond me. The phone rang and I let the moment pass. It was Helga reminding me of the meeting at Rose's house. They were waiting for me.

***

Rose greeted me with her usual secretive smile, a wordless greeting that, in spite of its aloofness, conveyed affection.

"Is André safe now?" I asked the group gathered in the living room. It included, besides the hostess, three of the original members: Carmen, Manuela and Helga.

"Safe," Helga confirmed.

I read the monosyllabic answer as a warning not to ask questions, and she looked at me to underline the message. That was all right. I didn't need to know what they had done with the kid. He was out of my hands. That was all that mattered to me.

"How is Chantal?" I asked Manuela. She shared the sofa with Helga. Carmen sat by herself on the loveseat and Rose sat sheltered in one of two vast wingback chairs that flanked the sofa. I headed for the other.

"Tu tia, she's with the niños right now. She's OK," Manuela assured.

I took the "OK" assessment with a grain of salt. The French aunt would be OK as long as she enjoyed mayhem. Manuela had about a million grandchildren, all of them full of beans.

I set my purse on the floor and leaned back in my chair, taking the time to test the temperature in the room. It wasn't warm. The four women sat apart, as if careful to maintain their personal space.

"I went to see your aunt," Carmen said from her seat across

from the rest of the group, facing them like an accused in the witness box. She glanced at her friends briefly before transferring her gaze to me. "We admitted we were the ones who made the decision to bring the boys here and we told her we were sorry. And we apologize to you as well, Claire. But honestly, we never meant to involve her. And we still don't understand why she was involved."

"I told you. She took over for Bernard. Did you know he was coming?"

"Yes. We asked him to."

"*You* did? Or was he the one who came up with the idea?"

"It was us, Claire." She was firm. "We always hoped to get you and your father back together. A while back the organization that helped Manuela's brother took charge of two young Haitians running from human traffickers. The organization gave them shelter and found a French-speaking volunteer to work with them, but the man ended up in the hospital after a car accident. That's when we suggested using your father instead. It was as if Fate was giving us the chance to bring him back."

"Suerte," Manuela agreed, saying the word in Spanish. "It was a sign, Chiquita."

If Helga was of the same mind she didn't say so, but I took her silence as good as a denial. She was far too practical to be ruled by superstition. Rose irritably shuffled her embroidered slippers on the carpet with a sibilant whisper.

Carmen glanced briefly at the two dissenters. "Elena, the woman who looked after the boys, knew Bernard from the time he helped Eduardo so she was glad to have him."

"We feel bad because you feel so bad, pobrecita, when he go," Manuela said, reaching for my hand.

I never blamed them for what happened. Forgiving them for interfering was another matter. "Maybe so, but since it didn't end well the first time he was involved, what made you think it would work this time?"

Carmen looked pained. "But the situation was entirely different, Claire, and we were so careful. We had no reason to believe something would go wrong. Elena's group is very reliable."

"Apparently not."

She shook her head impatiently. "You don't understand. We planned everything down to the last detail. Your father was to go straight to your house, and while there call my house using your landline. It would be just a call, no message, to let us know he had arrived. Elena cautioned us to have no direct contact with him until after he had taken the young men across the Canadian border. The call came—I have caller ID—so we dropped the box with the money and clothing at your door as arranged."

The call came but it wasn't Bernard who made it. It was Ruth who had dialed the number scrawled on one of the Haitians' cryptic messages to ask what they meant.

"We had no idea there was anything wrong until we heard about the wreck and the survivor taken into custody," Carmen went on. "Then we saw your aunt on the news. We couldn't understand why she was there instead of Bernard. Elena hadn't heard from him either, but they keep communication to a minimum for safety and she thought he was just late going to Canada. We still don't know anything about the men who attacked Chantal. What were they after?"

I decided not to tell them, not until I found out who alerted Howard to Bernard's return. It could have been one of the women innocently mentioning the fact to someone who knew him, or it could have been a member of the group voluntarily passing the word to the two guys who waited for him outside my house.

"Not knowing makes it hard on all of us, Claire," Carmen

said. Her cell phone buzzed and she reached for her purse. "I hope it's Sam texting to let me know he brought the van back. He drove it down to the cabin to work on the roof and came back without it. I don't know what he was thinking. We need it here."

Manuela muttered a word that sounded like estupido. "Talk, talk, talk about Sam all the time," she complained. "What we care? He no like us. We no like him. How he got back then?" she asked, forgetting she'd just told Carmen she wasn't interested in what he did.

"Not now," Helga cut in before Carmen had a chance to respond. "You can check with Sam later." There was an edge to her voice that warned Carmen not to challenge her. I knew Manuela wasn't the only one who resented Sam. The group had long been a captive audience for the saga of his and Carmen's rocky relationship.

Elena, Helga went on to say, had talked to the men who drove the Haitians to Clayton. They left them at the house, the backup drop point, when Bernard failed to meet them at the arranged time and place. They didn't report this immediately, and by then the trail was cold and one of the boys was dead, the other in the hospital.

FRANÇOISE BARTRAM

"Elena said they discreetly checked local hospitals," Carmen said, claiming back her role of spokesperson. "He didn't fit the profile of any gunshot victims. She thinks Bernard is in hiding and will resurface when it's safe. Your father is resourceful, Claire," she assured.

I didn't see her confidence reflected on her fellow members' faces. The three others looked troubled. They would have felt even worse had they known he had been shot.

CHAPTER THIRTY

It was dark when I left the townhouse. Moths mobbed porch lights and fireflies blinked a silent Morse code against the hum of traffic. The air was soft and smelled of dried grass.

Something about what had been said at the meeting had caught my attention, something that could be important, but the thought had been fleeting and now it was gone.

I drove to Sally's house before going home. Norma's van was in the driveway.

Norma sprawled on the living room sofa clad in striped pajamas, legs rolled up to the knees, bare feet resting on the coffee table. Her feet were as square as the rest of her, the nail on each stubby toe painted a glistening black. The room reeked of nail polish. Sally sat in a side chair wrapped in her old pink robe. Her toenails matched Norma's. An empty stem glass rested on her middle.

FRANÇOISE BARTRAM

"About time you showed up, Claire," Norma said when she saw me. She flapped a limp hand in the direction of a half-empty champagne bottle resting in an ice bucket on a side table. "Have a drink," she invited, making a grab for the bottle and almost knocking it over. She giggled, a sound I would never have associated with her, but then I never thought I would see her drunk either.

"That's the second bottle. Or is it the third? I can't remember. Norma's a bit tipsy," Sally informed, stating the obvious—a case of the pot calling the kettle black since she seemed to be having trouble focusing.

"Good stuff," Norma said, refilling her glass. "Sal got it for 'you know who.'"

"He never minded spending other people's money," Sally said. I was glad to see she could talk about him without emotion. "I would've bought a cheaper brand, but he had to have the best."

"May he drink rotgut for the rest of his life," Norma intoned, raising her glass.

I got up to refill Sally's glass and filled one for myself.

"And burn in hell for stealing my Cadillac," Sally added.

I took a sip. The wine was a dry Moët & Chandon, the total opposite of the sweet stuff sold in drugstores for the New Year.

The taste, clean and cold, lingered in my mouth. Who had driven the Cadillac back to Sally's house? Howard, because he didn't want her to report it stolen? Possibly. Next I thought of someone who had no reason to do it, yet *could* have done it because he was in the vicinity and returned to Clayton without using his own vehicle. I remembered Manuela wondering aloud how *Sam* got back after Carmen mentioned he had left the van at the cabin.

I knew his cabin was near the Ohio River. The river snaked along the state's entire southern border, so I was taking a leap of faith thinking Sally's park and the cabin were close. But it wasn't impossible.

If Sam and Howard were connected, it would explain how Howard learned of Bernard's return. Who knew how long he had been eavesdropping on Carmen's calls? He could have been feeding information to Howard for years.

Sam's possible involvement made me wonder if he had lured me to the bookstore to pick up *The Mystery of the Vanishing Clerk*, not to annoy Carmen, but to make it possible for Popeye to pick up my trail and follow me to the motel where Chantal was hiding.

Sally drained her glass and said, "I'm hungry again."

"You missed a couple of meals," Norma reminded. "We could order pizza. What do you like on yours, Claire?" she asked, looking at me.

I got up. "Nothing for me, thanks. I'm going home." I was feeling lightheaded, but I didn't think it had anything to do with the wine.

"You're no fun," Norma grumbled, but her disappointment didn't last long. She turned to Sally. "What about you, Sal?"

"I like everything except anchovies."

Norma made a face. "Who does? I want pepperoni and sausage."

"And plenty of cheese. What about bacon?"

They were so busy discussing topics they didn't see me leave.

At home, I parked in an empty garage. Joe's car was gone. I woke up when he came in at three, walking with the foot-dragging gait of a Frankenstein. He flopped down on the bed without bothering to take his clothes off and fell asleep, blowing beery breaths that made my head swim. I looked at his slack face, at the bristles on his jaw, at his shirt creased and stained. He came across as old and dissolute, the opposite of the fastidious man who buffed his nails, had his teeth whitened and went to a fancy salon for a haircut. Joe, whose father died an alcoholic, drank sparingly, terrified at the thought of following the same path.

What had happened to make him go over a cliff?

***

He was still sleeping when I got up the next morning. The phone rang while I ate breakfast and I grabbed it before it woke him up.

"...damn the girl to hell," Gladys said, her foghorn voice booming in my ear.

I got up to shut the door between the kitchen and the hallway and asked, even though I knew the answer, "What girl are you talking about, Gladys?"

"Who do you think? Lucie, of course."

"I thought she was gone."

"She is. But I just found out she stole Lamont's credit card. He left it with me after I told him I was through paying it off. Her badass boyfriend just got caught using it. His name is John Little. A clerk at one of those quick stops off I-64 thought it was strange for a white dude to be called Lamont and asked for ID. Little made a run for it and an off-duty cop who happened to be nearby went after him. Lucie tripped the cop. Now both she and Little are in jail for assault and resisting arrest. Someone from the card company called here for Lamont wanting to know how they got hold of it. I told them Lucie had to be the one who took it. Now she's been charged with carrying a stolen card across state lines."

I later found out that Texas had a warrant out for a John Little. The white man who died in the wreck was someone named Mayfield. Both men had been wanted on weapons charges and drug dealing.

Joe walked into the kitchen as I hung up the phone. His eyes were bloodshot but he had shaved and his hair curled down on his forehead, damp from the shower. "I have one hell of a headache," he said.

I refrained from bringing up cause and effect. "You want coffee?"

"Please."

I poured some into a mug and handed it to him. He took it but didn't drink.

"Would you rather have tea?"

"No, coffee's OK. Nothing's going to make me feel better right now, Claire. I lost my job."

I just looked at him. No way had I seen that one coming. Joe

FRENCH LEAVE

was the top salesman in his outfit, a business he had been with for ten years. "The company is downsizing. They're closing our office."

"Didn't they offer to relocate you?"

He shook his head numbly. I tried to think of something encouraging to say but my mind was blank.

"Who am I without my job, Claire?" he murmured, his voice so low I had trouble hearing him. "It's like somebody wrote my name on a board and wiped it clean."

I understood the feeling. "But you're good at what you do, Joe. You've been consistently good for years. Surely that counts for something. Some company is bound to snap you up." The empty promise got the scorn it deserved. "OK, maybe you won't, not right away anyway. But trust in what you know, in what you've accomplished. Confidence makes a huge difference when looking for a job." I was giving him the same argument Lisa leveled at me every time she tried to talk me into leaving Sally. It hadn't worked with me either.

"...won't need one for a while, not until the unemployment runs out," Joe said, breaking into my thoughts. "And then I'll have to find a place to live."

I blinked. "What for? You can live here."

"You haven't been listening. I said that if I land a job, it probably won't be around here. Last night I got together with the other salesmen and we talked about what we would do. We've known since last Monday. I guess I could've called and told you but I didn't feel like talking." I nodded to show I understood. He rarely called when he was on the road. "Anyway, the three other salesmen, Rob, Matt and Gordon, they all have plans. Rob is married and has two kids. They'll be moving. His wife never liked it here and she wants to go back to Idaho where she's from. Matt is young and he wants to finish college. Gordon's uncle offered him a job. And me, well..." Joe hesitated. "I've been thinking about going back to West Virginia and getting a job in Elmer's garage."

Stupid, stupid idea. Cousin Elmer was a Sally in pants, a bully and an egotist. He paid Joe a slave wage for two years under the pretense that his younger cousin was an apprentice, even though it was Joe who ran the garage. "Come on, Joe! Aunt Lou worked like a demon to get you out of his clutches; got you enrolled in community college, supported you until you graduated, and now you say you want to go back? Don't do that. The man's a user."

Joe turned on me. "And Sally isn't? I admit going back to West Virginia is a crappy idea. And you're right. I should make use of my experience instead of running to the nearest bolt hole. But you aren't exactly bristling with courage either. Here you are, banking on Sally to recognize your worth even though she pays you next to nothing for writing books that don't bear your name. You complain constantly, the two of you fight like cats and dogs, yet you don't want to leave. What does that tell you?"

"It tells me you have a point." I could hardly shame him for digging a trench to cower in when I had been doing the same for years. "Tell you what. I'll leave Sally if you promise not to go back to Elmer."

"You first," he said. And he walked out.

CHAPTER THIRTY-ONE

Chantal moved back to the house the next day. With Lucie and Popeye tucked in jail, she probably felt safer, but Howard was a loose cannon. I would have to keep an eye on her. Joe made her a cup of what he called his world-famous coffee before leaving for his usual Saturday meet with Steve. Chantal perched at the island savoring her drink. "Manuela's coffee, it is very good, but my hands they shake after two cups. I like Joe's better."

"Don't tell him that. He's vain enough already. You're looking better," I said, studying her face.

She touched her cheek. "Yes, the mirror, it is kinder to me. And now that I look like an old woman with ugly gray hair I do not have to worry about the police knowing who I am."

FRENCH LEAVE

"I don't think they'd recognize you, no, but keep a low profile just the same."

"Manuela says the man who took me is in jail. Is this true?"

"Yes. The girl was arrested as well. It's too bad you can't testify against the guy, but since Texas has a warrant against him, John Little will be locked up anyway."

"What about the girl?"

"She's been charged with stealing a credit card and carrying it across state lines. And she made things worse by assaulting a cop."

"So she will be punished, too. That is good. Now if only your father would call."

The phone rang. Chantal jumped and turned sharply as if she expected her brother to crawl out of the handset. But it was just Sally asking to see me.

***

I parked at the end of the driveway and entered the house through the kitchen. It didn't look as if she had moved since she called. The cordless was in her hand. She sprawled at the kitchen table with her head down on the place mat.

"Where's Norma?"

Sally slowly raised her head. "She went home."

The party girl had the pale, sweaty look of the severely hungover. She dropped the phone to support her head with both hands. "I feel terrible, Claire. Norma's even worse. She took a sick day."

I sat across from Sally. "I'm not surprised. What can I do for you? I can run to the grocery store if you need something."

She squinted in my direction even though we were barely two feet apart. "The only thing I need is for my head to stop hurting and there's nothing you can do about that. But before I go back to bed there's something you need to know."

I was curious. "About what?"

"I want you to know how Howard made a fool out of me."

"You don't owe me an explanation, Sally."

She started to shake her head, changed her mind and waved a hand instead. "I had a reason for doing what I did, and I need you to know it." She leaned her head in her hand. "God, I feel like my eyes are going to fall out! Can you get me an aspirin? And after that go up to my room and bring back the silver frame on my nightstand."

She was sitting up looking a bit more alert when I came back with the picture of the stern man with the preteen Sally.

FRENCH LEAVE

I looked at the girl with the tight braids and the bleak eyes. "Is that you? You don't look happy."

"I wasn't. My dad wasn't easy to live with. He hardly ever smiled and there were times he was downright mean. I think it was because he didn't know what to do with me."

"What about your mom?"

"She was dead by then. He would've been OK raising a son. But girls confused him. He always acted as if I was too weak or too dumb to handle life. It didn't do much for my self-esteem, I tell you."

"But you have self-esteem now."

"That was Aunt Bea's doing. Aunt Bea was my mother's sister. I went to live with her when I was twelve. She offered to take me in right after Mom died, but Dad said no. He despised her. She was everything my mother was not: brash, loud and fiercely independent. So he hired a housekeeper. Mrs. Severn." Sally's mouth hardened. "She dressed me all in brown and braided my hair so tight it made me cry."

"Good mothering skills."

Sally shrugged. "She didn't like kids. I didn't like her either. When I hit puberty I turned wild and she told Dad she'd had enough. That's when he sent me to live with Aunt Bea. I was glad. But I hardly saw him after that. Six years later he sent word that he had lung cancer. I went to the hospital to see him. He was no longer the man I knew. It wasn't so much his physical appearance that shocked me—he had lost a lot of weight. It was the fact that he had lost his authority as well. In his work as the CEO of his own company, he was competitive, even ruthless. No more. There he was, scared, unsure of himself. He clung to me. He promised to build a new house just for the two of us. He would take me to Europe. He would send me to college. I saw him every day for a week. Then he died." Sally's eyes darkened. "A week's worth of approval was all I got. That and his money."

She set the picture, glass down, on the kitchen table. "I was attracted to Howard because he was the same kind of man: demanding, self-assured and well-spoken." She placed her hand flat over the frame. "I wanted him to approve of me the way my father never did. So when Howard imposed change, I went along so I could be the kind of woman my father admired. I didn't realize I had this need until he came along." She pushed the picture away. "But I found out Howard wasn't after the ideal woman after all. All he wanted was my money. He called, you know."

FRENCH LEAVE

I felt a chill. "Howard did? Where from?"

She shrugged. "I don't know, but he asked me for money. For his daughter. I laughed at him. What daughter?" Sally snorted. "He never told me he had children. He claimed she'd been arrested by mistake and needed money for bail. Right!"

Funny how Sally swallowed every lie Howard told. But when he told the truth, she didn't believe him.

She went back to her room when I left. My cell pinged as I walked to the car. It was a message from Joe.

"Heads up! Some guy named Randy called asking for you. Chantal took the call. He said Bernard'll be at your house today."

CHAPTER THIRTY-TWO

Today? The announcement took me by surprise.

I was glad to hear he was safe, but I wasn't really looking forward to meeting him. It had been a long time since I had been Dad's little darling.

Chantal would expect me to share her joy. I couldn't do it. So instead of going home I drove to a park on the river's edge and sat down on a bench to watch the flow. The current was strong, forcing the bronze-colored water past the arches of a nearby bridge.

I liked to go my own way and I was afraid he would want a part of me. As a stranger he had no right to ask. Was he close to his sons? I had no idea what to expect. What kind of man was he? Was he as dedicated to his job as Chantal claimed? What was his day-to-day life like? Did he live in an apartment, a house?

What kind of books did he read, what kind of music did he listen to? The span of what I didn't know about him, what I should know, overwhelmed me.

I sat for an hour and watched the river rush past until I felt calm enough to go home. When I got there I realized I didn't have to worry about hiding my feelings from Chantal. She barely noticed me. She and Ruth were in a frenzy of activity. They were best buds now, allied in their effort to welcome the prodigal dad. I doubted Ruth really looked forward to seeing Bernard again. It was the celebration she enjoyed, planning the menu, cooking the food, setting the table with the good china.

The house was theirs, and they occupied every inch of it, searching for dishes, tablecloths, silverware. They slammed drawers, rattled pots, banged doors. I was so spooked by the upheaval that I went looking for Joe—he had taken refuge in the garage—and took him out to lunch. He didn't resist.

"So your dad is finally coming," he said over burgers and fries at a nearby fast food restaurant. He tore open a salt packet and dumped it over his fries. "The man named Randy is dropping him off. From what I heard they'd been on a fishing trip. I wonder if Chantal knows why he was off the radar for so long."

I bit into my chili dog. "I didn't ask. Even if I had I doubt she would've told me. She's too busy killing the fatted calf." The old resentment toward Bernard surged back. Even if I accepted him in the future, I suspected the resentment would stay. "What gets me is that nobody bothered to ask if it was OK to invite him for dinner. I would've liked time to think about it. It's my house after all."

"How much time do you need?" Joe asked, upending the ketchup bottle over his fries. "A day? A month? You're running from the inevitable, Claire. Meet him and get it over with."

I sank my teeth into what remained of the chili dog. "Why is it inevitable? I managed fine without him."

"It's not just about you. Like it or not, Bernard is your father. It's done. He's here. Deal with it."

I put the hot dog down. "You don't understand, Joe."

"What's to understand? He was gone a long time and now he's back. It's a decision that was a long time in coming, but he made it."

"Taking a long time *is* the problem. I grew up without the man. I don't know him at all. What will I say to him, what will I do? I don't even know what I should call him. Bernard, Dad?"

"How do you want him to greet you?"

I pictured myself being hugged. "God, I hope he doesn't kiss me!"

"Yeah, violating your personal space would be a terrible thing," Joe said sarcastically. I was, he once said, a walking bug zapper and he the mosquito suffering a thousand deaths.

He moved the fries out of my reach after I filched a couple. "If you don't know what to say to him, Claire, why don't you wait for him to make the first move?"

"What would *you* do, Joe? Picture your dad coming back, wanting to talk to you. He hasn't changed that much, but you have. Would he approve of what you turned into or would he be critical? Would he pick you apart?" Maybe that was my problem. I was afraid I couldn't live up to expectation.

Joe pondered over a mouthful of fries. "He wouldn't dare pick me apart, not after what he did. He died because he drank too much, and as a result took my mom with him. I'm guessing he would be more likely to be afraid of my judgment, not the other way around. The same argument applies to your dad."

We stayed gone over two hours. When we came back we found the table set on the back porch with Lisa's plates, my best tablecloth and matching napkins. The buttery, milky fragrance of Ruth's signature corn pudding mixed with the scent of roasting meat. Ruth had gone home to change, Chantal said, pointedly looking at my T-shirt decorated with a blob of chili. She had swapped her apron for a crisp sleeveless blouse and pressed jeans. I went to shower and change, not because she wanted me to, but because I figured she would take my refusal to dress up as defiance.

At six we gathered on the back porch making small talk waiting for the doorbell to ring. I sat at the table against the railing, Joe on my right. Ruth was across from me. In Bernard's honor she had traded her loose cotton pants and top for her best housedress. But comfort took precedence over elegance when it came to footwear. She had kept the rubber clogs she tromped in for garden work. When the doorbell rang, Chantal went inside to let her brother in.

We waited in silence. I heard the blood beat in my ears. A vein pulsed on my wrist. Joe traced patterns on the tablecloth with the tines of his fork. Ruth kept her eyes down.

Footsteps rang on the hardwood floor, French voices grew in volume. The screen door opened and Chantal came out. She was smiling. Next came the thin man in cargo shorts and Birkenstocks.

FRENCH LEAVE

"Lord have mercy!" Ruth exclaimed, laughing. "You've changed but I should have known it was you, Bernard, whistling to beat the band."

"You remember the whistling? I, on the other hand, knew you right off."

"Of course you did. I was standing on my own porch. And here you are without a scratch. How did you manage to get away from the men who shot at you? We figured you were dead for sure."

Chantal froze. "Someone shot you?"

"Shot at," her brother corrected. "It happened before you came. Two guys went after me as I approached Claire's house. They winged me. It was no big deal, just a flesh wound. It's fine now."

"Why didn't you tell me?"

"I never had the chance. Now you know why I took off. Once they made me, I knew I couldn't take the chance of leading them to the Haitians. Or to you, Claire," Bernard said, looking at me.

It was the first time he had done so directly. I liked the fact he didn't zoom in on me when he first came in.

"You had no idea who I was, did you?" he asked, cocking his head, his eyes meeting mine, holding them.

I returned the look. "Not a clue."

And I still didn't. In my mind the Whistler and Bernard were still poles apart. For years the image of my father, cobbled from memories, hadn't come with knobby knees and khaki shorts. I had imagined him taller, more formal, the kind of man who wore a business suit with ease.

"And I assume this is Joe," he said, turning to Joe, hand extended.

He was giving me space.

CHAPTER
THIRTY-THREE

We sat down to eat. Chantal came from the kitchen bearing a quiche as big as a cart wheel, fluffy and golden, its dome rising past the fluted edge of the tin. It collapsed when she cut into it, releasing an aroma of hot cheese. "I want to know what happened," Chantal demanded without looking at her brother. "I want to know who those men are."

"From what I heard, you know them better than I do."

She looked up. "There was only one, and a girl."

"One of them died in the wreck of the pickup. I'm sorry you had to go through that, sis. I didn't have time to warn you. The battery on my phone was almost out when I called."

"And later?"

"There was no signal at the cabin where Randy and I stayed.

FRANÇOISE BARTRAM

Look, why don't we wait to talk about this until after we've eaten? Give me the time to get reacquainted. I can't even remember the last time I saw Ruth."

"It was a week before you went south to fetch that man," Ruth said, referring to Eduardo. "We ate dinner at Gin's house. You, Cora, the two girls, Raymond and me." She looked at the wedge of quiche Chantal had just dropped on her plate. "How do you get the top to brown so nicely, Tchantall?"

Bernard's mouth quirked at the pronunciation of his sister's name. "Lots of cheese is the secret, Ruth. Not to mention eggs and cream. Chantal thinks low fat is a sin."

"If that's the case, Bernard, you never sin. You use cream in your café au lait, and the boys say you eat more hamburgers than they do when you take them to McDonald's," Chantal fired back.

He laughed.

"Is that what they told you? That was when I was young and I wanted to impress them. Now that I am a senior citizen I watch what I eat."

"So you say."

The exchange was good-natured and without heat; the evident familiarity suggested a long and comfortable relationship.

339

It made me envious. I couldn't remember the last time I was at ease in my sister's company.

Silence fell as we started eating. I glanced at Bernard. Gray frizzy hair rising above a thin face gave him the look of an aging dandelion. I doubted he had ever been handsome, even before the appearance of wrinkles and crow's feet. His eyes were his best feature, as large as Chantal's and the same deep brown, but whereas hers often reflected anxiety, his expressed warmth. His mouth, wide and flexible, easily broke into a smile, but there was vulnerability there as well, perhaps not a desirable trait in a man. Still, I liked that better than Cora's backbone certainty.

All in all he wasn't as bad as I had imagined. But I still had trouble merging the man Chantal described—twice-divorced and father of two boys—with the Whistler, a happy-go-lucky guy with a spring in his step and songs in his head.

The boys, my half-brothers. I should have asked Chantal how old they were.

After the quiche, after the capon roasted with herbs and Ruth's corn casserole, after the cheese course served with more wine and more baguettes crisped in a hot oven because Chantal insisted that bread should have a hard crust, we pushed back from the table and waited for Ruth and Chantal to serve coffee. They brought the carafe and a tray with cups and saucers.

"Carmen, she told me much yesterday," Chantal said as she passed cups around the table. "She said she asked you to come, but you did not tell me about this, Bernard. I do not like for you to keep things from me."

"I wasn't. You were away when Carmen called, off on a cruise, remember? So when she said Elena needed my help, I went."

Chantal didn't speak. Bernard poured sugar into his coffee and stirred. The clink of the spoon filled the silence.

"I owed Elena. Ease up, Chantal." His voice was gentle. "I realize how much you worried about me, and I'm sorry I landed you in such a mess, but I had no idea what I was getting into when I left."

Chantal still didn't meet his eyes. He sighed. "Elena's group not only helped me find Eduardo, but she also found an attorney to represent me when I was arrested. I couldn't turn my back on her. And I didn't think it was a big deal anyway. Her organization has been feeding and clothing migrants for years. She knows what she's doing. But communication with the Haitians was a problem. That's why she needed me."

"Why? You are not the only man who speaks French, Bernard."

"Possibly, but the only one she could trust on short notice."

Ruth broke in, "Was it you who had those boys staying at Claire's house?"

So she knew the whole story. Chantal must have told her.

Bernard finished his coffee and pushed his cup away. "No. I never meant for Claire to be involved. Carmen and her group dropped the box of clothes at her house because they assumed that's where I was. In fact I was already gone. I also missed the rendezvous to pick up the boys. So the two guys who brought them dumped them on Claire."

"They'd been given Claire's address," Bernard continued, "in case something went wrong. Everyone involved made mistakes. Had I been able to get to Claire, had I not been hurt, I would have taken charge. As it was, I was lucky to get hold of Randy. He's the one who patched me up after I was shot."

Chantal asked, "Is that when you called me? After he picked you up?"

"Yes. I couldn't stay at his place. His family would've asked questions. So he took me to his cabin. It's no more than a shack. No running water, no electricity. And no phone. We couldn't get a signal."

FRANÇOISE BARTRAM

"And later? What took so long?"

Bernard hesitated. "Well, for one thing, we were afraid the guys who shot me would try to track me down. Plus, I was in a bad way for a while. Infection set in. Fortunately Randy knew what to do. He trained as a medic, like me."

Ruth clicked her tongue and Chantal turned dark tragic eyes on her brother. "You could have died."

He shook his head. "No. It wasn't that bad. Randy offered to take me to a hospital, but I would've had to explain how I got shot. Still, it wasn't a good situation. The old pickup we drove up in broke down after we got there. We eventually got it running and by then I was over the hump."

Night had fallen when Bernard stopped talking. Bats swooped down, skirting the porch. We went back inside. I carried the coffee cups to the kitchen so Joe could put them in the dishwasher; Ruth was at the sink scrubbing the roasting pan.

I walked over to the window overlooking the street. I needed to be alone for a few minutes, to forget about being a daughter or a niece, to just be me.

Marlene's house was lit up. A group composed of mostly men had gathered on the porch to watch Craig, Marlene's husband,

FRENCH LEAVE

crouch on the sidewalk. Every year, the guy's passion for rockets and sizzlers carried the Fourth of July through fall. Craig ran to the porch. A rocket shot up with a sizzle and a sigh and exploded overhead. The group on the porch cheered. The fireworks always drew a crowd. Cars lined the curb on both sides of the street and more were coming. A beat-up Chevy crawled past followed by a white commercial van.

I took a better look. The van was similar in size and age to the one Sam kept at the shop. I couldn't see the driver. It was too dark. As it passed under a street lamp I noticed the windshield was covered with dust except for two half-moons cleared by the windshield wipers. It looked as if it had been on dirt roads. I followed it with my eyes until it turned right at the next corner. Could it be Sam?

A patrol car came next, slowing as it went past Craig's house. The gatherings sometimes turned rowdy and the local cops liked to maintain a presence. I was glad to see it.

Chantal called my name then and I turned away from the window.

She stood near the door that led to the living room, her hand on her brother's shoulder. "Your father will be leaving soon, Claire. His friend Randy is coming back for him."

Her eyes grew misty as she watched me approach. "I dream, yes? I did not think I would ever see you and your father together. Oh, I am so happy!" She reached for me and Bernard at the same time and gathered us into an embrace. I ended up pinned against his shoulder, my face squashed against a scratchy patch of fabric that smelled of dust and engine oil. I pushed back but Chantal had us in a firm hold.

"Whoops!" Joe said. The crash that splintered what turned out to be the meat platter as it hit the floor put a stop to the group hug.

"It slipped out of my hand," he explained as we turned around to look.

"I just washed that," Ruth complained.

"Then it was clean when it hit the floor. It was a garage sale find," I told Joe to console him. He was looking sheepish. "I only paid two bucks for it."

He offered to clean up the mess and Ruth herded the two guests into the living room.

I kneeled to gather shards of pottery into a dust pan. Joe stood with his back to me pushing a broom in half-hearted sweeps. I figured that the meat platter had died a noble death to get me out of the group hug. Joe was well aware of my personal space issues, but I didn't realize he was so attuned to my feelings.

A few minutes later we gathered on the back porch to say our goodbyes. It had been a long day for Ruth. She was worn out. Chantal said she was tired but too keyed up to sleep so she was going to take a sleeping pill. She kissed her brother on both cheeks before heading back to her room. Bernard laughed. "You won't hear a peep out of her until morning. Sleeping pills put her out for hours."

Joe and I stayed with Bernard as he waited for his ride. "That will be Randy," Bernard said as we heard the squeak of the garden gate. "I told him to go in the back."

But it wasn't Randy.

CHAPTER THIRTY-FOUR

It was Howard.

So it hadn't been Sam at the wheel of the van crawling past earlier. Sam must have left the store van at the cabin for Steele's use.

Howard now stood at the top of the steps holding a huge Colt, most likely the weapon involved in the death of his father. I saw Bernard looking at it.

The look wasn't lost on Howard. "That's right, Palmer. It's the same gun."

Bernard didn't say anything. He faced Howard, his face impassive under its cloud of dandelion hair.

A nerve jumped in Howard's jaw. "Aren't you going to say anything? Surely you know who I am." He kept his eyes trained on Bernard and never once glanced in my direction or Joe's.

The two men stared each other down like two china dogs on a mantelpiece. Bernard finally acknowledged the other man's presence. "Yes, I know who you are."

"I thought you might. You don't look surprised to see me."

"That's because I heard you were looking for me."

"You know why, don't you? I want to see justice done, Palmer. You cheated me of the chance to see you in court. The only reason you didn't go to jail back then was because the organization you were with bribed the sheriff."

"There was no bribe, Steele." Bernard sounded weary, as if he had heard the accusation many times before. "The charges were dropped because the witness who claimed we attacked your father admitted he lied."

"He was bullied into it!" Howard countered swiftly. "I told the sheriff what happened. He didn't believe me either. I guess it was easier for everyone involved to blame my father for causing his own death. No court case and everybody walks." He stopped to catch his breath, closed his eyes and inhaled deeply, his chest expanding as his lungs took in a bushel of air. "But I didn't come here to talk about the witness," he added after a long exhalation restored his calm. "We don't need a judge or lawyers or law enforcement to settle the matter. It's just between you and me now. You may not have pulled the trigger, Palmer, but I still hold you responsible for my father's death. The wetback had no business being in that field. You led him there. You were trespassing. My father had every right to stop you."

"I agree." Bernard's admission caught Steele off balance. He had expected a fight. "We shouldn't have been on his land, but we strayed off course. Still, crossing that field shouldn't have turned into a death sentence. All he had to do was tell us to get off his land and wait for us to leave."

"How could he? You attacked him!"

"No, we didn't."

"Not you, the wetback. I *saw* him."

"You remember seeing what you wanted to see, Steele. You want to blame someone. I realize that it was a traumatic experience for you. You were young. But it's time you faced the truth. I'm not denying the fact that your father's death was tragic. But it was an accident."

Howard stood his ground. "*No*! It was murder."

The two men stared each other down for what seemed a long time, oblivious to what was going on around them. A dog barked, the beat of a rock song drifted from Craig's party, a train hooted in the distance. The sounds made no impact on them. They had reached an impasse.

It was Howard who blinked first. "It was a death you could've prevented," he clarified, and I wondered if he was offering a bargain, hinting that he would be satisfied if Bernard took responsibility for Eduardo's actions and apologized.

Bernard didn't bite. "I couldn't have prevented it, no. Could *you*?" he challenged, stressing the pronoun and leaning forward in expectation of the answer, making it important enough to perhaps settle the argument. The way he worded the question gave it a secret meaning, something unstated and yet obvious to both.

Howard blanched. Emotions flickered across his face, shock at first, then fear and finally anguish, the latter so intense it was difficult to watch.

Caught in the moment, I paid little attention to the squeak of the garden gate or to Joe standing at my side. I was in a bubble where seconds stopped ticking and time froze. My whole being focused on Howard's anguish and the way he held the Colt, his fingers tightening on the grip.

The bubble burst when Craig fired another rocket. The boom was sudden, the flash that followed blinding. As I blinked to clear the dazzle out of my eye I saw a hand reaching for Howard's gun. He turned. The gun went off and a second later the light over my head exploded.

I ducked from under the shower of broken glass. The darkness was intense. People were moving around, stumbling into each other. It was chaos until a light came on, streaming from the open porch door and outlining Joe's tall form.

I scanned the porch. Howard was nowhere to be found and a stranger stood in his place. It was a big man with a round face and sharp gray eyes. He was reaching for Bernard. I gasped when I saw my father. Blood flowed from between the fingers of the hand he was pressing against the side of his face.

"Let me see," the stranger said, prying the hand away from the wound. "You're one lucky son of a gun, Bernie boy. Looks like the bullet ricocheted and nicked your ear before hitting the porch light."

Bernard let his breath out. His shoulders slumped as he relaxed his body. "It may not be bad, but it hurts like hell. Damn, Randy! I'm not looking forward to another of your patching jobs."

FRENCH LEAVE

"Well, at least this time I don't have to dig the bullet out. What happened to you?" Randy asked, looking at my arm. It was bleeding from a myriad of shallow cuts.

The sound of a stampede on the cement walk leading to the porch kept me from answering. "Are you guys OK?" Craig asked as he came up with two other men in tow, all of them red of face and short of breath. One of Craig's sidekicks clutched a beer can, the other was empty-handed but his florid face suggested he had drunk his share. "We heard a shot. Oh my God!" Craig said when he saw Bernard, shock creasing his broad face. "You've been hit."

Bernard waved off his concern. "It looks worse than it is. It was an accident."

"Was it?" beer-can man questioned. "Then why was the guy with the gun in such a hurry to get away?"

"Some guy in a white van was waiting for him," the other man cut in. "It took off real quick but we got a partial plate and called it in. There was a patrol car hanging around earlier. They probably got him."

That last bit was probably meant to make us feel better, but I saw the way Bernard and Randy looked at each other. Better for Howard to disappear and claim the shooting was unintentional than to have to tell the police the truth. Because it was a given they would come asking questions. Too bad Howard hadn't fired the gun as the rocket went up. No one would've heard the shot and Craig's crowd would've been too busy looking up to see a gunman running out of the backyard.

When a couple of patrolmen showed up at the house, I was thankful Chantal was safely tucked in bed, dead to the world after taking a sleeping pill. She had even slept through Craig's fireworks. The cops told us the occupants of the van Craig's friend described had been placed under arrest for failure to stop, illegal possession of a firearm and resisting arrest. Occupants, plural. I guessed Sam had not only agreed to loan his van, but had volunteered to drive it as well.

Those were serious charges. Hard to dismiss the seriousness of the incident when Bernard, who by then had cleaned up and was wearing one of Joe's tops instead of his gory vest, displayed a bandaged ear and a chalky white complexion. Not knowing if Howard had given the police a reason for threatening us with a gun, Bernard told the truth, or at least a partial truth—that he knew the shooter had been looking for him to settle a score after an accidental shooting in a Texas field years ago. Luckily one of

FRENCH LEAVE

the cops, who had been a rookie at the time of the Eduardo incident, remembered the case.

"I live in France and this is the first time I've been back to Clayton. I came to see my daughter," Bernard told the patrolman who was familiar with the case. "I barely recognized the man, but he knew me."

We later learned that Howard refused to enter a plea. Sam, on the other hand, pleaded guilty to driving the van and resisting arrest, and aiding and abetting in the commission of a crime. He posted bail until sentencing, but Howard remained in jail awaiting trial.

"So the guy was the son. Not the forgiving type, is he?" Randy commented as we drifted to the kitchen after the patrolmen left. Joe took cans of beer out of the refrigerator and passed them around. I opened a bag of pretzels and a can of mixed nuts. I wasn't hungry but I figured food would help us decompress. Every time I thought the day was over something else happened to extend it.

Bernard popped the tab on his beer. "No, but you can't entirely blame him. It looks like the shooting shadowed his whole life."

"It didn't have to. It's clear the old man overreacted. He didn't like border crossers?"

"Hated was more like it. So did his son. But that's not what matters here. Steele junior came here to hear me say I was responsible for his father's death. He needed me to do it because deep down, he blamed himself."

Randy crunched down on a pretzel. "Why?"

"When Eduardo reached for the gun, instead of rushing forward to help his father, Steele stepped back. He did it instinctively and who can blame him? He was scared. I never said anything about it until now."

"Would it have made any difference if he had stepped forward?" Randy asked, reaching for more pretzels.

"No, there was nothing any of us could've done. The old man dropped the Colt and it discharged when it hit the ground. The bullet got him square in the chest. Eduardo felt so bad about what happened. But he came from a violent country where men mean business when they point a gun. Eduardo really thought Steele Senior was going to shoot him, and the old man thought the same when Eduardo came for him. Misunderstandings all around."

"Isn't it always?" Randy philosophized. "Pass the nuts, Bernie boy," he said, extending a massive arm across the table. "I'm starving."

CHAPTER THIRTY-FIVE

The bookstore only had one customer when I came in. I waited for him to leave before approaching Sam. We were alone in the store. It was Carmen's day off.

"You really screwed up, didn't you?"

He looked at me without speaking, his face with its heavy-lidded eyes Buddha-like in its stillness. He hadn't shaved and the stubble stood out against his pale skin.

"I did, and I'm sorry," he finally said, spreading his hands, palms up in a gesture of surrender. "Howard was obsessed with your father, Claire. He just couldn't let go. I realize it wasn't a good idea to tell him your dad was coming back, but he's my friend. We've known each other since boot camp."

"Has he always been so hateful?"

"Not hateful, just unhappy. What happened back then changed him. You must realize that in less than a year he lost everything that mattered to him—his father, his mother who died of cancer a year later, and the farm his mother had mortgaged to pay for her medical bills. He enlisted at the same time I did. Since neither one of us had a home anymore we spent the holidays and our leave time together. Even after we left the service, we kept in touch. But from the very beginning, when Howard heard I came from the same town as your father he asked questions about Bernard and asked me to keep him in the loop."

"Didn't you realize what he was after?"

Sam shrugged. "Not really. I figured it was normal."

Only up to a point. But I couldn't dismiss the fact that Sam, after his wife's fling, was no lover of border crossers, therefore no friend of the man who helped them. He didn't like Hispanics any better than Howard did, neither did they like the bleeding hearts who let them in.

"Didn't you know Howard was capable of violence?"

Sam shook his head. "He gave me no reason to suspect it. I was the one who planned everything, and at no point was violence involved until he brought in his daughter."

"Really? What about Sally then? Was it your idea to dump her at the park?"

"No!" He was adamant. "It was Howard's. I put him on to Sally because you worked for her, but at no time did I intend for her to be involved. Everything went wrong after the daughter and that John Little showed up. They changed the rules, got into a mess and had to leave. Howard knew his time was short. He was anxious to meet with them, but he didn't have a car and I wasn't home. I was at the cabin already. So he used Sally's. When I found out what happened I talked him into going back for her, but she was gone. That's when I took the car back."

"He was after her money, wasn't he?"

Sam hesitated. "Yeah, he was. He's broke. He thought that if he could keep her books, he could skim some off the top and she would never know."

She would have. Money and sex—Sally was expert at both.

***

I called Chantal just to talk. It was the second call for me since she'd gone home. After she left, I found myself missing her. She sent me a picture of her son Alexander. He was tall and wiry with a shock of dark hair, wide-spaced eyes and his mother's chin, hinting at an obstinate nature. Except for the obstinacy and wide-spaced eyes, we didn't have much in common, but those shared traits were enough to spark a sense of kinship I never felt for Mirabelle. Funny how hard I fought to be different from my mother and sister, but turned clannish when it came to a cousin I had never met.

Bernard didn't send pictures of his sons, but he said they wanted to meet me. He called once in a while, though I usually took the initiative. I liked being in charge of our relationship. I still had trouble merging the Whistler with the boogeyman of my childhood, but I came to appreciate his discretion and his patience. During one of our phone conversations, as he recalled the years he taught at Clayton High, he said, "I should've insisted on getting my job back, Claire. I should've stayed at your side. I regret letting your mother intimidate me."

"Then why did you?"

He didn't answer directly. "My father always said I let people push me around because I was afraid to test my strength. He was half right. I have been and can be strong for others, but when it comes to defending myself, I cave in. Not pretty, is it? I'm glad you didn't inherit that from me."

I kind of did, but I was working on it.

FRENCH LEAVE

***

Two weeks after Howard left, Norma called me to the kitchen for coffee.

"You and Sal done with the book yet?"

"Just about. It's not one of Sally's best, but it improved after Howard left. She changed the character he originally inspired into a bigger-than-life villain and pitted him against a Jake Satterwaite equivalent. Guess who got the girl?"

Norma flapped a large hand. "I don't care as long as Sal gets paid. You know Jake is taking her to Europe, don't you?"

"He mentioned it the last time he came. How long will they be gone?"

"About a month, I think he said. I really like the guy, Claire. It took a while for her to warm up to him, but he finally won her over. After Howard, he's a class act."

***

The day after we finished *Mischief in Michigan* Sally asked me to come by to pick up the check for the work I had done on the manuscript. We sat on lounge chairs on the patio just off the office. It was a nice day with the September sun angling low on the horizon, bathing us in warmth.

"I'm going to Europe with Jake," she announced and looked at me expectantly, probably waiting for me to congratulate her. But I merely nodded, thinking it was best not to let on that I already knew. I wasn't sure why she felt the need to tell me unless it was to make me think men were still at her feet.

"I may want you to write another book for me and again I may not," she said, maybe to punish me for not commenting on Jake Sattherwaite's generosity and the depth of his feelings for her. The more money spent, the deeper the love. "I'll let you know when I get back. We'll be gone for two months, possibly three."

I leaned back in my chair and closed my eyes. Norma had said a month. Sally hoped to spook me with the specter of months of unemployment. She could stay a year for all I cared.

She didn't know I was about to move into my own office in Lisa's building. I now had a website and ads in several magazines.

"Did you hear what I said?" Sally asked when I didn't respond.

I opened my eyes. "Every word. Three months, you say?"

Vertical lines creased the space between her eyebrows. "Well, no more than two probably," she amended. "I'll let you know."

"No rush." I started to get up. "I have work that will keep me busy until then."

FRENCH LEAVE

Her lounge chair creaked as she sat up. "What kind of work?"

"Editing. I have three new clients. Knowing I can no longer count on a regular paycheck gave me the push I needed. I want to thank you for letting me go, Sally. I couldn't have gone forward without your help."

She glared at me. I smiled and wished her a pleasant trip. I could feel her eyes boring into my back as I walked to the house. I stopped by the office to clear it of my belongings. Then I went to the bank to deposit my last paycheck.

ACKNOWLEDGMENTS

I thank my first readers: Bill Bartram, Donna Bartram, Josephine Bates and Monica Durbin. Thanks also to the members of Writers' Satellite: Peg Hanna, Rose Ann Kalister, Brenda Layman and Rosalie Ungar. I couldn't have written *French Leave* without their help and encouragement.

I am grateful for the support of Brad Pauquette, publisher at Boyle & Dalton, and copy editor Emily Hitchcock, for their keen insight and patience.

Thanks to Sandy Cathey, my faithful go-to person for computer mishaps and other disasters.

Finally, many thanks to my husband Bill for his love and support.

ABOUT THE AUTHOR

Françoise Bartram was born in France. She lived near Paris until she moved to the United States to join her husband, a member of the US Air Force. She now lives in Columbus, Ohio. *French Leave* is her first novel.

CPSIA information can be obtained
at www.ICGtesting.com
Printed in the USA
FFHW02n1333210918
48516243-52392FF